Who Murd﹍
Dr. Damien?

The Mystery of the Deadly
Asylum

By C.M. Blackwood

"We all go a little mad sometimes."

– Robert Bloch, *Psycho*

Contents

Chapter 1

The prisoners were screaming. Again.

Katrina Throckmorton threw her blanket off, and sat up in bed. She could have sworn that she just saw a demon with a red face, dancing at the end of the room.

She put her hand to her face, wiping off the sweat, and shivering a little. This sort of thing had been happening a lot lately.

As soon as she sat upright, however, it seemed that the whole thing had passed, as if it had never happened. She squinted into the darkness, and then began to grimace.

No – it hadn't passed. The demon was still there. Still there, but standing motionless now. It was watching her intently, its eyes looking like black holes in its red face.

"What do you want?" Katie asked, trying to stop her voice from shaking. "Why do you keep coming here?"

But the demon didn't answer her. It never answered her.

She passed a hand across her face again, breathed deeply in and out, and then looked up. The hellish figure was gone, now. It hadn't simply disappeared, though. Katie had heard its footsteps as it walked out of the room.

She even thought she could hear them now, going down the staircase. Then the sound died away.

Before she woke up, Katie had been having a terrible nightmare. She had been trapped in that old asylum again. The chipped, dirty bricks that formed the walls almost seemed to have voices. They whispered in her ear, and on top of that, the prisoners were screaming.

The prisoners in the countless rows of filthy, narrow beds. Even narrower than twin-size beds. It was a good thing all the prisoners were so thin: almost anorexic-looking, with sallow skin, stringy hair, and shadows under their eyes. They didn't do much sleeping in those narrow beds.

Off to the side, silhouetted in a lighted doorway, there stood a tall, thin man. Thin, but not in the same way as the prisoners. You could tell that, unlike them, he had access to food. He was pale, but not sallow. There weren't any rings under his eyes, either.

What he did to the prisoners didn't cause him to lose any sleep at night.

***

When Katie got up later in the morning, she felt groggy, and she was in a black mood. It was always like that when she woke from nightmares.

She put her feet on the chilly floor, and sat on the edge of the bed for a minute or two, staring at the closed door. It was strange, but she thought that she had seen it open, in the night.

She thought she had seen the demon come through it. But no – that was impossible. She hadn't seen the demon since she was a teenager. She'd left it behind a long time ago.

She tried to convince herself of this, but she still couldn't shake the remnants of the nightmare. She knew that the red-faced monster had come to her in the night.

With this certainty in mind, she looked slowly and warily all around, wondering if maybe the demon was still there. In the closet? Under the bed?

No, that was stupid. There was no one there.

"You're twenty-eight years old, Katie," she said to herself, as she stood up on her feet. "When are you going to grow up?"

Since she didn't really know how to answer herself – and since this made her mood even darker – she grabbed her black silk robe from the hook on the back of the door, and started out into the corridor towards the bathroom.

The robe was a gift from Mallory Kent. One of many gifts, in fact. It often occasioned disagreeable expressions on the faces of the other members of the household: quiet concern and embarrassment on Axel's, unbridled disgust on Queen Regina's.

Axel Throckmorton was Katie's father. He had divorced her mother, Linda Cleary, when Katie was young. Her mother remarried and moved to Florida, but she and Katie still had a good relationship.

As for Axel – well, despite the fact that he rented an enormous two-floor flat in one of the most recently built high-rises of Boston's West End, he was nowhere near rich. He was a traveling salesman, and he hated his job. He'd been wanting to quit for a long time, since Katie was grown, and off on her own.

But then he met Regina. Regina MansfieldWhitehall, to be precise. When they met, she'd just turned forty, having spent the past twenty years married to a rich man named Leonard Whitehall. Then old Lenny met a new twenty-year-old, and married *her.* So Regina found herself kicked to the wrong side of the gleaming BMW parked on the curb.

Then she found Axel. She was impressed by his manners, his fancy suit, and his shiny briefcase (maybe it reminded her of the BMW). But, most of all, she was impressed by the fact that he wasn't destitute. He decided to keep the job he loathed, just so she'd marry him.

Katie, for one, couldn't see the real merit of the trade. She was inclined to think that her father was on the losing end of it, but he didn't like it when she said that.

Regina made no money, but she hired a woman named Rosa to clean the flat twice a week. Every Tuesday and Friday. Regina hosted a book club every Tuesday afternoon, and she liked for the place to be exceptionally tidy at that time. She liked it even better when Rosa was still cleaning while her club discussed their current inane volume. It made her feel superior to sit there talking about nonsense, while a poor sixtyyear-old woman dusted the television behind her.

A year after the wedding, Regina gave birth to a daughter. They named her Lockwood, after Regina's family mansion. Her family had gone broke a long time ago, and Lockwood Mansion was now owned by an unassuming British family called the Prescotts, but Regina's recent dabbles with misfortune had led her to cling to the glory of bygone days.

For most of Lockwood's childhood, Katie only visited the flat sporadically. But she got to understand, even during those infrequent visits, that she hated the child. She was spoiled; she was bad-tempered; she was occasionally violent, and almost definitely evil.

Katie was allergic to shellfish. Once, Lockwood hid half a dozen cocktail shrimp in her spaghetti, and sent her to the hospital for two days. When her father brought her to visit, insisting that Lockwood hadn't really known what she was doing, the little girl just hovered under their father's arm, assuming a stance of contrition. At the same time, she smiled a devilish smile that only Katie could see.

Back in the present moment, Katie shook these disagreeable thoughts away, and stepped into the bathroom. She practically slammed the door behind her, wishing that the rest of the house would fall away on the other side of it. Maybe, when it disappeared, she'd find herself back in the familiar town house, with its feather bed and its state-of-the-art appliances.

For the past five years, Katie had been what you'd call a "kept" woman. Her home was the lavish residence of a wealthy middle-aged woman. Her name, as you already know, was Mallory Kent. But then, Mallory kicked Katie to the same unfortunate curb that Leonard Whitehall had thrown Regina over. Hence her return to her father.

The worst of it was, all of Katie's books were still at Mallory's. She had an enormous collection of volumes, some of which Mallory had bought for her, but most of which she'd already owned when she moved in. It had been horrid of Mallory to refuse to give them back.

She hadn't given anything back, actually. She'd shoved Katie out the front door, while Katie was wearing nothing but the black silk robe. Bare feet and everything. She'd had to walk up and down the street several times, trying to beg enough change to call her father from a payphone. It was one of the lowest points of her life – but probably not *the* lowest.

Now, she let the robe fall to the floor, turned on the shower head, and stepped into the little glass cube, sliding the semi-transparent door shut behind her. She stood under the shower head for a long time before she even started washing her hair. She tipped her face up towards the warm jet of water, and covered her nose with it so that it was difficult to breathe.

She wondered if it was possible to drown yourself in the shower.

Probably not.

***

After her shower, Katie returned to the guest room, where she'd been sleeping since she moved back into her father's house.

It was the perfectly bland, perfectly *perfect* sort of room one would have expected Queen Regina to design. Cream-colored walls and a cream-colored ceiling. Boring, pale bedspread that would be badly stained if Katie accidentally tipped her merlot over it.

Boring, boring, boring. Well, then again – the room would have been pretty enough, if it had been anywhere else.

Anywhere other than in the immediate vicinity of Regina Whitehall-Throckmorton.

Katie shuddered involuntarily, and sat down on the little white bench in front of the vanity. It wasn't to say that Regina wasn't attractive. She was just – well, she was just so . . . *horrible.*

Satisfied with this simple phrasing, Katie looked at herself in the mirror. She had a habit of looking at herself objectively, not thinking too highly of herself, but not trying too hard to be modest, either. She knew that she was good-looking. If she hadn't been, she could never have snagged a rich woman like Mallory Kent. She was five-eight, what some might call tall, but not too tall. She had nice white skin, clear blue eyes. Pleasant features.

Not that any of this was doing her much good *today.* She sighed, and started brushing her hair. It was a cascade of tight curls that didn't need rollers, or perms, or anything. They were part-brown, partyellow, almost as if she'd dyed them that way. But she hadn't. That's just what color they were. Sexy, some people called it.

Psychotic, other people called it.

Whatever, Katie thought, as she brushed out her curls. She brushed them out, morning, noon and night – and they never got any looser. She didn't mind it, though.

Her mother used to call her Shirley Temple. She'd liked that.

Come on, Shirley! Mom had yelled, sliding the porch door open, and holding a soccer ball up in the air. *Let's go kick a few around the yard.*

Katie had liked outdoor activities, and some sports, when she was young. She'd never really learned the rules to anything, but she still liked to play. Liked to play with Mom, anyway.

She kept on brushing her hair, thinking about the recent past. She was glad Daddy had taken her in – but she wished she could skewer Mallory Kent through the heart.

Damned old vampire, she thought bitterly.

The most beautiful vampire she'd ever seen, though.

She just went on brushing her hair, growing a little more bitter by the second, and even starting to take it out on her own scalp – *ouch,* she thought – when a knock sounded at the bedroom door.

She looked up to see her father standing there, and she smiled.

Axel Throckmorton was a very handsome man. He was tall, a regular skyscraper, just like Rock Hudson or Cary Grant. He made Katie, who was tall for a woman, feel almost short. His hair was coppercolored, thick and wavy. It was sort of like Edward Cullen's hair from *Twilight.*

Katie had always told him how much she liked his hair.

"Hi, Daddy," she said.

"Hi, Punkin," he replied. He stepped through the open doorway, walked across the room, and perched himself on the edge of the bed.

Katie smiled at him in the mirror. He smiled back, and gave her a cheerful little wave.

"You look sad, Punkin," he said. "What's the matter?"

"Nothing, Daddy," she answered, as she went back to brushing her hair.

"You think too much, baby girl," Axel said, frowning deeply. "You've got to look on the bright side!"

Katie looked at him questioningly in the mirror. "The bright side of what, Daddy?" she asked in a glum voice.

He leaned forward with a smile, and planted his elbows on his knees. "There's a bright side to everything, kiddo," he said. "It might not seem like it right now, but everything's going to be all right."

He held up his hands, and looked all around. "You've got a roof over your head," he said. "You've got a warm bed, and food to eat."

He grinned at Katie in the mirror, and added, "Not to mention your wonderful talent. It won't be long before your name's in magazines again. It might have been a few years, but they'll remember you. They'll remember how good you are."

Katie sighed, and threw down her brush. "That's the thing about this business," she said. "People don't remember anything. If you don't show them something better than the last thing you showed them, every few months or so – they'll forget you're alive."

She sighed again, and hung her head. She remembered how proud her father had been when her essay on themes in Russian literature was published in the *New York Times*. But, then again – he'd always been proud of all her work. Every essay, every paper. Even the ones that weren't published.

"It's been years, Daddy," she said. "No one's going to remember me."

But Axel's grin didn't fade.

"Listen, baby girl," he said, rising up from the bed, and moving forward to lay his hands on Katie's shoulders. "Life is hard, I'll give you that. But it's nothing we can't overcome, if we keep our spirits up."

He smiled cheerfully, and leaned down to kiss the top of Katie's head.

"It's all going to work out for you, Punkin," he said. "Just wait. You'll see."

He gave her one more kiss, and then started towards the door.

"Off already, Daddy?" Katie asked.

"I'm afraid so, baby girl," he replied. "Duty calls – and I must answer."

He turned to give her a soldier's salute, and then disappeared through the doorway.

Katie sighed, and went on brushing her hair.

Chapter 2

Less than a month ago, Katie had celebrated her twenty-eighth birthday.

But then, maybe "celebrated" was the wrong word. Yeah – there was a cake. Yep, there were candles. But then Lockwood had a total meltdown, thrust her hand into the cake (burning herself pretty badly), and yanked out some of the candles, which she threw onto her mother's white damask valances in the kitchen.

Then the seven-year-old girl started jumping up and down, her face crimson with fury, her eyes shining like those of a demon. Sometimes Katie wondered if she *was* a demon. Everyone had stared at the little girl for a few moments, unsure what to say or do. But Lockwood didn't care. She never cared.

Now it was Halloween night. Katie got stuck babysitting, because Lockwood didn't want to go trickor-treating, and everyone else in the house was out for the evening. But, then again, Katie thought – if Lockwood had wanted to go out, *she* would have been the one forced to take her. And she couldn't imagine anything more disagreeable than taking Lockwood Throckmorton trick-or-treating.

What would the kid dress up as, anyway? A bunny rabbit? A princess?

Yeah, right. Maybe if bunnies and princesses had the eyes of homicidal maniacs.

Axel and Regina were out at a charity event. It was the sort of thing that cost five hundred dollars a plate – "And, trust me," Katie's father had once told her, "there's hardly anything *on* the damned plate."

Having grown accustomed to the life of a rich wife while she was married to Leonard Whitehall, Regina didn't seem to know how to let go of all the pomp and circumstance that had gone hand-in-hand with her first marriage. So she forced her second husband to spend money that he didn't have, in order to boost up the reputation that she couldn't bring herself to toss out with the weekly garbage.

Not eager to spend any time with Lockwood, Katie locked herself in her room with a boom-box and a bottle of wine. She could hear Lockwood downstairs, doing something very noisy. She was probably defacing the living room walls again.

Whatever, Katie thought. Let her write all over Regina's eggshell walls with her markers. It was Axel and Regina's fault for buying her the markers in the first place.

Katie took a sip of her wine, staring at the ceiling. Her head was propped up on a stack of three soft pillows, and the wine was taking effect. The bold notes of Tchaikovsky's "Souvenir de Florence" were issuing from the little speakers of the boom-box, and wafting around Katie's head in a perfectly lovely manner.

Only one thing would make it even better. Katie looked to the bedside table, and opened the topmost drawer. She took out a little orange prescription bottle, and fondled it for a moment in her fingers. The label read NEMBUTAL. It was only one of many from Mallory's town house.

When Mallory threw Katie out, she'd had nothing on her but the black silk robe. And, of course, it wasn't as though she'd been walking around on that fateful day with bottles of Nembutal in her pockets. No – she'd stolen the prescription bottles later.

It was an evening in early spring. Spring had always been Katie's favorite season – very similar to autumn, but without the pervading sense of death that fall brings with it. She was walking through the city at the eight o'clock hour, wearing a long, light trench coat to ward off the intermittent rain, and pondering her circumstances.

It wasn't fair, she thought. She'd never done anything to purposely hurt anyone. She hardly ever even lied. It wasn't necessary to lie to Mallory, anyway. The woman barely listened enough to detect a falsehood. All Katie asked for was a quiet, comfortable place to eat, sleep, drink, and study.

Though it certainly hadn't hurt to have a ravishing woman lying beside her in bed every night. No – that was an added bonus.

But what had she really done to occasion the loss of it all? Spoken her mind? Let it be known that she had more feelings than a rag doll?

"It's not fair," she muttered into the darkling evening, where the rain was beginning to fall again, *pitter-pat* against the concrete sidewalks and stoops.

She wanted her books back. She didn't care about all the clothes, all the jewelry that Mallory had given her over the years. Clothes were clothes, and she'd never really cared for jewelry, anyway.

But those books! They were her life. They told the *history* of her life, in terms of other's people's pasts. In addition, she had dozens upon dozens of notebooks filled with meticulous memorandums and essays. She'd left off publishing essays after moving in with Mallory, because the older woman considered it stuffy and pretentious. But before that, she'd been a regular contributor to the local Boston papers. She'd been published more than once in the *New York Times,* including that essay on Russian literature.

Her father had been especially proud of the *Times* articles. He'd had them framed, and he mounted them on his office wall.

Those notebooks were filled with years' worth of future work. Without them, Katie felt that she'd be nothing. Just as she was nothing at this moment.

She began straying away from the streets of the West End, veering towards Charlestown. It was more than a two-mile walk, but she hardly even thought about anything along the way. Her mind was blank, and her legs were mostly numb. She couldn't even feel the ground beneath her feet.

The rain began to fall harder as she came into Charlestown. The Charles River flowed directly beside her, and she looked down into it, watching it run. She remembered seeing the sailboats that floated over it on Sunday mornings, while she sat next to her father on a park bench.

She wondered how many dead bodies were at the bottom of the river.

She shook her head, as if trying to rouse herself from a daze, and went back on her way. On Pleasant

Street, she stopped off at the Warren Tavern, feeling all of a sudden that she required some sort of sustenance to go on with her errand.

She walked into the old building, and found a large area of modern comfort and convenience. Off to one side was the dining room, with its many pictures and placards along the walls, and on the other side was the shining bar, equipped with the huge, sparkling beer tap.

Not that she wanted any beer. It didn't do the trick fast enough. What she wanted was vodka.

She'd taken to drinking vodka while she was with Mallory. No matter how much vodka you drank, you never seemed to gain any weight. Mallory had grown perturbed, at first, when Katie's belly became a little less flat than it had been when they met, and she told her so.

"I don't care how much you spend," she said, "and I don't care how much you drink. You may be high as a kite every time I come in – I don't mind it. But I expect you to stay thin. I don't want you lying on top of me with jelly rolls hanging off of your sides."

Katie had thought this was a little dramatic, seeing as she'd only gained five pounds, but there was nothing she could do about it. So she limited herself to two meals a day, and switched to vodka. Red wine didn't seem to hurt much, either.

The tavern was full to bursting, tonight. The dining area was crammed, and there were people waiting at the door for a seat. Men and women jostled at the bar for the bartender's attention. He was a short young man, with spiky hair and a little paunch that pressed against his tucked-in black shirt. He seemed overwhelmed, and very cross.

Katie pushed through the crowd, ignoring several indignant outbursts, and waved her hand in the bartender's face. "I want vodka," she said. "Just bring the bottle, and save yourself the trouble."

"You'll have to wait your turn," he said gruffly. His voice was deeper than you'd expect a little man's like his to be.

"What is this?" Katie demanded. "The deli counter at Stop and Shop? Get me a damned drink."

He glowered at her, and grabbed a bottle of vodka from one of the glittering shelves behind him. He put it on the bar, and then practically threw a tumbler at Katie.

But she'd forgotten about him already. She was gazing desperately at the shining surface of the bar, thinking over her predicament, and twisting furiously at the cap of the vodka bottle. She splashed a generous amount into her tumbler, and took a long swig. It burned like rubbing alcohol. It tasted horrible, yet it tasted like nothing at all. She was accustomed to mixing it with diet soda, but that was for slow evening sipping, not for urgent matters of business.

There was an annoying sound at the edge of her awareness, and she turned irritably to see what it was.

There was a long, thin young man sitting on a stool at the edge of the dining area, strumming a guitar that was set on his knee, and singing a song that Katie hated.

"And rain falls angry on the tin roof

*As we lie awake in my bed
You're my survival, you're my living proof
My love is alive and not dead . . ."*

"Goddamn it," Katie muttered. "Fucking Edwin McCain."

*"I'll be your cryin' shoulder I'll
be love suicide . . ."*

Katie clenched her teeth, and took another drink.

*"I'll be better when I'm older
I'll be the greatest fan of your life."*

She slammed her glass down on the bar, and probably only very narrowly avoided breaking it. She took the glass in one hand, the bottle in the other, and marched off towards the young guitar player.

Then she threw a shot of vodka in his face. His playing subsided with a discordant *twang*, and he looked wonderingly at her.

"If you're going to sit there and make a spectacle of yourself," she said, "don't you think you should at least play your own music?"

His brows knitted in confusion. "I don't have any music," he said.

"But you still call yourself a musician?" she asked.

"Well, I –"

His voice trailed off, because it didn't seem like he could think of anything to say.

"Nobody likes that fucking song," Katie hissed. *"Nobody.* If they do, it's either because they're ignorant, or they're still six years old."

She peered at him with a hard eye. "You don't look like you're six years old," she observed. "So you must be ignorant."

She sprinkled a little vodka from the bottle over his head, and began to march away. But the bartender had emerged from behind the bar, and was running after her.

"You have to pay for that!" he cried.

Katie looked at him viciously, and he balked a little. "Well, now," she said. "A bottle goes for eleven or twelve bucks at the package store, yeah? Twenty or twenty-five for the nicer stuff?"

She looked down at the bottle she was holding, and frowned. "Not the nicer stuff," she observed. "So what's the price? About a hundred bucks?"

She threw the bottle at him, and he tried to catch it before it went spilling over the floor. Then she took a twenty-dollar bill from her pocket, and threw that at him, too.

"That should cover what spilled," she muttered.

"I should call the police!" the bartender shouted.

"Go ahead," Katie said sullenly, starting on her way out of the tavern, oblivious to the hundreds of eyes fixed on her.

From there, she walked purposefully to Mallory's town house. The whole time, she was picturing herself lying in Mallory's bed, with one of Mallory's legs thrown over her waist, and her beautiful face buried in her neck. She could smell her. A scent like honey and milk, a warmer scent than you'd imagine such a cold woman would have.

"I'll Be" by stupid Edwin McCain was playing on the radio. Mallory liked that song, even though she'd never admit it. When it played, she became more sensuous, and she kissed Katie more passionately. Something about that song made her want to snuggle.

Katie wiped an angry tear from eye, and kept walking. When she got to Mallory's house, she didn't even knock, since she knew that Mallory usually left the door unlocked. She just walked right in.

The moment she came through the door, she could hear the sound of many feminine voices, raised up in merriment in the living room. Her expression soured, and she started in their direction.

Mallory was sitting with all of her girlfriends, sipping champagne and laughing idiotically. Katie stepped into the wide doorway of the living room, standing motionless, and watching the raucous celebration of the drunken women.

The room was an enormous one, a truly grand one, with all the most modern furniture and hangings, but with a few choice antiques thrown in for what Mallory called "cohesion of atmosphere." The walls were covered in beige-and-white striped wallpaper by Candice Olson – one hundred dollars per roll.

Mallory was sitting in her favorite indigo chintz armchair – but she wasn't sitting directly on the cushion. Instead, she sat on the long, thin lap of a very young woman. Her height was obvious, even while she was seated. She was even taller than Katie. Her hair was the color of burnished gold, and her eyes were bright blue, a perfectly clear hue, despite the billows of cigarette smoke wafting through the living room.

"Is she the new me?" Katie asked, stepping forward into the room. No one had even noticed her standing in the doorway.

The question wasn't sharp, wasn't bitter like she'd thought it would be. Rather, she only sounded curious.

Mallory looked up in surprise. Not shock, no – she was too disinterested and disaffected to ever be truly shocked by anything. In another moment, she'd even begun to grin wickedly.

"The new and improved version!" Mallory announced. "She does as she's told – and she's nine years younger."

A few of her friends giggled cruelly. But many of the others were silent. They remembered very well when Katie had been the one sitting with Mallory in the chintz armchair – and they felt uncomfortable to see her, now, standing dripping with rain, with a tortured look on her beautiful face.

"Ah," Katie said simply, nodding as if she'd just figured out something that she hadn't understood before. She stood for a moment, still and silent, while Mallory reveled in her victory. But then she stepped forward confidently, picked up Mallory's highball from the little table beside her, and splashed it all over the front of her pastel lavender party gown.

Mallory leapt off the young woman's lap, glaring at Katie with eyes caught on fire. "This is silk!" she screamed. "The stain will never come out!"

"I hope not," Katie said in an aloof tone. Then she looked down at the pretty young woman in the chair, who wore a good-fitting dress of blue paisley, but who hardly seemed to mind having been splashed by the highball. *She* hadn't paid for the dress, after all.

"You know," Katie said to her in a serious voice, "it's all well and good for you now – but watch yourself. Where do you think *you'll* be, nine years from today?"

She started out of the room, and didn't even look back as she added, "If it takes that long."

Mallory chased Katie across the dimly lit foyer. She looked down at the huge oriental rug beneath their feet, which covered nearly the entire length of the foyer, from the front door to the staircase.

Her face twisted in rage and disgust. "Look what you've done to my five-thousand-dollar carpet! It's tracked all over with your muddy footprints! This might never come out!"

"So many things seldom do, my dear," Katie said absently, starting up the staircase towards the room that had served as her library for five long years. Only now did she begin to wonder, how was she supposed to get all those books out of the house? In the pockets of her trench coat? She'd need a much bigger trench coat.

Suddenly, she heard Roy Scheider's voice in her head. *We're gonna need a bigger boat.*

She laughed out loud, and continued on her way up the stairs. That's the thing about movies like *Jaws*. You can never watch them too many times.

"What are you doing?" Mallory cried shrilly. "You're tracking mud everywhere! You have no right to be in my house!"

"Ah," Katie repeated softly. "Anyone and everyone but me, I suppose. But then – that's the way it's been for a long time. Hasn't it, Mallory?"

She cast a quick glance back at the older woman, and the depth of meaning in her expression even caused that spoiled, ill-mannered tart to pause for a moment. She stared into Katie's face, almost as if she were trying to decide whether she had anything to reprove herself for.

But then, suddenly – the fog cleared from her face, she shook her head briskly, and Katie knew that she'd decided in her own favor. Just as she always did.

"Don't try to make me feel sorry for you," she barked at Katie. "You foul hussy!"

Katie just shook her head lightly, and went off on her way again.

"Where are you going?" Mallory cried. "What are you doing? Come back here!"

"I want my books," Katie said plainly.

"Well – you can't have them! They belong to me now."

"It must get very tedious," Katie said thoughtfully, "when everything in the world belongs to you. There's nothing to wish for anymore –

nothing to hope for." She looked deeply, once again, into Mallory's face, pausing at the open door of the library.

Then she asked: "Don't you think that's so, Mallory?"

Again – and for an even longer space than before – Mallory paused. It took more effort, this time, for her to shake off the strange spell Katie was involuntarily casting on her.

But, in the end, she said nothing at all. She just watched Katie, as she walked on into the library, shaking the beads of water off her coat as she twirled all around in rapture.

"My books!" she cried. "How I've missed you!"

"I suppose you brought a U-Haul to get them all out of here?" Mallory asked sourly.

Katie stopped twirling, and looked at her blankly. "I don't suppose you'd want to hire one for me – would you?"

Mallory couldn't seem to tell, for a moment, whether or not Katie was joking. Then she realized she wasn't, and she frowned severely.

Katie looked around at the books again, shelved along the walls in that magnificent room, whose floor was made of Brazilian walnut covered in hard, shining lacquer. The hangings at the windows were of the finest linen, colored a rich crimson. There were several choice pieces of artwork on the walls, none of which Katie actually knew by name, but all of which Mallory had picked out for her over the years.

"A woodland scene by Ivan Shishkin," she'd once announced, while presenting Katie with a muted panorama of trees and shadows. "I know how you love the forest."

Then she frowned, and added, "Though of course I can't understand why."

Katie had hung the picture on the wall directly in front of her desk. She'd looked at it often, thinking of how Mallory had once had the presence of mind to remember what sort of things she liked.

She realized, now, that she'd never get her books back. Mallory wouldn't let her take them.

She turned slowly to the older woman, examining her striking appearance in the moonlight that flowed through the open drapes. Everything was exactly the way Katie had left it – Mallory hadn't even bothered to draw the crimson curtains.

It wasn't hard to see why Katie had fallen so hard for her. She was regal, elegant, majestic and practically queen-like. A crown would have been fitting atop her well-shaped head. Her dark hair shone like diamonds in the light from the tall windows, obscuring Katie's vision.

Katie forgot, for a moment, what a horrible person she was. She just remembered how lonely *she* was – and she flew towards Mallory.

"Oh, Mal," she sighed, laying her head gently against the other woman's bosom, and wrapping her arms around her slender waist.

Mallory seemed touched, for a moment. She laid an uncertain hand on Katie's rain-damp head, and even bent down slightly to breathe in the scent of her hair. She seemed to forget her pride, and to remember that, above all the young women she had ever prized, she had prized Katie most of all. She was still no more than a trophy, of course – but a lush, enviable trophy, one she doubted she'd find anywhere else. The one downstairs was a poor replica, but it was the best she'd been able to find.

"You're too proud," she said simply, her full lips moving lightly against Katie's hair. "If you'd just do as I tell you – I'd let you come back."

For a lengthy moment, Katie savored the feeling of Mallory's arms around her. But then, she started thinking about what she'd said. Maybe that was her problem – she thought too much.

"And what does that mean?" she asked, looking into Mallory's face. "That I have to come to your bed when you call – but lie alone when you don't want me? Is that it?"

"Essentially," Mallory said brusquely.

Katie pulled away from her, and stood up to her full height, which was about three inches above Mallory. "Not a lover, then," she said flatly. "Just a plaything."

"A very comfortable and well-provided-for plaything, you might like to add," Mallory said in a dry tone.

Katie looked desperately around at the books. "You'll never let me have these," she said, "will you?"

Mallory looked sharply into Katie's face, and saw that she wasn't game. "No," she said simply.

"You'll give me nothing," Katie said, her voice rising a little wildly, her heart beginning to hammer, "after all these years? Not even what belongs to me?"

"Nothing belongs to you," Mallory snapped. "You

belonged to *me*. Now you have flitted away –" (she made a violent motion with her hand through the air) "– like some daft little bird. I don't care if I never see you again."

"Don't worry," Katie said, looking into Mallory's face with an unwavering expression. She held it for so long, Mallory seemed to grow uncomfortable. Then she added: "You won't."

She stormed out of the library, down the corridor to the bathroom. The light was on. It was an enormous bathroom, with a porcelain claw-foot tub, and a mirror nearly the whole length of one of the walls. The floor was made of pristine white tiles interspersed with golden diamonds.

Katie went to the great mirror, which was actually an optical illusion, and which opened up in the center to reveal a wide medicine cabinet. It was filled with prescription bottles.

Mallory Kent was a notorious pill-popper. Her bathroom cabinet was filled with all sorts of little treats: barbiturates and benzodiazepines of all varieties. Nembutal – Seconal – Valium. And so much more.

Mallory caught up to Katie, and grabbed hold of her arm. "What are you doing?" she demanded. "Get out of there!"

"If you won't give me anything," Katie said airily, "I'll *take* something."

She reached out, and began to sweep all the bottles off the shelves. She ran to the bathtub, and turned on the tap, allowing a prodigious jet of water to gush out into the porcelain vat. Mallory tried to keep on her heels, but directly afterwards, Katie dashed back to the floor under the cabinet, scooped up some bottles, and flew to the toilet. She threw up the seat, and started emptying the bottles out into the bowl.

"No!" Mallory cried. She sounded like a banshee watching her *true* lover being beheaded. "Stop that, Katie!"

Katie moved so fast, Mallory couldn't keep up with her. She dashed from the toilet, to the cabinet, and then to the tub, where she poured more bottles out into the warm bath water. Then: back to the toilet, back to the cabinet, back to the tub. Toilet, cabinet, tub; toilet, cabinet, tub, over and over, until it seemed Mallory might lose her mind.

At one turn past the cabinet, Mallory grabbed a pair of hair-trimming shears, and dove after Katie with them. She caught her in the back of the hand, opening up a wide gash. Blood splattered down onto the white tiles, like angry Englishmen against a snowy American hillside.

"Oh-ho!" Katie cried. "It's the Siege of Boston! The redcoats are coming – the redcoats are coming!"

She laughed hysterically, and started off on her rounds again.

Eventually, the people downstairs caught on to the noise, and started drifting upstairs in search of the cause. They clustered together in the bathroom doorway, watching the unfolding scene in bewilderment and awe. Mallory's new toy stood at their head in her blue paisley dress, looking on in astonishment. It was clear she was beginning to wonder whether she hadn't bitten off more than she could chew.

"Mallory, dear," one of the women said cautiously. "What in the world is going on?"

"Don't just stand there, Victoria!" Mallory screeched, turning on the woman in fury, and looking at her as if she were every bit as responsible for the fiasco as Katie herself. "Help me!"

But Victoria didn't seem to appreciate this generous slathering about of guilt and blame. Why, she'd only been sitting innocently downstairs, sipping at her chardonnay. Who was Mallory Kent to look at *her* that way?

"Well, I don't know about the rest of you ladies," she said pointedly, "but I've had enough of this little party. I'm going home."

Some of the other women *harrumphed,* and began to follow Victoria down the staircase. A few hung back, looking uncertainly from the distraught Mallory to the departing entourage. But, finally, they all opted to follow after the escapees.

All except Miss Blue Paisley, that was. She stood open-mouthed in the bright doorway, obviously unsure as to what it was she was supposed to be doing. It seemed she was considering diving after Katie in an attempt to restrain her; but after thinking about it for a moment, she appeared to doubt the wisdom of the attempt. She was a little longer, but Katie was a little heavier, and much lither. It didn't seem to be a choice match-up.

"Are you just going to stand there?" Mallory screamed at the young woman. "Aren't you going to help me?"

The young woman looked from Mallory to Katie, then from Katie to Mallory, back and forth until it seemed she might get whiplash. Then, her voice issued from the top of her throat, so soft it could scarcely be heard. "What do you want me to do?" she asked.

"Heart of a lion, that one," Katie said with a wild laugh, pouring another bottle down the toilet, and flushing it in satisfaction.

This left many bottles still untampered with – but Katie felt that she'd done enough. She'd caused Mallory a good deal of unhappiness, and that was sufficient. So she staggered back to the cabinet, scooped up a dozen or so of the bottles, and crammed them all into the pockets of her trench coat.

There was blood everywhere. The wound on the back of Katie's hand was more serious than she'd realized, and it wept red tears all over the shining white floor, creating an even more perfect picture of disorder.

Mallory didn't say anything else. She just watched Katie with hatred, as she tripped towards the bathroom door, nodded cordially to the young woman in blue paisley, and then went laughing out of the house.

Chapter 3

A particularly loud note from the boom-box called her back to reality, and she lay staring at the prescription bottle in her hand.

I shouldn't, she thought. *Not while I'm watching the brat.*

She vacillated for a few moments between the right and the wrong of it – but finally, she shrugged it all off, and popped off the bottle cap.

She'd already downed half of the merlot, and was feeling rather light and airy. Now she popped two Nembutal, and then lay back against the pillows.

Her heartbeat slowed, but her eyes remained open, staring up at the cream-colored ceiling. There were no images on the ceiling, no cloistered memories painting themselves against the plaster in this particularly subdued moment. She was lying flat, but at the same time she was floating, nearer to the ceiling, nearer to a little black hole that was yawning open in its center.

It was like the dark spiral in a YouTube video on how to hypnotize yourself. It opened up there in the middle, very small at first, but then it grew wider and wider, encompassing more and more of the creamcolored ceiling.

There was nothing showing in the spiral. There was nothing but the darkness.

But then, quite suddenly, Mallory Kent's face appeared in the middle of the spiral. It sneered cruelly, and held up a pale, fine-boned hand to wave one of Katie's books around.

Katie screamed loudly, and threw her glass at the ceiling. It shattered into hundreds of miniscule pieces, and then fell down in a shower, over the floor and the bed. Katie averted her face just in time to avoid getting glass in her eyes.

She should've known the little brat would hear it. There was a sudden pounding at the door of the guest room – *bang bang bang!*

Who knew a little kid could knock that loudly?

"What do you want?" Katie hollered.

"What are you doing in there?" Lockwood shouted.

"It's none of your damned business!"

"I'll tell Mom and Dad!"

"Go ahead!"

"Just try me, you haughty bitch!"

Katie stopped dead at those words. What in the world kind of seven-year-old *says* something like that? What sort of movies was she watching, anyway?

Katie went to the locked door, and leaned her head down against it. "Look, Lockwood," she said. "I'm tired. Just go to bed."

"I don't want to go to bed," the little girl said in a wheedling voice. "I want to play."

She paused for a long moment, and then added in a sinister tone: "Come and play with me, Katie."

She sounded like the kid in *The Omen*. Or creepy little Gage in Stephen King's *Pet Sematary*.

Either one was just as bad.

"No, Lockwood," Katie said firmly. "Go to bed."

"If you don't come and play with me," Lockwood stated, her voice rising significantly, "I'll whack my face against the corner of the coffee table, and say that you hit me."

Katie was stunned. She didn't know what to say.

"Please come out, Katie," the little girl said quietly.

A long moment of silence. Katie was almost beginning to doubt that she'd correctly heard what the kid had said, when she started pounding on the door, shouting, "Let me in, you nasty lesbian whore!"

Katie had had it. She swung the door open, and stood towering over the little demon, five feet eight inches to Lockwood's four-foot height.

"What is the *matter* with you?" she demanded. "Did your mother teach you to say that?"

The little girl stood with her feet planted crookedly, and her small hands twined behind her back. She looked innocently up into her half-sister's face. "I don't know what you mean, Katie," she said.

"Whatever," Katie said. Her voice was a little shaky. Lockwood had thrown her for a loop, and there was no concealing it. The kid seemed to know it, too.

"What's the matter, Katie?" she asked sweetly. "Don't you want to come and watch TV with me?"

"No," Katie replied. "I want to go to bed. You can – you can do whatever you want."

"Can I have a bowl of ice cream?"

"Sure."

"Can I sit in Daddy's chair?"

"Knock yourself out."

"Can I watch the show about the blood?"

Katie had just been about to shut the door in the kid's face – when that last question made her pause. She pulled the door open again, and looked down at Lockwood in astonishment.

"What did you say?" she asked.

Lockwood kept her hands behind her back, and pulled her arms tight, swishing her little feet like a young hussy trying to get a shot of whiskey from her prohibitionist aunt.

"Daddy keeps the TV locked up," she said. "All that's on right now is stupid SpongeBob SquarePants."

"What's wrong with that?" Katie asked.

"That's for babies," Lockwood answered, twisting her face in disgust. "I want to watch something else."

"What do you want to watch?"

Lockwood stared with unblinking eyes up into Katie's face. "I want to watch the show about the blood," she repeated plainly.

"So go and watch it," Katie said quickly, trying to shut the door again.

But the kid stuck her tennis shoe in between the door and the jamb. If it hurt to have her foot caught like that, she showed no sign of it.

"You have to unlock the TV," she said. "You have to punch in the code."

"If Dad set up that code," Katie said, "it was because there were certain things he didn't want you to watch."

"Daddy doesn't know me," Lockwood said in an ominous voice, swishing her little feet around again. "No one does."

"Go and watch cartoons," Katie said. "Have your ice cream. Then go to bed."

She tried to shut the door once more – but this time, Lockwood stopped the door with her arm. It caught in the jamb with a sickening crunch, but she never made a sound. She just kept looking up at Katie with that same blank expression.

"I want to watch my show," she said. "Go put in the code."

"No," Katie replied.

"Do it," Lockwood said, "or I'll tell Daddy you hit me."

"He won't believe you."

Lockwood watched Katie for a long moment, searching the depths of her eyes for something. It made Katie uncomfortable.

"People will believe anything," Lockwood stated in a clear, calm voice.

Katie stared at her. She was still dumbfounded, still at a loss for words.

But Lockwood remedied the situation for her. She threw the door open, smacking Katie in the chin with it, and stomping her tiny feet.

"Damn it!" she cried. "Damn it, damn it, damn it!"

Katie watched her in disbelief. "What are you *doing?"* she demanded.

"You make me sick!" Lockwood cried. "You make me sick, you nasty whore! You nasty lesbian!"

She stopped stomping for a moment, and looked with unblinking eyes up into Katie's face. "I know what you nasty lesbians do," she whispered. "Mommy told me."

Katie couldn't take anymore. She hauled back her arm, and slapped the kid across the face. She must have done it harder than she meant to, because an angry red welt sprang up immediately on Lockwood's pale cheek.

"Oh, my God," Katie spluttered. "I'm – I'm sorry, Lockwood."

The child was silent for a moment, staring straight ahead of her at the wall. Then, all of a sudden, she began to scream, stomping all around again.

"Nasty lesbian!" she shouted. "Nasty lesbian whore!"

"Stop it, Lockwood!" Katie pleaded, stepping out into the corridor to try to lay her hands on the unruly child. "Calm down!"

The kid quit stomping, and started hopping up and down, up and down, like a kangaroo on cocaine.

"Nasty lesbian whore!"

There was a large doll lying on the carpet nearby. It had been lying there for days – lying there looking up with its dead glass eyes. Axel had asked Lockwood to pick it up, and she'd refused. So he'd left it there, trying to teach her a lesson.

And there it was – looking up with its dead glass eyes.

While Lockwood was hopping all around in a rage, she tripped over the doll. It was bigger than her two feet put together, and it knocked her off balance.

She was extremely close to the staircase. She teetered to the right, and Katie sprang forward to grab hold of her arm.

But she wasn't fast enough. She narrowly missed snatching the purple fabric of Lockwood's Tshirt. The child continued to teeter, farther and farther to the right, like a speeded-up stop-motion animation video.

Katie snatched at her again, but it was too late. The kid had already fallen.

Katie watched in horror as she tumbled to the bottom. Even worse were the sounds that her little bones made. *Crunch, crunch, crunch – snap, snap, snap.*

In what seemed like less than a moment, Lockwood was lying in the entryway at the foot of the stairs. Several of her limbs twisted out at unnatural angles. A dark red pool spread out around her small head.

Katie stood motionless at the top of the stairs. She thought of calling for help – but she couldn't move. Two violins, two violas, and two cellos swelled their magnificent notes through the darkened, gloomy corridor behind her, and the red pool around the little girl's head continued to spread.

***

They found her there, more than an hour later. Everything was quiet. The CD had stopped playing a long time ago.

Axel and Regina came into the flat. Regina started screaming. She flew up the stairs, and tried to wrap her hands around Katie's throat, but Axel pulled her off. He kept her at bay until the police and the paramedics got there.

There was a cop on Katie's left-hand side; a paramedic on her right.

"What happened here?" the cop demanded.

"How are you feeling?" the paramedic asked.

"Did you have anything to do with this?" the cop shouted.

"Do you need medical attention?" the paramedic inquired.

In the end, the cop trumped the paramedic. Katie had been catatonic since they came in – and in the absence of an explanation, they arrested her. The cop slapped a pair of handcuffs on her, led her out of the flat, and hauled her down the corridor to the elevator.

Out in the chilly October night, the cop pushed her into a squad car, while her father watched miserably from the front doors of the building. A little crowd of tenants was gathering in the front lobby, wondering what was going on. Regina was glaring down from the living room window two floors up.

Katie knew Regina had always hated Lockwood. She suspected she was only grateful for an acceptable reason to show her hatred for *Katie*.

The squad car pulled away from the building, with its lights flashing, but its siren off. Katie looked wistfully back at the high-rise.

She wondered if she'd ever see it again.

It turned out that she wouldn't.

***

The night Katie spent in jail was the longest of her life. There was this one woman named Martha Jane – and she turned out to be Katie's worst nightmare. She was big as a quarterback, and she had a wooden spoon she'd gotten from a cook named Emma Dee.

Martha Jane took a liking to Katie right away, and herded her over into a corner of the cell, where she got way too friendly with the wooden spoon.

Katie thought she might have internal bleeding. There was a fierce, fiery pain shooting from her rectum to her abdomen – and she thought she was going to bleed to death out of her ass. It was the most humiliating way she could have thought to die.

But, by the time old Martha Jane was snoring in the top bunk, Katie realized that she'd stopped bleeding. Her sweatpants were stained beyond repair – but what the hell.

The next morning, one of the guards came to unlock the cell. "Katrina Throckmorton," he said. "You've been released on bail."

As it turned out, the mayor of Boston himself had had a hand in Katie's release. Regina's former husband had been extremely wealthy, and when he left

Regina, Marty Walsh made a habit of checking on his ex-wife. In this way, he became friends with Axel Throckmorton.

Axel begged for Walsh to help Katie. Walsh was skeptical, but he was fond of Axel. So he pulled a few strings.

Next morning, Katie was free. Her trial was scheduled for the following Monday.

The judge was named Wallbecker. He was a hard-ass – but with Marty Walsh's suggestion, and Axel's heartfelt testimony, he ruled that Katie would be sent to Greystone Asylum for at least six years. There was no jury present. Another string pulled by Walsh.

Official verdict: Third degree murder. Katrina Throckmorton was responsible for the death of her half-sister Lockwood, but the murder was not intentional. The incident was caused by Katrina's drug and alcohol abuse, which stemmed from some longignored disorder of the mind.

Walsh's suggestion was pointed, and Axel's testimony was complicated. Even better, Regina never showed up. She was probably at home drinking martinis and watching Real Housewives.

Chapter 4

The November morning was fresh and brisk – the perfect sort of morning to don one's coat, and take a long walk beneath the colorful leaves.

But Katie wasn't taking a walk. She was sitting in the passenger seat of a police car, traveling at a steady speed towards Greystone Asylum.

Her chauffeur was Officer James Humphreys, the head guard of the jail where she'd spent the night. He was a good man, she could tell. He kept shooting apologetic glances towards the side of her face, clearly hoping she'd understand how sorry he was. Sorry, she knew, because he didn't think she'd killed Lockwood. Slapped her, that was for certain; was probably a drug addict, and a drunkard more likely, but not a *murderer*. There was a bit of a difference, so far as that was concerned. At least – so far as Officer Humphreys was concerned.

He was a very different sort of man, and Katie liked him immensely. It was hard to realize it, considering her current predicament – but she figured it out later on. Humphreys was a tall, stout African who hailed from Nigeria, whose mother was a native, and whose father was a white politician. Officer Humphreys could have had a career in politics, if he'd wanted one, but he didn't much care for the things his father did. He preferred to watch over the half-mad, half-high delinquents in one of Boston's busiest jails, for a very modest salary, making it so he could say he left more behind him than he took away.

Though he'd been brought to America when he was very small, his mother had taught him English, and he had a mild Nigerian accent. He spoke to Katie, now, and in spite of her terror and despondency, his compassionate voice made her smile.

"I'm sorry, Miss Throckmorton, for what's happened to you," he said earnestly. "I don't believe you deserve it. Many things that happen to us in life, we do not deserve – but they happen, anyway. I hope you will be strong enough to overcome it."

"Thank you, Officer," Katie said in a slightly tearful voice, turning her face abashedly towards the window.

"I say that I hope you will be strong enough," he said, in a more meaningful voice, "because I know what kind of place Greystone Asylum is. It's a hard place – a dark place."

Katie looked at him with narrowed eyes. "Aren't all asylums what you'd call *dark* places?" she asked.

"Ah," he said, trying to laugh it off a bit, "of course they are, Miss Throckmorton. I only beg you to tread carefully, in *this* place. It is not such a remote, outof-the-way place for no reason at all. It's a hard place."

With the repetition of these four words, he fell silent, and Katie couldn't find the courage to ask any more.

The road they traveled was a narrow, rutted road, full of potholes, with asphalt that looked more than fifty years old. It led into the farthest reaches of Hyde Park, where the thick woodland claimed its reign, and the sounds of the city were all swallowed up. There were the calls of birds in the trees overhead, and the chirping of the early-morning crickets – but other than that, the world was in a hush, with only the tall trees to remind you that you were still alive.

Katie usually loved woodland areas like this one, but today, of course, she got absolutely no enjoyment from the surrounding trees and shadows. Today, it all looked very sinister, and very cruel. Today, it all looked wrong.

The road wound and wound, in and out. Bend after bend, Katie expected to see the asylum looming out of the bright, clear light. But, even though she was expecting it, its actual appearance startled her more than she could have anticipated.

Whatever she'd expected – she hadn't expected *this*. All of a sudden, from out of nowhere, there appeared an unbelievably vast structure, innately Gothic in design, and looking like something out of a Charlotte Brontë novel. Black ravens – wouldn't you know it – whorled all above the building, some settling on the roof, but most simply flying in dizzying circles, and crying out violently.

"Here it is," Humphreys said softly. "Greystone Asylum."

Katie looked at the building with a pinched face, her fists furled in her lap, her left eye twitching slightly. "I didn't know places like this still existed," she muttered.

"Oh, they do," Humphreys assured her. "They're few and far between, but they're there. Judge Wallbecker made sure you weren't headed to any plush resort, poor girl. He sent you to Greystone – and he knew what he was doing."

Katie shivered horribly. She wrapped her arms around herself, but tried to do it subtly, so that Humphreys wouldn't know how scared she was.

The officer pulled off the rutted asphalt road, and into the wide gravel lot that stretched across the front of Greystone Asylum. He positioned the car sideways in front of the broad double doors, and shifted into park.

"Here we are," he said ruefully. "It's time to go."

Katie nodded absently, looking towards the steering wheel. "You know," she said, "I used to love to drive. It's not easy to do, in Boston – but I still loved it." She paused, and her face darkened like a storm cloud. "I'll probably never drive again," she added softly.

"Don't say that," Humphreys said encouragingly, chucking her under the chin with his beefy finger, and trying to smile warmly. "You'll drive again, my dear."

He looked seriously into her face, and added, "You'll live again."

"Thank you, Officer," Katie said in a broken voice, pushing open the car door, and planting her feet in the loose gravel of the lot. With her back to him, she said: "I appreciate your saying that – but you'll forgive me for not wanting to hope."

"Hope," Humphreys said clearly, in a significant voice that made Katie look back at him, "is being able to see that there is light despite all of the darkness."

So said Desmond Tutu, the South African civil rights activist. From anyone else, the quote would have made Katie sneer. But coming from Humphreys, it filled her with a flickering flame that lasted until she reached the doors of the asylum, and then, for a long while, went out.

"Thank you, Officer," she said quietly.

"This is a hard place," he repeated. "But it is also a place of wisdom. If *you* are wise, you might find more than you bargained for."

"What do you mean by that?" Katie asked.

"I'm referring to the warden," Humphreys said. "His name is Karl Diederich. He is a German, and he is very brilliant. He was educated at all the best schools, and he is extremely liberal in his opinions. If you make a friend of him – as I feel you might do, considering how intelligent you are – you might have an easier time of it."

"You think well of Diederich?" Katie asked wonderingly.

"For the most part," Humphreys replied. "Yes, I do."

"I suppose that's *something*," Katie murmured, glancing back towards the formidable building.

So they started on their way. Humphreys got out of the car, and Katie followed suit. She opened the door to the backseat, and pulled out her suitcase.

They had made it halfway to the steep front steps, when suddenly Humphreys stopped in his tracks, and smacked his forehead.

"I forgot the cigars," he said.

"What cigars?" Katie asked in confusion.

"I said before that I know Dr. Diederich," Humphreys explained. He clearly had much more to tell; but he hesitated before saying anything else. He looked at the old asylum for a long moment, his face covered with a strange cloud. It was clear he was brooding over something that affected him profoundly.

"The doctor and I have not seen one another in years," he finally went on, "but we have met two times before. On the first occasion, he offered me a fine Italian cigar, as well as a glass of what he called *Obstwasser*. Fruit water. But, let me tell you – it was hardly fruity, and there was nothing like water about it. The doctor seemed to enjoy my company, and we sat for a long while, talking about his asylum.

"I had come to deliver two young sisters who were found in an abandoned van on the side of the highway. The van was covered with blood, but the girls themselves were unharmed, and there was no one else to be found. No one else ever *was* found.

"I brought the girls, who were twins, about thirteen years old at that time – and I handed them over to Dr. Diederich. They had been acting very strangely, ever since they were taken out of the van. Even before that – they were found in the van's middle seat, side by side, their bloody hands in their laps, their bloody hair hanging down in their faces, looking straight ahead out of the bloody windshield. I never heard them say a single word.

"It was decided that they should be brought to Greystone. I was the one assigned to do the job. I was a very young man then. I was shaken by what I had seen, but the doctor braced me up with a drink, and then sat me down to talk. He is very amiable, and very down-to-earth, for such a prominent physician.

"Two years later I made another delivery: a young man who had tried to kill himself in his jail cell. Somehow he'd managed to swallow one of his shoelaces before they locked him up. When he was alone, he made himself vomit, and then attempted to hang himself from the window bars."

He paused, and passed a hand over his face. "By that time, though," he went on, "I was used to seeing things like that. It was obvious I didn't need comforting, but it seemed that the doctor wished to speak with me, anyway." He smiled a little proudly, and added, "He said he had appreciated my conversation during our previous visit. So we sat down again, and talked even longer, this time. It was that second talk, I think, that had the greatest impact on me. It was like talking with some great figure whose words can change your very life! Someone like Gandhi, or Mandela."

He looked away into the trees for a moment, and his eyes glazed over with the memory. But then he cleared his throat, and looked back at Katie.

"Let me just go and fetch the cigars," he said hastily, shaking his large, dark head in a perturbed fashion. "Italian cigars," he added, as if searching for something inconsequential to say, so as to draw attention away from his obvious infatuation with the doctor. "The doctor favors Italian cigars," he explained. "There are no German cigars, really, so he settles for what is at least European."

He ducked back towards the car without another word.

Katie watched him for a moment, as he opened the passenger door, and got into the car. He sat for a long moment, with his fingers outstretched towards the glovebox, but not quite connecting with it. It seemed he might stay that way for a few long moments, so Katie turned back towards the great asylum, and took a few cautious steps towards it.

The dry gravel crunched like broken bones under the soles of her sneakers. At the sudden sound, a huge crow *cawed* in a high tree nearby. He looked accusingly down at Katie, as if he were asking why she had come to disturb his peace.

She would have told him she would much rather be – well, *anywhere* else. But soon, he lost interest in her, and flew away. She wondered, for a moment, where he was going; but then she lost interest, too, and went back on her way.

It was a peculiar circumstance. She spent a brief moment contemplating it: that here she was, a lone woman sentenced to imprisonment in Greystone Asylum, and there was her escort, a kindly police officer who had been delayed by a box of Italian cigars. Cigars he intended to share with the director of the asylum, an alleged German intellect called Karl Diederich.

Katie wondered about Dr. Diederich. What had Humphreys said, about making friends with him? About things going easier for her?

All of a sudden, she couldn't remember – for the broad, grey face of the asylum was looming before her. The wide steps were mere feet away.

She stepped forward, once, twice, and then mounted the first stair. She stepped again, and again, climbing the steep stone staircase. It was like the staircase of a Roman temple: just as ominous, and just as vast.

Finally, she came to the top. She looked back, and saw Officer Humphreys, still meditating in the passenger seat of the police car.

She looked down, and saw a rectangular steel buzzer beside the door. She stared at it for a moment, and then stretched out a finger to push it. She heard the soft sound it made, like an angry bumblebee wrapped in linen.

All she could think was that it was a peculiar circumstance. Very peculiar indeed . . .

The door clicked, and she reached to pull it open. There was a small glass vestibule before her, about the size of two phone booths side by side. In front of her there was another door, but no more buzzer. She pulled the door open, and found herself in a chilly entryway tiled with dirty beige squares. Perhaps the dirty beige squares had even been white, long ago.

The walls were the color of misery. It was an inexplicable color, somewhere between the eggshell hue of Queen Regina's living room, and the sickly color of a cue ball in a very old tavern that had seen a lot of cigarette smoke.

Katie looked up. She saw a large desk, oblong in circumference, attached to the wall so that no one on the outside could get in. It was very high, and had Plexiglas windows that reached to the dingy ceiling.

A very small woman in a nurse's uniform sat behind the Plexiglas. She looked up at Katie as she came in, and smiled at her. Obviously, she thought Katie was someone very different from who she actually *was*.

"Hello," she said to Katie, through a little speaker that was set on the desk in front of her. "How can I help you?"

Katie didn't know what to say. What was she supposed to tell the woman? *Oh, hi. I'm the new loony.*

She shouldn't have come in by herself. What had she been thinking?

There was just something about the strange old place. It had called her forward like an unwary spider into a Venus flytrap.

She hefted her suitcase in her hand, and shifted her weight uncomfortably from foot to foot.

There was the sudden sound of clicking shoe soles on the hard tile floor. Then something buzzed. Katie looked up, and saw a door behind the Plexiglas swing open. A fifty-something-year-old woman walked into the little space the nurse occupied, said a few words to her, and then passed her a clipboard with a sheaf of papers attached to it.

The nurse nodded, and then gestured towards Katie through the Plexiglas. She said something to the other woman.

The other woman looked up at Katie, and watched her for a moment. Katie stared back.

The woman punched a code into a keypad beside the door to the nurse's cubicle. There was another buzz, and then the door swung open. The fifty-something woman stepped out into the lobby, and smiled professionally at Katie.

A doctor, Katie thought with a sinking feeling.

"Hello," the woman said. "May I ask your name?"

Katie didn't answer. She couldn't think of what to say, despite the fact that the question had been a fairly simple one.

She was saved from her momentary dumbness, however, when the door opened behind her, and Officer Humphreys came in.

"Ah!" he exclaimed in his deep, booming voice. "Dr. Halstead! What a pleasure to see you again."

The doctor smiled lightly, and nodded. "Hello, James," she said familiarly.

Humphreys walked up to her, and held out his hand. She shook it warmly. It was clear that she liked him.

"Now tell me, Cora," he said in a confidential tone. "How have things been?"

"Nothing to complain about, I'm sure," the woman replied, still with that same light attitude.

"That's very good," Humphreys said. "I'm glad to hear it. But now – I must carry out my duty."

He smiled a little sadly, and gestured back at Katie, who was standing a few feet behind them.

"Dr. Halstead," he said, "allow me to introduce Miss Katrina Throckmorton. Checking in for your first-class accommodations."

Katie couldn't help but smile, and neither could the doctor, apparently. She laid a hand on the officer's arm, and then stepped forward to meet Katie.

"Miss Throckmorton," she said. "It's a pleasure to meet you. I was fairly sure who you were, because you're the only arrival today. And, aside from that, you're my new patient."

Katie looked into the woman's face. Not an old-looking face, but a tired-looking one. Her dark eyes were burned out. There wasn't much luster left in them. But her skin was beautiful, pale as powder, with just enough color of life in her cheeks to remind you she still had some fight in her. Her black hair shone brilliantly, perhaps with pomade, bound up behind her head like the hair of an English schoolteacher. She wasn't very tall, maybe about five-four.

She smelled like rose water and lavender, powder and aloe. Almost like a garden at the height of spring.

Katie shook herself, realizing that the woman had said something to her.

"I beg your pardon," Katie murmured. "What did you say?"

"I asked you if you'd like me to show you to your room," the doctor said with an uncertain smile.

Katie looked away from the woman, suddenly sensing the reality of the situation, and feeling as if a load of rocks had been dumped down over her shoulders. This doctor, and this police officer – they weren't her friends. No matter how kindly the officer spoke, and no matter how pleasantly the doctor smelled, it wasn't of any consequence.

Katie was about to be imprisoned. Maybe she'd never see the outside world again. Six years, the judge had said – but once they locked you away in a place like this, who was to say they'd ever let you out again?

"I won't say that I'd like it," Katie stated in response to the doctor's inquiry. "But I don't suppose I have any choice, so I won't argue with you."

She looked at the doctor with a blank expression.

"Well," the woman said, "that's as good an attitude as any. But I'm afraid I have to ask for your suitcase."

"What?"

"Someone's going to have to go through it, before it can be brought to your room. Just to make sure you don't have any prohibited items."

"Oh," Katie returned in a dull voice. The idea that someone would be going through her suitcase made her feel very oppressed. "So I suppose they're going to take the box of wine I've got in here?"

The doctor didn't reply. She was obviously too used to people's bitterness to even let it faze her.

Katie didn't offer any argument when the doctor came to take her suitcase. She gave it to the woman behind the Plexiglas, and then came back to Katie.

Officer Humphreys seemed to realize that it was time for Katie to go. He came near to her, and appeared to want to lay a hand on her shoulder; but she just looked at him with a pair of dead eyes, and his hand fell away.

"Goodbye, Katie," he murmured. "I know we will see each other again someday."

"Maybe you'll be first on the scene," Katie replied absently, already starting after the doctor, "when they come to haul my body away."

She looked back over her shoulder, and added in a clipped voice, "Enjoy your cigars with the doctor."

***

Katie left Humphreys staring after her with a dumbfounded expression, and followed after Dr. Halstead, as the older woman passed through a door in the glass wall between the lobby and the adjoining corridor.

"The South Corridor," she explained. "If you look this way, you'll see that it opens up onto the cafeteria and the Community Room."

She pointed to two wide doorways, one leading to a large area filled with lunchroom tables, another leading to a big room crammed with comfortablelooking chairs.

Katie didn't care how comfortable they looked. She never wanted to sit in them.

"The East and West Corridors house the patient dormitories," the doctor went on. "The North Corridor is where you'll find the doctors' offices."

She looked back at Katie, and said, "The women's rooms are in the West Corridor. Follow me." She started off to the left, and Katie followed after her.

The doctor led her to the end of the South Corridor, and then took a right. They went about halfway down the second corridor, until the doctor stopped at an open doorway on the left-hand.

"You're allowed to close the door, if you like," she said. "Lydia just likes to hear the sound of the people passing."

Katie furrowed her brows, and followed the doctor into the room. It was medium-sized, not claustrophobic, with two twin-beds made up with thin white blankets. The windows were covered with iron bars.

There was a young woman sitting cross-legged on the bed nearest the door, with a large sketchpad laid on the blanket in front of her, and a charcoal pencil in her hand. Her whole hand, and parts of the blanket, were covered with charcoal. She even had black smudges on her small, pixie-like face.

She had short black hair, and pale white skin. She looked up at Katie with a start, and then glanced questioningly at Dr. Halstead.

"It's all right, Lydia," the doctor said. "This is your new roommate. Her name is Katrina."

The pale young woman looked so frightened, Katie forgot her surliness for a moment. "You can call me Katie," she offered.

The dark-haired girl looked up at her, and smiled shyly. Her cheeks flushed bright red, and she went back to drawing in her book.

The doctor looked back at Katie, apparently surprised. But Katie certainly hadn't been trying to win *her* approval. She looked away, and lugged her suitcase over to the second bed.

When the doctor realized that Katie didn't intend to say anything more to her, she cleared her throat quietly, and said, "All right, then. If you need anything, just make your way down to the nurse in the South Corridor."

She paused, waiting for Katie to respond. But she didn't.

"I'm sure you won't be feeling up to much of anything today," the doctor went on. "We'll leave you alone for now. Tomorrow morning at nine, an orderly will come to take you to group. After that, though, you'll be expected to show up every morning on your own. There are wireless alarm clocks on your night stands."

She waited for a moment, obviously thinking that Katie might say something. But she didn't, so the doctor turned and left. Her shoes clacked loudly against the tile, the sound growing fainter and fainter as she moved away, until everything was quiet.

Katie sat down on the second bed, and glanced at the pale young woman. "How long have you had this room to yourself?" she asked.

"A few months now," the girl answered quietly. "The last girl said I was weird. No one wants to share a room with me."

She hung her head, and made some violent strokes on the paper in front of her.

"Your name is – Lydia?" Katie inquired. "That's what the doctor said?"

The young woman looked up quickly, clearly surprised that Katie had remembered her name. "Yes," she said softly.

"Well," Katie said with a smile, "you look pretty normal to me. And, if you ask me – everyone in this world is weird. No one should be judging anybody else. Don't you think?"

The dark-haired girl smiled cautiously, and then nodded.

"Good," Katie said. "We're on the same page, then. I think that means we're going to make good roommates."

The pale young woman smiled more brightly, now, and blushed again. She looked away quickly, and went on with her drawing.

Chapter 5

Next morning, Katie sat upright on her hard little bed, waiting for the orderly to come and fetch her. The doctor had said he'd come at nine.

Lydia had left early in the morning. Apparently, they started letting people outside at seven-thirty. Lydia said there was a small garden in the back, only full of dead things at this time of year, but still a bright, fresh place that was better for thinking than anywhere else in the hospital.

There was a pamphlet lying on Katie's night table: a schedule of her daily appointments. She hadn't really bothered to look at it yet.

She glanced at the wireless alarm clock on the bedside table. It was almost nine.

She'd slept terribly. Every time she drifted off, she was startled awake by a horrible nightmare, and then wary to fall asleep again, for fear that the dreams might come back. But eventually, she got so tired that she dozed off – and a few minutes later, she woke with a start, trying to forget the horrid images that were painted behind her eyelids.

There was a knock at the open door, and Katie jumped. She looked to see a tall, thin young man standing in the doorway.

"Hi," he said. "You're Katie?" Katie nodded.

"I'm here to take you to your group," he told her.

Katie didn't like the way he was looking at her. Too much like the way Mallory's friends used to look at her: coveting her while she sat on Mallory's lap.

Not much left to covet, Katie thought bitterly. *What the hell is he looking at?*

Katie hadn't showered yet. She still had a little powdered foundation smudged over her cheeks, though the bridge of her nose was shiny. She'd wiped the smeared eyeliner from under her eyes, but there was still a dark outline around them, making them pop a little. She should've washed it all off when she got up that morning, but she'd known that once she did, there'd be no more makeup for the foreseeable future.

So she'd left it.

"Well, come on," the young orderly said with a smile.

Katie stood up warily, her slip-on sneakers moving quietly across the tiled floor. She met the orderly at the door, but kept her distance. "I'll follow you," she said.

"All right," he said with a self-assured grin. Katie's stomach rolled.

He led her down the dim corridor, only faintly lit at this early hour. The fluorescent lights had gone off, but the sunlight wasn't shining properly through the windows yet. The light was still down at the east end of the building.

Katie had gotten pretty used to those fluorescent lights, the night before. It seemed that Lydia liked to leave the bedroom door open at night, as well as in the daytime. She liked to have the light, as well as the occasional sound of a nurse's footsteps in the corridor.

Not that the light from the corridor was enough for her. She was terrified of the dark, and she was in the habit of leaving the bathroom light on, too. It was kind of annoying, but Katie didn't want to be mean. She figured she could get used to it.

When she and the orderly came to the end of the women's hall, they turned left, into the South Corridor. The orderly led her down the passage, past the cafeteria, and past the door that led out into the lobby. He stopped at the doorway that led to the big room with the comfortable-looking chairs.

"The Community Room," he announced.

Katie looked around, and saw dozens of people. Some of them were standing, just looking blankly out the windows in the far wall. Some of them were sitting, and quietly watching the television that was bolted to an anchor above their heads. Some just sat and talked to themselves.

Katie tried not to look at *them*.

She followed the orderly across the room, to a circle of different-colored saucer chairs beneath what seemed to be the brightest window: the one least smeared by dirt and bird dung.

It was a circle of seven chairs. Seven saucer chairs, strangely modern additions in a place like this, a place that would have been the perfect setting for a Gothic horror story. Six of the chairs were occupied. One was empty. The orderly gestured to the empty chair, still grinning smugly.

Katie shot him an icy look, but he didn't flinch. She would have elbowed him in the gut if she could have gotten away with it.

One of the patients in the circle was Lydia Brock. She was doodling on her sketchpad, her knees drawn up in front of her. She was drawing with a frantic hand. Suddenly, her pencil flew away from her, and landed next to Katie's foot.

Katie picked up the pencil, and handed it to Lydia. The young woman smiled shyly, and looked away.

Katie took her place in the empty chair. A pink one. Fairly comfortable, yes – but the thing with saucer chairs was that you could always feel the metal bar under your thighs.

Katie had picked out a black faux-fur saucer chair for her reading room at Mallory Kent's house. It was her favorite kind of reading chair. She just laid a cushion over the hard metal bar.

She sat for countless hours in that chair. Winter nights, when the windows were frosty, and the baseboards were clicking as the heat came on; summer nights when the air was regulated by central airconditioning, and filled with the scent of Mallory's flowery perfume. Spring nights when the windows were thrown open to the noise of the city, and fall nights when the leaves spiraled down in orange cyclones.

Katie looked towards the asylum window. Leaves were falling, now. They fell slowly, as if they were in no hurry to get where they were going. Up in the trees, or down on the ground, it was all the same to them.

Mallory had often come in while she was reading. She said she liked to watch her read. She looked very *erudite,* she said. She often leaned down to kiss her. Sometimes she took the book away, and threw it aside, so she could sprawl in Katie's lap, and occupy the whole of her attention.

Katie shook these thoughts away, and tried to return her attention to the present moment. She couldn't quite decide which was more unpleasant: the memory of Mallory Kent, or the realization that she was stuck in a mental asylum.

Directly in front of her was the woman she'd met when she first came to Greystone. She remembered her name perfectly.

Dr. Halstead.

The woman smiled at Katie when she sat down. Her eyes lingered for a moment on Katie's face, as if she were wondering about something, but she soon looked away, and paid recognition to each of the other patients in turn.

The first was a young olive-skinned man. He looked Puerto Rican, possibly Mexican. He wore a faded black suit that looked like it had been washed many times, with a red shirt and tie underneath, and a dark grey bowler hat. He had a thin mustache above his lip.

"Good morning, Lamberto," Dr. Halstead said to him.

"Good morning, Dr. Halstead," he returned in a very friendly tone. Katie thought it was extremely odd, though, that he spoke with a British accent.

Accent's not bad, she thought, *just a little off.*

"There goes Sherlock again," said a young white man in a green polo. He shook his head in disgust, and passed a hand across his face.

"I resent that comment," Lamberto replied politely. "I am not Sherlock Holmes. My name is Lamberto Esplanade – though I admit that I am a very able detective. No doubt I could give the great Mr. Holmes a run for his money." He smirked in a debonair fashion, and then added, "Shall we say a hundred pounds?"

"Don't snap at Lamberto, Eric," Dr. Halstead said to the young white man. She spoke in a protective voice, and then smiled kindly at the young gentleman in the bowler hat. But then she looked away, and sighed almost imperceptibly.

She looked tired, Katie thought.

"Sorry, Dr. Halstead," Eric muttered.

The doctor nodded, and then looked back to Katie. Katie thought she noticed, once again, that the woman's gaze lingered for a little longer than was usual. But she may have been imagining things.

"No doubt you've all noticed that we have a new arrival," the doctor said. She looked back to Katie, and met her eyes. "Hello, Miss Throckmorton," she said with a soft smile. "Do you mind if I call you Katie?"

"No," Katie replied.

"There are forty patients here at Greystone," Dr. Halstead said. "That's not much in terms of individual asylums – but it's more than you'd usually find in a psychiatric ward of a multi-level hospital. You'll find, though, that everyone keeps pretty much to themselves."

She looked directly into Katie's face, as she said this, and Katie thought that she was lying. She suspected that she only said it because it would be a comforting thing for Katie to hear.

"The patients are divided into eight groups, at the moment," the doctor went on. "Five in each group. We try to separate all of you based on age, similarities, and whatnot. The people you see in this circle will be your personal group, not necessarily for as long as you're here, but for the foreseeable future. So try to get off on the right foot."

She smiled in what Katie knew was supposed to be an encouraging way. But Katie just looked from her to the other five patients in the circle, and she felt cold.

"Well," the young white man said, grinning wolfishly at Katie, "since you've probably already heard all you want to about Sherlock, I'll introduce myself. The name's Eric Conley."

"His dad's the DA," scoffed a twentysomething-year-old black man.

"So what?" Eric retorted.

"You almost killed that girl," the young black man said quietly, staring into the other guy's face with a venomous expression. "What I'm saying is, if your daddy wasn't Daniel Conley, you'd be in prison."

Eric leapt up from his chair, his chest heaving, his pale face flushed bright red. "I didn't do that!" he cried. "That wasn't me!"

"Sure it wasn't."

"Marcus," Dr. Halstead said warningly, looking from one young man to the other with an anxious expression.

"Fine," Marcus said curtly. "I won't talk about it, if that makes psycho white boy feel better." He leaned back in his seat, and shrugged. "But we all know he did it."

Eric lunged forward, but the doctor stood up, and positioned herself between him and Marcus. She laid a hand on his shoulder, and looked into his face. "Stop it, Eric," she said quietly. "You know you don't want to do this. Do you remember what happened last time?"

Eric froze, and a look of fear passed across his face. Katie wondered what he was thinking. Solitary confinement, maybe? Yeah, that seemed like a bummer for a narcissist like him. It would be torture not to have anyone around to admire him.

He nodded fervently, and then sat back down. The doctor watched him for a moment, then took her own seat.

Katie looked around at the three young men whose names she now knew. Then there was Lydia, and one other young woman.

The second woman was a slight Latino with raven-black hair and angry eyes. She was watching Katie suspiciously.

"It's funny that Marcus brought that up," she said. Her voice had a heavy Spanish accent. Whether she used it to make herself seem more like a tough girl from the *barrio,* Katie didn't know. She sounded like a Latin rapper.

Katie watched her carefully. She knew that she was about to start trouble.

"Eric's daddy getting him out of trouble, I mean," the young woman added in a hostile tone, staring at Katie with accusing eyes. "Because I think I know who *you* are."

"I'm sure you think you do," Katie returned quietly, looking down at the floor.

"You killed your sister," the young woman said with a cruel grin.

Katie didn't say anything.

"But *your* daddy's friends with the mayor," the young woman went on. "Marty Walsh got you out of jail – even though you broke your little sister's neck."

Katie wasn't sure whether she should protest, or keep silent. Either choice seemed to have its drawbacks. If she spoke, she might say something she didn't mean to say. She might make the whole situation worse than it already was. If she kept quiet, though, people might think she was guilty. She didn't know what to do.

The circle was quiet for a long moment after the young Hispanic woman spoke. But finally, someone said something.

It was Lydia. She had been drawing up until the point when the young Hispanic woman started badgering Katie. Then she lowered her knees, which had been serving as an easel for her sketchpad, and she started looking from Katie to the hostile young woman.

"Cut it out, Carmen," she said in a tired voice. "Why do you have to judge everyone all the time? Why can't you just leave people alone?"

Carmen looked at her viciously. "You're just mad because nobody loves you," she spat. "No one even cared when you jumped off that stupid building."

Lydia hung her head. Then she drew her knees up to her chin, and hid her face.

Eric grinned smugly. He'd recovered quickly from his brief fit of anxiety.

"You're one to talk," he said to Carmen. "You slit your wrists in the middle of a convenience store, and your boyfriend left you there to die."

He laughed with sincere amusement, while Carmen scowled darkly.

Eric looked over at Katie, and said, "She and her boyfriend *Ignacio* were going to rob a gas station. They hadn't even gotten the money from the clerk yet – and Latino Bonnie over here starts yelling at numbnuts Clyde, something about how he didn't really care about her, or some crap like that. All he cared about was the money, though, and he told her to leave him alone. So she tried to kill herself – right under the fluorescent lights, right in front of the security cameras!"

He laughed wildly, slapping his hands on his knees. Finally, he sat back in his chair, and wiped the water from his eyes.

"Ah," he said lightly. "I never get tired of telling that one."

"You piece of shit," Carmen hissed.

"Let's watch our tempers," Dr. Halstead advised.

"Why?" Eric asked with a broad smile. "I want to see what happens when she gets *really* mad. Maybe she'll cut herself up again! Will you do that, Carmen? Will you carve yourself up like a Thanksgiving turkey? I doubt they'll make us turkey in this place. We can eat you instead!"

He started to laugh again: that same manic, wild laughter. But eventually, he began to choke, and he had to quiet himself. He straightened up in his chair, breathing deeply, his eyes shining with a feral light.

"You're a damned mess," Carmen said. She frowned in disdain, and looked away towards the grey windows.

Everyone in the circle looked miserable. Eric, Carmen and Marcus were strung taut as piano wire; Lydia was sobbing into her knees; and Lamberto was sulking in his chair, upset that everyone was ignoring him. As for Dr. Halstead, she looked more tired than ever.

Katie watched all these people with a deep frowned etched across her face.

What in the world was she going to do?

She was just asking herself this imperative question, and feeling as if she didn't have the slightest hope of answering it, when one of the doors to the large room swung open, and a tall, thin man walked in.

He wore a long white coat, had short, fair hair, and a very erudite expression.

She would have bet a million dollars – if she had a million dollars – that *that* was the head of the hospital. Dr. Karl Diederich.

He laced his hands behind his back, and meandered in and out of the eight circles, sometimes stopping to listen, or to smile gently. Every now and then, he reached down, and squeezed a patient's shoulder.

When he passed by Dr. Halstead's circle, he nodded to the doctor, and then ran his eyes quickly over the patients. His eyes lingered on Katie, because he'd never seen her before.

He stared at her for a moment, then tipped his head politely, and went on his way. But something about the gesture made her shiver.

Chapter 6

After the group meeting, the patients were released from the Community Room, and given leave to go wherever they wanted. They could go to their rooms; they could go outside; or they could stick around and watch TV until lunch.

Katie was one of the last people to leave the circle. After everyone else had gone, only she and Lydia Brock were left. The other girl had retreated into herself again, and was sketching furiously.

Katie walked up to the young woman, feeling hesitant.

"Lydia?" she said.

The dark-haired girl looked up at her shyly. She made a few violent motions on her sketchpad, and then looked back at Katie with a sigh.

"Hi," she murmured.

"Want to take a walk?" Katie asked.

Lydia looked at her questioningly.

"In the garden," Katie added. "Don't you go there in the mornings?"

Lydia was still looking at her doubtfully. "It's all full of dead things," she said. "There's nothing pretty to see."

"That's okay," Katie said with a smile. "Can't we just talk?"

The dark-haired girl beamed brightly, and leapt out of her seat. She threw her sketchpad aside, and said, "Let's go."

So they went outside. The air was cold, and everything was perfectly dead. The dry leaves were spinning, and there wasn't a single spot of green to be seen.

"I told you," Lydia said regretfully.

"That's all right," Katie replied. "Let's just walk."

So they walked. There was a path that wound beneath the tall oaks, golden and brown, crunching beneath their feet.

When Katie arrived at the asylum, the trees had looked ominous. She certainly wasn't any happier now than she'd been then, but there was something less unpleasant about the trees, something more like what she was used to seeing in them. Something wild, something free. Something that had nothing to do with her current situation.

"So," she said to the other young woman as they walked along slowly. "What's up with this place?"

Lydia looked at her shyly. "Well," she said, "there are four doctors besides Dr. Halstead. There's the warden, Dr. Diederich. Then there's Dr. Damien. The two Doctor Dees." Katie smiled thinly.

"I don't like talking to Dr. Diederich," Lydia said. "*He* likes to talk, but I hate him. He's a little – he's a little bit mad."

Katie frowned, and asked, "What do you mean by that?"

Lydia shivered, and shook her head. "I don't know," she said. "I guess I'm just being silly. Anyway, what was I saying? Oh, yes. I mentioned Dr. Damien.

He's nice enough, but he doesn't really care about anybody except his own patients. I've never even talked to him. But he's awfully handsome."

She looked a little wistful for a moment, but then she went on to say, "Anyway, as for the other two doctors. Dr. Salvador is a good doctor, I guess. Otherwise she wouldn't be here. But I see her winking at the boys all the time. And once, I thought I saw one of them in her office . . ."

Katie waited for her to say more about the boy in Dr. Salvador's office, but she didn't.

"Then there's just Dr. Wilkins," she said. "He's sort of plain, and sort of shy. But he seems nice."

Katie waited for a moment. Really, she was just fishing for information, but she wanted to make a good impression.

"And what about you?" she asked. "What brought you here?"

Lydia tried to hide her face. She ducked her chin down into the corner of her jacket, but then, as if she realized that this wasn't really doing any good, she said, "I hope you won't think badly of me, if I tell you." "Of course I won't," Katie replied.

Lydia took a deep breath. Then she puckered her mouth, and said: "I jumped off of a building. But my jacket got caught on a flagpole, and then somebody pulled me inside."

She heaved a sigh, and Katie listened intently. This was pretty interesting stuff.

"I was there to work out my student loans,"

Lydia added. "But they didn't really care about the job I'd gotten waitressing at Denny's, and they were going to report me. I would've had to file bankruptcy."

She paused, and inhaled sharply. "It's probably not *that* big of a deal," she said. "But it was to me. I knew I could never pay back all that money. I thought I might be rich someday. I thought I might be an artist."

She sighed deeply, and Katie could just make out the hind-end of her breath, as it plumed out into the autumn air.

"But that didn't quite work out the way I thought it would," she said.

She laughed wildly, and added: "What ever works out the way we think it will? Not much, I guess. But whatever. No one ever said it'd be easy."

She shivered in the cold breeze, and pulled her sweater closer around her.

"Well," Katie said, "it seems like I've heard about almost everyone. But what about Marcus?"

Lydia looked at her sharply. "What?" she asked.

"Marcus," Katie said slowly. "The other guy from group."

Lydia's face darkened. She looked like Marianne Dashwood after she caught a cold in a rainstorm, calling for Willoughby on a green English hill.

"He's not a bad guy," she said quietly. "He saw his father kill his sister when he was ten years old. His father beat his mother for years. But after little Willa died, Mrs. Bickford shot herself."

Lydia was quiet, looking out into the landscape of dry autumn leaves with a numb expression.

"Marcus has had problems ever since," she explained. "It's not his fault."

"I'm sure you're right," Katie said, reaching to press Lydia's hand supportively

Lydia looked at her shyly, and then turned her head away in embarrassment. They walked along for a while longer under the trees, watching the leaves spin down, and wondering about the insanity of their lives.

***

After she came in from her walk with Lydia, Katie went to her room. She thought she'd lie down for a few minutes before lunch, and try to forget where she was.

When she went into the room, though, she found that it wasn't empty. And of course it was supposed to be.

She was even more surprised when she recognized the visitor. It was the tall, thin man in the white coat.

Dr. Diederich.

He was standing at the window with his hands behind his back, looking out over the barren grounds. When he realized that someone had walked into the room, he turned around, and smiled widely.

"Hello, young lady," he said in a thick German accent. "I had a feeling you'd stop in after your walk." Katie looked at him suspiciously.

"Ah!" he exclaimed with a little laugh. "I saw you through the window. You were walking with Miss Brock."

He hung his head, and made a *tsk-tsk* sound. "The poor young woman," he said.

Then he looked up, straight into Katie's face. "Do you know what brought Miss Brock to Greystone?" he asked curiously.

Katie narrowed her eyes at him. She thought the question was extremely inappropriate.

"Ah," he repeated with a knowing wink. "You think it's bad form of me to ask. Well, for most doctors – maybe it would be. But you'll soon find I'm not like other doctors."

He was smiling, but there was something ominous in his tone.

"I care very much about my patients," he said. "I do everything I can for them. For Miss Brock –"

He shook his head, and sighed. "I've tried to help her, of course," he added with a despairing look. "But, in order to help a person – well, that person must have at least a small spark, the faintest ember of a will to live. I'm afraid Miss Brock has neither."

His melancholy look disappeared in the briefest instant, and then he was smiling again. "But of course that's not what I came to say. I make it a habit, you see, to visit each of our new patients. So here I am!"

He gazed at Katie with that same smile, and the silence was uncomfortable.

"Have you found your stay pleasant so far?" he asked.

"I suppose so," Katie said slowly.

"Very good!" he exclaimed, clapping his hands loudly. "I'm glad to hear that. Of course I'm very busy – but if you ever need anything, please don't hesitate to pass the message along."

He smiled again, and waited for Katie to say something. But she didn't. He cleared his throat in a superior manner, and his smile faded.

"But now," he said, looking nonchalantly towards the window, "I think I'll leave you in peace. I'm getting hungry. Time for a bit of *Kaffee und Kuchen.*"

He nodded courteously, and went out of the room.

***

Katie lay down on her bed, then, and tried to sleep. Meanwhile, Karl Diederich walked through the hospital, till he came to the North Corridor, where Abel Damien's office was located. He knocked softly at the door, and was invited to enter.

He went into the room, and closed the door behind him. "Good day, Dr. Damien," he said politely, inclining his head towards the other physician.

Abel Damien stood to acknowledge Diederich, and straightened his black tie. As Lydia Brock had claimed, he was an extremely handsome man. He was more than six feet tall, lean, and packed with muscle. His clean-cut hair was dark; his eyes were dark. His mouth was blood-red.

Diederich walked into the room, and Damien sat down behind his desk. The two Dr. Dees.

"And a good day to you, doctor," Damien said with a broad grin. It was almost a smug grin. Very selfassured, at the very least.

Diederich went to a chair in front of the desk, and sat down comfortably. Damien opened the top desk drawer, and pulled out a long box of cigars. He shook one out, and offered it to the other doctor. "I know how you like them," he said with another grin.

"Thank you, doctor," Diederich said graciously, reaching out for the cigar with his long, graceful fingers. He took a book of matches from the pocket of his white coat, struck one, and lit the cigar. He took a deep puff, and smiled in satisfaction. "Have you finished the preparations for this evening?" he asked.

"Everything's set," Damien replied, lounging back in his chair, and lacing his fingers behind his head. "Will you bring the boy – or do you want me to get him?"

"I think I'd better fetch him," Diederich said. "He'll be less likely to resist me."

Damien nodded, and began to whistle. He propped his feet up on the desk, and gazed at the ceiling, as if there were something painted there that interested him. He stopped whistling, and smiled widely.

"You are always very content, Dr. Damien," Diederich observed. It was hard to tell whether he made this remark in admiration, or in criticism. "Does nothing faze you?"

"Not much," Damien replied candidly. "I think of myself as a very capable man, Dr. Diederich. There's very little I can't accomplish when I set my mind to it. So why would I ever need to feel sorry for myself?"

He made his grin even wider, and then began to whistle again.

"Sound logic," Diederich remarked, taking another puff of his cigar, and tapping some of the ash out into a black ashtray on the corner of the desk. "I can't argue with it. But someday, my friend – you may find that it's not as sound as you suspect."

"That may very well be, doctor," Damien returned with that same smile. "But why worry about tomorrow, when today is so splendid?"

"Have you had a good day, dear Abel?" Diederich inquired. "I'm glad to hear it."

"I've made great strides in my research," Damien replied. "I think we may be fairly successful tonight."

"Is that so?" Diederich asked. "I'm glad to hear it."

"I'm sure you are," Damien said with a wink.

Diederich gave another one of his courteous nods, and rose from his chair. "Until tonight, Dr. Damien," he said.

"Until tonight, my friend," Damien returned with a smirk.

Diederich nodded again, stubbed his cigar in the ashtray, and went out of the room.

Chapter 7

After Katie stretched out on the bed, she lay thinking for a long while, feeling as if she were trapped in some surreal rock CD. The music was creepy, it was flowing through her head, and she couldn't escape.

Eventually, she fell asleep. She woke up about fifteen minutes before her scheduled appointment with Dr. Halstead. She was supposed to meet with her every day at one-thirty, right after lunch.

She had slept through lunch. So now it was time to go and meet the doctor.

Room 303, the schedule read, *in the North Corridor.* She found Room 303 with little difficulty, but it wasn't as easy to make herself knock.

For some reason, the little hairs on the back of her neck were standing up. It was an annoying prickling feeling. She lifted a hand to rub them back into their usual places.

She raised her fist to knock, but hesitated for a long moment. She let her hand fall once, and then brought it back up. Finally, she knocked. Weakly, without any conviction.

A few seconds after she knocked, a voice called out for her to come in. Dr. Halstead's voice.

Katie pushed the door open, and stepped noiselessly into the room, her tread muffled by the thick beige carpet. Cora Halstead was sitting at her desk, her eyes roving restlessly over a pile of paperwork in front of her. The phone was hanging off the cradle.

Katie could hear the dial tone from her place across the room.

It was a large room, perfectly square in shape. The walls were painted that same color of misery as every other wall in the God-forsaken place. It was a color like moldy tapioca pudding.

The wall to the left was made up of numerous bookshelves, stuffed with countless volumes. Katie saw mostly medical books, of course – but she also saw other books, travel books, history books, volumes of classic literature. She would have liked to have an hour or two to browse those shelves uninterrupted.

The wall that held the door, and the wall behind the doctor's desk, were completely bare. But the wall to the right, which contained two tall windows on opposite sides, had a large picture hanging in the middle. It was an oil representation of Vermeer's *Girl with a Pearl Earring*.

When the doctor called for Katie to enter, she hadn't looked up. She was wearing a puckered expression, and carefully examining a stapled sheaf of long papers. She flipped one of the pages, and made a hasty note.

"Dr. Halstead?" Katie said quietly.

The woman looked up, obviously flustered. She seemed surprised to see Katie there.

"Hello, Katie," she said quickly. "You'll have to forgive me for looking perplexed. I thought it was time for Carmen's session, that's all."

Despite what she'd thought, the doctor looked relieved that it *wasn't* actually Carmen's session time.

Who wouldn't have been? That Carmen was a real peach.

The doctor smiled thinly at Katie, still looking perturbed. It didn't just seem to be on account of the paperwork, though. No – it was more like something had happened. Very recently, probably not more than a quarter of an hour ago, judging by the freshness of her aggravation.

She gestured to a comfortable chair in front of her desk, and said, "Please sit down."

So Katie sat. She felt a little uncomfortable, sitting there, and knowing that she was expected to talk about herself – when the woman in front of her was so obviously in a state of emotional disorder. It made her feel very awkward, like she was doing something improper.

But Cora Halstead was apparently a fine physician; and though she was admittedly disordered, she immediately set about putting the physical space in front of her into its proper order, so as to make herself feel more in control of the situation. She had just cleared the papers away, and filed them into a large manila folder, when all of a sudden an agitated look came into her face, as if she knew that something was still off, but she couldn't tell what.

Katie could still hear the dial tone.

"It's the phone," she said.

"Ah," Dr. Halstead said, mastering herself right away, and nodding to Katie in thanks. She hung up the phone, and then sat back in her chair, folding her hands over her middle, and taking a deep breath.

Next second, though, she was all business. She looked into Katie's face, and smiled professionally. "How are you today?" she asked.

"Just fine, thanks," Katie answered. But that was all she had to say, for now.

She wondered how this usually worked. With crazy people, that was. Did they feel a different sort of feeling, when they sat down in this chair? Did they start automatically spewing all the messy thoughts inside their cluttered heads? Was it a relief to them?

Katie thought about it for a moment, but then sighed inwardly. It probably wasn't right to classify people into two categories: Crazy and Sane. There were more crazy people than sane people, she thought. Even the sane ones had a touch of madness to them.

Just look at Mallory Kent.

She shivered in disgust, and looked towards the window. It was a windy autumn afternoon, and the half-bare trees were swaying mournfully. They seemed to call out for help. Or for a change of location, at least. Who knew what unspeakable things they had witnessed, over the years, here at Greystone Asylum?

"Are you all right?" Dr. Halstead asked.

Katie looked at her sharply. "I beg your pardon?" she asked.

"You looked as if you had a sudden thought," the doctor explained. "One that upset you."

"No, it was nothing," Katie replied. Her voice was short and clipped, yet not impolite. She spoke like a businesswoman trying to get out of a meeting as quickly as possible.

Cora Halstead noticed. She watched Katie for a moment, while Katie's face was turned towards the window. But of course Katie *knew* that she was watching her, and it made her uncomfortable. She felt like she was being deceptive, keeping her face turned away like that. But it was only because she knew that, when she looked back, the doctor would stop watching her.

And, for some reason, Katie liked the feel of the woman's eyes on her.

She shook the thought away, and swiveled her head towards Cora Halstead.

"Are you *sure* you're all right?" the woman asked with a smile.

"Quite," Katie replied.

Neither of the women said anything for a few moments. The doctor was still leaning back in her chair, and apparently trying not to make Katie feel as if she were scrutinizing her. But of course she was.

"I've examined your file," the doctor said finally, looking directly into Katie's face. "I think it would be an insult to your intelligence to pretend that I know less about you than I really do."

Katie looked at her in alarm. What sort of things did she know? What *could* she know?

"You received a good education," the doctor went on. "Harvard University. Major in English, minor in ancient history. You worked as a freelance writer after you graduated."

She smiled lightly, and added, "That's not an easy job to get, as I'm sure you know. People fight tooth and nail for those freelance positions. But you made it look easy."

"Just good luck, I guess," Katie said stiffly, watching the doctor with a cold expression.

"I'm sure that's not true," Dr. Halstead returned. "In my own experience, at least – I've usually found that luck has very little to do with it."

Katie didn't reply. She really didn't have anything to say.

She wished she had a magic lamp with a genie in it. Robin Williams was dead – but maybe when you're dead you can still be a genie. She would have loved to have a big blue Robin Williams right about now.

She wouldn't even make him wait until the third wish to be set free. She'd just make him get her out of this damned place – and then he could do whatever the hell he wanted with the other two wishes.

"May I ask what you're thinking about?" the doctor asked.

"I can't stop you," Katie replied flatly. "But I probably won't answer you."

"Hostility isn't uncommon in this situation," the other woman said. "But it doesn't help."

"I'm sure it doesn't."

Cora Halstead sighed, and leaned forward in her chair. "You can be angry if you want," she said plainly. "But like you just said yourself – it doesn't help. I admit, I read a few printed words on a piece of copy paper. But that doesn't mean I know you. The only way for me to help you is to understand you better. Only you can help me to do that."

Katie stared at her for a moment; but then, in spite of herself, she started to laugh. The doctor looked surprised.

"I admit," she said with a smile, "that wasn't the reaction I was expecting."

"How many times have you recited that spiel?" Katie asked, still laughing, and wiping the water from her eyes.

"More times than I can count," the doctor replied, still smiling. "Was it that obvious?"

"Very much so," Katie said with a sigh.

Another moment of silence; and then: "Despite the fact that you seem more amiable now," (the doctor said), "I'm sure you're still unwilling to answer my questions."

She was watching Katie with a knowing expression. She had played this game before – like she'd said, too many times to count. She was trying to find the quickest route to the exit.

Katie was suddenly perturbed. She wasn't sure why.

"If you're so sure of that," she said shortly, "maybe I should just go. I wouldn't want to waste your valuable time."

The doctor looked at her carefully. "Is that what you think?" she asked. "That you're wasting my time?"

Katie felt like a fool. She wasn't sure what she'd been thinking about this doctor – but whatever it was, she'd been wrong. Halstead was a hack. She asked the same questions every other psychiatrist asked.

She was a joke.

"Look," Katie said quickly. "I'm sorry if I was rude before. There was no reason for it. But I feel I should tell you – I have no interest in answering your questions."

She looked steadily into the doctor's face. "I didn't kill my sister," she said in an authoritative voice. "I might not have liked her – hell, I might have thought she was crazy – but I didn't kill her. Send me to prison if you don't believe me."

She got up from her chair, pushed it back roughly, and turned away from the doctor without another word or glance. Then she marched to the door, and walked out of the room.

***

That night, Katie lay awake in bed, staring at the ceiling. It was covered with strange shadows cast by the bathroom light.

Lydia was embarrassed about being afraid of the dark, so Katie tried not to make a big deal about it. But the damned light was shining right in her eyes, and it was driving her nuts. She thought about stealing the lightbulb while Lydia was sleeping, but one of the nurses would probably just give her another one.

As Katie lay sleepless, comparing the bathroom light to the moon, and remembering the curve of Mallory Kent's breasts against the silver evenlight, she thought she heard something.

It sounded like screaming. But it was faint, and she wasn't sure.

She hadn't undressed before bed, because it was cold in the asylum. Maybe she'd get used to it after a while. She was still wearing her khakis and her sweater. She threw off the thin blanket, and shivered. She swung her legs over the edge of the bed, and shoved her feet into her sneakers.

Then she heard it again. The hollow sound of screaming from far away.

She stood up, and walked towards the open door. She didn't argue, when Lydia said that she wanted to leave it open.

Katie glanced at Lydia, and saw that she was sleeping peacefully. For someone who left the bedroom door open just so she could hear the various noises of life, she was surprisingly oblivious to this strange screaming.

Katie sighed, and turned back to the doorway. She was about to step through it, but then she thought, was it really a good idea? What business was it of hers? It was probably just a hostile patient. Why get herself into trouble?

She kept listening, and the screaming drifted back into her ears. Still from very far away, but loud enough to let her know that the screamer was in pain. Serious pain.

She thought about it for another moment or two. What would happen, if she got caught outside her room at night? She just got here. Could she really afford to get into trouble now?

She took a deep breath, and listened. More steady screaming.

She couldn't help it. She had to go.

She went out into the corridor, stepping quietly. The corridor was illuminated by dingy fluorescent squares, set up at the top of the walls at intervals. The light was dirty, caught between blue and grey.

Katie went slowly down the hall, listening carefully.

Could it really be that no one else heard that screaming? Or were they just afraid to leave their rooms?

What about the nurses? Couldn't *they* hear it?

But then Katie had another thought. What if it was all in her head?

She remembered the red-faced demon from her bedroom. No one would have believed *that* was there, either.

It had seemed real. But had it been?

She stopped in the middle of the hallway, and thought about going back to her room. She could pull the covers over her head, and pretend that she hadn't heard anything at all.

The asylum had fallen silent for a long moment. But then the screaming started again. How could she just ignore it? She had to find out what was going on.

She went on down the hallway, until she reached the bend that turned right into the North Corridor. The sound was coming from that direction.

She started down the second hallway, listening carefully. The dirty blue-grey light illuminated the scuffed tiles, glinting against the shiny paint slathered across the walls.

The horrible sound was getting closer. She kept walking, until she came to a door that was standing partway open.

There were lights inside the room. She could just make out the name plate on the door.

Dr. Abel Damien.

She took a deep breath, and put her eye to the open space between the door and the jamb.

She saw a man kneeling on the carpet, completely naked. There was a hooded figure crouching in front of him, inserting a shard of glass into the skin of his abdomen. The figure drove the glass in deeper, and deeper, while the man continued to scream. Then he pulled out the glass, and took hold of the skin. He dragged it upwards, separating the upper layer of skin from the flesh beneath. Blood dripped down onto the beige carpet.

It was obvious that the person beneath the hood was a man. Katie could make out his masculine muscles, rippling beneath the black fabric of the cloak.

It looked as if he'd been working at this gruesome task for a while now. The greater part of the victim's body was blood-red, with the topmost portion of the skin peeled away.

The screaming was horrible. Katie wished more than anything that she hadn't come.

She must have made some sound, given some indication that she was there — because suddenly, the figure in the hood shot to his feet, and looked towards the door. The man was tall and thin, but that was all Katie could make out. She shrank back into the shadows, but it was too late.

The door flew open, and the hooded figure came hurtling out into the corridor. But it seemed as if he didn't care who'd been watching him. He just wanted to get away. He sprinted towards the opposite end of the corridor, where there was presumably some sort of exit.

The figure disappeared from Katie's sight, and she fell back against the wall, sinking down, and breathing shallowly. She felt as if she were about to have a fit.

But the fit never came. She just slipped down to the floor like a pile of rags. She wanted to get up, to go for help – but she couldn't move. She was immobilized by fear.

Then she passed out.

Chapter 8

She woke to the pressure of gentle hands on her shoulders. She opened her bleary eyes, and saw Cora Halstead's face in front of her.

The dirty grey light was gone, now. The corridor was filled with morning sunshine. Katie blinked against it, feeling dazed.

"Katie," the doctor said urgently, trying to snap her awake. "Katie! Can you hear me?"

Katie stared at her, and frowned, wondering if her recent memories were only nightmares. But then she realized that she was lying on the floor. She glanced back, and saw the door behind her.

She saw the name plate.

Dr. Abel Damien.

She felt as if she were going to be sick. She hurled herself forward, flailing on the floor, slapping her palms against the tiles.

"It's not real," she whispered, staring down at the dirty tiles. "Please tell me it's not real."

"Katie," the doctor said gently, pulling at her upper arms. "Come on. Let me help you up."

Katie allowed herself to be hauled up to her feet, but then she fell against the doctor, feeling lightheaded.

"Sorry," she murmured, putting a hand to her head.

"It's all right," Dr. Halstead said kindly, putting her arm around Katie. "I'll help you."

Katie blinked her eyes rapidly, trying to clear away the fog that was wrapped around her brain. Then she looked up and saw the orderly. The orderly who'd come to her room the morning before.

What was he doing there? Had he been called in to stand guard in case Katie flipped out? Dr. Diederich was standing behind him, watching Katie carefully. Both men wore blank, solemn expressions.

Dr. Halstead noticed Katie staring at the orderly. "Tim was the one who found you," she explained. "He was making his rounds this morning, and he saw you lying on the floor."

Katie narrowed her eyes at the orderly. Likely story. She examined him a little more closely, noting his build. Tall and thin. Just like the man in the hood.

"Come on," Dr. Halstead said to Katie. "We're meeting in my office."

She led Katie down the corridor, and they turned into her office. The doctor guided Katie to the couch, and then sat down beside her.

"They'll be coming soon," the doctor said softly. "Try to calm down."

Katie tried to take a deep breath, but it caught in her chest, and she began to cough. The doctor laid a hand on her back. Katie leaned towards her slightly, and inhaled the scent of rose water and lavender.

Dr. Diederich was standing off to the side. He had followed Katie and Dr. Halstead into the room. But he'd sent the orderly away.

Soon afterwards, more people began to come into the room. There was a man and a woman, presumably the other two doctors of the asylum.

Wilkins and Salvador, Katie thought.

The man was short, with longish grey hair that really could have used a trim. His face was slightly wrinkled, but innocent-looking. He wore thick glasses that looked like 1975 had thrown them up.

The woman was stunning. She was tall, slender, and shaped like an hourglass. She was like JLo on steroids. Her cream-colored blazer pinched her shoulders, and hugged her breasts. Her short skirt nearly played peek-a-boo with her crotch.

Salvador glared at Katie, and then looked pointedly at Dr. Halstead.

Katie frowned, and glanced over at Halstead. But the doctor didn't meet her eyes.

Trailing behind the doctors was an ordinarylooking man. He wore khakis and a beige trench coat. When he walked, the side of his open coat moved back a little, and Katie saw the handgun holstered to his belt.

He must have been a cop.

Katie knew she was in for a world of hell.

"Miss Throckmorton," Diederich said politely, coming to stand in front of the sofa, and lacing his fingers behind his back. This was the first time he'd spoken to her that morning. He'd been watching her for a while now, but he'd never said anything. Katie wondered what he was thinking.

"I know you must be very distraught," he went on. "But I'm afraid –"

"We have to ask you a few questions," the cop interrupted. He looked sharply at Diederich. He didn't plan on playing nice.

Katie looked back at the cop with an equally stalwart expression, but she didn't say anything. She just waited for the first question.

"My name is Detective Morgan," the man announced in a booming voice, "and I'll be handling this investigation."

He watched Katie carefully before going on.

"You were found just outside the room where a man was killed," he finally added.

He was a short, stocky man with salt-andpepper hair and a curious expression. He sort of looked like Sheriff Tupper from *Murder She Wrote*.

Where was Angela Lansbury when you needed her?

"Yeah," Katie said in a flat voice.

"Can you explain what you were doing there?" Morgan demanded.

"I heard screaming," Katie replied roughly. "I went to see what was going on."

She felt Cora Halstead's hand on her back again. She was warning her to take it easy.

"You heard screaming," the detective said, nearly rolling his eyes. "Can you think of any reason why no one *else* heard the noise?"

"No," Katie replied, trying to soften her tone. "I'm sorry, but I can't."

"You'll forgive me for finding that hard to believe."

Katie couldn't help glaring at him. "I don't know what else to tell you," she said slowly. "I was in bed. I heard screaming. I went to see what was happening."

"Yes, yes," the detective said wearily. "You said that already. You followed the noise to Dr. Damien's door, and found that it was partially open. You looked through the crack to see Dr. Damien with an unknown assailant. Someone in a black hood, who was – peeling away his flesh."

Katie looked at him with hard eyes. "Yes," she snapped.

"But suddenly," Morgan went on, making his disbelief perfectly obvious, "the hooded assailant turned and ran from the room. For no reason."

"I must have hit the door," Katie said defensively.

"Ah," Morgan returned. "Of course. You alerted the assailant to your presence, and they fled. Then you – passed out?"

"Yes," Katie said through gritted teeth.

"You didn't think to go for help? Maybe Dr. Damien wasn't dead yet."

"This is ridiculous," Dr. Halstead declared in a loud voice. It surprised Katie that she'd spoken in the middle of the inquiry.

"A person doesn't have any power over when they lose consciousness," the doctor added forcefully. "Katie must have been overwhelmed by what she saw. She's been through a great deal lately – and it must have been too much for her."

"Ah," the detective repeated with a knowing grin. "I think I know what you're referring to. Miss Throckmorton only recently arrived, yes? She was accused of killing her younger sister."

The room fell silent. No one seemed to know what to say.

"Detective Morgan," Diederich said finally, "I think you'll agree when I say, it's rather inappropriate to discuss the reason for Miss Throckmorton's arrival at Greystone. All that has been decided by the courts."

"Of course," Morgan said grudgingly. "It was only an attempt to understand the doctor's comment, you understand."

Diederich nodded stiffly, and looked unhappily at Halstead.

She was sure going to get an earful later.

"I'm still not convinced," Morgan said stubbornly. "How do I know Miss Throckmorton didn't kill Damien?"

"You've got to be kidding," Halstead said with a half-laugh. "You can't be serious?"

"And why not?" Morgan asked with a frown.

"She was found at the murder scene," the doctor said slowly. "She was thoroughly unconscious, I assure you. And she didn't have a spot of blood on her! How could she have managed that?"

"Perhaps she changed her clothes," Morgan said with a shrug. Then his eyes lit up, and he added, "She mentioned a hood. Maybe she was referring to her own hood, and trying to make it seem like someone else's. An outer garment would have kept her clean."

He looked seriously at the doctor, and went on to ask, "How can you be so sure she wasn't conscious? Maybe she just thought that being discovered at the murder scene would decrease the chance of suspicion."

"That's ridiculous," Cora Halstead said firmly. "You're being ridiculous."

Dr. Diederich looked at her warningly. She turned her face away, and let out a quiet sigh.

"Well," the detective said significantly, "there's one more thing I haven't mentioned yet."

"And what's that?" Katie demanded. She felt as if she were being attacked, and her hackles were raised.

"There was writing on the wall," Morgan said, looking at Katie steadily.

"What?" Katie snapped.

"Writing," Morgan went on, "in the victim's blood. *Semper tecum,* it said."

He continued to gaze at Katie with hard eyes. "I suppose you know what that means?" he inquired.

"So what if I do?"

"Would you mind translating for us?"

"Always with you," Katie said slowly. "It means *always with you.*"

"Strange that you know it," Morgan said, shaking his head with a sigh. "Most people in this hospital probably don't."

"I'm sure some of the doctors do," Katie spat. "It's simple Latin."

"You mean to accuse the doctors, now?" Morgan asked. "Even the one who's trying to defend you?"

Cora Halstead's hand fell away from Katie's back. Whether it was because she didn't want anyone else to see, or because she disliked Katie's comment, of course Katie couldn't tell.

"You have a classical education," Morgan persisted. "You were schooled in Greco-Roman history – not a very popular field nowadays."

"Anyone with access to Google Translate could have written that," Katie snarled.

"Well, yes," Morgan agreed, "but why *would* they?"

"Why would I?" Katie asked. "Don't you think it would be a stupid thing to do?"

"Stupid, maybe," Morgan said, spreading his hands. "Or just insane. After all – I'm not the one in the asylum, Miss Throckmorton."

Katie nearly leapt at him. But when her muscles quivered, Dr. Halstead circled a hand round her arm to keep her in place.

"Ah," Morgan said in an amused tone. "You have a stalwart defender in Dr. Halstead, it seems. Very strange, considering you only arrived the day before yesterday."

"I didn't kill that man," Katie said firmly. "I've never killed anyone."

"Your younger sister might disagree with you, Miss Throckmorton," the detective said, almost tauntingly. "But, then again – she's not here to tell us what happened."

Cora couldn't keep her seated, this time. Katie jumped up from the sofa, and took a step towards the detective.

"Instead of blaming it all on me," she snapped, "why don't you go and question that orderly? What the hell was *he* doing there?"

"What orderly?" Morgan asked in confusion.

"Tim Reynolds." Dr. Diederich supplied the name quickly. "He was the one who found Miss Throckmorton this morning. While he was making his rounds."

"Well, that's perfectly natural," Morgan said. "He was walking his usual route, and he observed Miss Throckmorton lying on the floor. I'll question him, of course, but I'm sure he doesn't have much to add."

"You're sure about that?" Katie said indignantly. "You're sure about him, but you're perfectly willing to give *me* hell?"

Morgan held up his hands in defense. "I said I'd question him," he stated firmly.

Katie rolled her eyes, and turned away in frustration.

"You asked me why you'd kill Abel Damien," Morgan went on. "The simple answer to that question is: I don't know. I'm not saying you did or you didn't. Maybe you had a little crush on the doctor. Maybe he rejected an advance you made? He was a handsome man. I'd believe a young woman like you might be attracted to him." He smiled innocuously at Katie. "That would explain the writing," he added. "You have to admit, *Semper tecum* would be a strange thing for a simple orderly to scrawl across the wall."

"That's a little stereotypical," Katie said in irritation. "And besides, I've only been here for a day. You think it's strange for Dr. Halstead to say something in my defense after so short a time – but you don't think it's strange that I would have already tried to hit on some other doctor? Besides, I never laid eyes on Damien before last night."

"So you say," Morgan returned.

"Are you accusing me of lying?" Katie demanded.

"Again," Morgan said, tapping the side of his head, "I'm not saying I've worked anything out yet. I'm just presenting theories! One must have theories, of course, at the beginning of an investigation."

He looked around at the others in the room. "And I think," he said quietly, "that this is going to be an interesting investigation. Very interesting indeed."

He paused for a moment, and simply stood there. He looked at Katie with that same bland smile. "Anyway," he said slowly, starting to turn away, "the truth remains to be seen. So we shall see! We shall see."

He nodded gravely, and then went out of the room. The other three doctors were talking frantically with one another, so Katie whispered to Halstead, "I think he's read one too many Sherlock Holmes stories."

The doctor couldn't keep from grinning. She glanced into Katie's face, and held her eyes for a moment. Katie was just trying to think of what to say, when suddenly Karl Diederich's German cadences soared out from the other side of the room.

"This is a catastrophe," he declared, reaching up to run his long fingers through his short, fair hair. "What is happening?"

No one seemed to know how to answer him. Of course, Katie would have never even thought to attempt it, but the other three doctors were speechless.

Diederich whirled on Katie, and stared at her for a moment, his chest heaving. "I am not accusing you of anything, Miss Throckmorton," he said. "I have no idea whether you had anything to do with all this. But it is – it is a dilemma, and now I must go and think about it."

He ran his hands through his hair again, and stormed out of the room. Katie and the other three doctors were left alone.

Wilkins stood for a moment, his hands in his pockets, a thoughtful expression on his face. But then he started, as if waking from a reverie, and nodded curtly to the other two doctors. He went out of the room, his hands still shoved deep in his pockets.

Salvador lingered a little longer.

"A strange thing, Cora," she said in a sharp voice. "Don't you think?"

"Of course," Halstead returned flatly.

"What do you make of it?"

Cora jerked her head subtly towards Katie, and said, "Maybe now's not the best time."

"Ah," Salvador said with a soft smile. "Of course. Goodbye, then."

She cleared her throat in a superior manner – like a queen waltzing away from the execution of a pickpocket who'd tried to steal her jewels – and sashayed out of the room.

When everyone was gone, Katie didn't know what to say. It seemed like Dr. Halstead didn't, either.

Katie wondered if that meant it was time for her to leave. But she lingered for a few seconds, inhaling the scent of rose water and lavender. She closed her eyes for a brief moment, and imagined they were sitting on a couch somewhere else.

But then she started, and opened her eyes. That was a dangerous thought. No good thinking it.

She stood up quickly, and looked down at the doctor. "Thank you," she said quietly.

"For what?" Halstead returned with a soft smile.

"For standing up for me, I suppose."

"I was just telling them what I thought to be true."

"Ah," Katie said.

They were silent for a moment, obviously trying to think of something else to say. But they both failed, so Katie turned away from the doctor, and went out of the office.

Chapter 9

Later that morning, Katie's father arrived at the asylum. He hadn't planned to come until the weekend, but the police had called him with the message that Katie was "involved in a murder investigation."

He came at half-past ten, a long while after breakfast had ended. An orderly led him into the Community Room, where Katie had been sitting ever since she left Dr. Halstead's office.

She'd been too upset to eat breakfast. Besides – there was nowhere for her to sit. At dinner last night, she'd sat alone at a table in the corner. No one else sat alone. Even in this crazy place, everyone had their own clique – their own meal table. It was just like high school.

There were the "cool kids," who crowded into one long table in the middle of the room, talking and laughing noisily, and doing all they could to draw attention to themselves. Strangely, both Eric Conley and Carmen Rodriguez sat at this table. They might not have gotten along very well in group, but they didn't fight at the dinner table. Katie supposed it was some kind of loony bin etiquette that she hadn't yet deciphered.

In opposition to the cool kids, there were, of course, the weird kids, or just the quiet ones. Lamberto Esplanade and Marcus Bickford sat at that table, with an assortment of other docile young people, and even a smattering of middle-aged people. Katie had thought, at first, that this might be the table for her, but when she walked by, everyone at the table glared at her.

Maybe they thought along the lines of Carmen Rodriguez, and thought she was a child killer. In any case, and no matter the cause, Katie knew she wasn't welcome, so she continued on her circuit round the cafeteria.

There were three more big tables that were completely occupied: the one with the comparatively normal people, who discussed international affairs and the state of the stock market over their food; the old people, all over the age of sixty-five, who talked about gardening and various ailments of the body; and lastly, the exceptionally crazy people, who often screamed or cried while they were sitting at the table, and occasionally had to be ushered out of the cafeteria by an orderly.

Katie had no desire to sit at *that* table. There was someone at the end of it who looked like Norman Bates. Not that she could say she knew what Norman Bates looked like, unless she said that he looked like Anthony Perkins. But this guy didn't look like Anthony Perkins. He looked like Norman Bates.

It was something in his expression, more than anything else. He kept glancing at Katie, and smiling strangely. Even if he'd walked over to her, bowed slightly, and asked very politely for Katie to come and join him, she would have dropped her tray, and run away screaming.

She wouldn't have minded sitting with either the old people or the "news-o-philes." From time to time, she even heard the subject of literature pop up at the newsophile table, and she wished she could listen more closely to the conversation.

But when she passed by these two tables, both groups shunned her just like the weird kids had. They averted their faces, and pulled their trays closer. Whether they were afraid she was going to sprinkle poison on their food, she couldn't say for sure.

But God, crazy people were pretty damned judgmental. It sort of made her sick. So eventually, she went to sit alone at one of the empty tables on the far side of the cafeteria. Her food tasted like glue, and she had the distinct impression that everyone was staring at her. She tried not to look at anyone, but she was fairly sure she was right.

No, she didn't look at anyone else – but she couldn't help noticing Norman Bates. There was something evil about his eyes.

It was too bad Lydia Brock didn't come to dinner. As a habit, she ran away when the dinner bell rang, and went to hide someplace where the orderlies couldn't find her. She was anorexic, and she had an abject fear of food. Every now and then, when Dr. Halstead realized that she still wasn't eating, she ordered for her to be fed intravenously. But mostly, she survived on water and diet ginger ale, the latter of which was available in limited amounts in a small refrigerator in the Community Room.

Katie was disappointed that Lydia wasn't there. She felt sure that Lydia would have wanted to sit with her.

Anyway, on the morning after Abel Damien's death, Katie skipped breakfast. She wasn't hungry, and she had no desire to be surrounded by people who judged and despised her. She just wanted to be alone.

She wanted to be alone, that was, until the orderly showed her father into the Community Room. At the sign of movement, she looked up absently from a vapid magazine she'd been perusing. Her face brightened at the sight of Axel Throckmorton. He smiled at her warmly, and held his arms out to her.

Katie ran to hug him. Suddenly, she felt like a lost little girl who'd just found her daddy again. The thought that he'd leave her soon filled her with a terrible fear. She clung to him as if her life depended on it, and buried her face in his shoulder.

"It's all right, Punkin," he said. "Here – let's sit down."

They seated themselves in two saucer chairs side by side, and Axel took Katie's hand.

"How are you doing, sweetie?" he asked in concern.

"I don't know, Daddy," she answered honestly. She lowered her voice, and added, "One of the doctors was killed last night. I heard him screaming, and I went to see what was happening. I saw – I saw the whole thing."

Axel looked as if he were about to be sick. "Oh, Punkin," he murmured.

"I guess I passed out," Katie said, shaking her head in confusion, and looking down at the floor. "I'd been hoping it was all just a nightmare – but I woke up to find out that it was real. There was a detective, and he seemed to think that I . . ."

"That you what?" her father asked with narrowed eyes.

"He thinks I had something to do with it."

"That's ridiculous!" Axel exclaimed, nearly shouting.

"Thanks, Daddy," Katie said with a sigh. "But not everyone agrees."

Axel looked livid. But soon, he composed himself, and squeezed Katie's hand. "I'm going to make some calls," he said. "I'm going to fix this."

Katie smiled sadly, and replied, "Marty Walsh can't fix this one, Daddy."

He looked away for a moment, his dark eyes shining with tears. But then he cleared his throat, and tried to smile. "All right, Princess," he said. "Let's not talk about it. Let's pretend you're a little girl again, and we're playing in your tree house. Remember the tree house, Punkin?"

"Of course I do, Daddy," Katie said quietly.

Axel sighed heavily. "I talked to your mother," he said.

"Did you?" Katie asked, her voice sounding a little brighter. "That's great. They won't let me make long distance calls."

"She's awfully worried about you, of course," Axel said. "I told her she should come up – but she gave me some second-rate excuse, just like always. Some art show, or some stupid thing –"

"It's all right, Daddy," Katie said. "Please don't worry about it."

She looked at him pleadingly. She hated it when he let Linda upset him. All these years, she'd put her work before her family, and Katie had come to terms with that. But Axel never had.

To lighten the air – or just to change the subject – Katie asked: "How's Queen Regina?"

"Oh, Punkin," Axel said with a sigh. "I wish you wouldn't talk about her like that."

"I'm sorry, Daddy," Katie said. "I didn't mean anything by it. I guess I just don't know how to make you laugh anymore."

"Even if I'm not laughing, sweetie," Axel said with a smile, "just being with you makes me happy. But you have to understand, Regina's all I have now. Everyone's gone."

He hung his head, and stared at the floor for a moment.

"I'm sorry, Daddy," Katie repeated, with a note of desperation in her voice. "Oh, Daddy . . ."

"What is it, Punkin?" Axel asked, gripping Katie's hands.

She took a deep breath.

"You don't think I killed her – do you, Daddy?"

Tears started up in her eyes. She wasn't sure if she could hold them back.

Her father looked at her in disbelief. "Are you talking about Lockwood?" he asked.

"Yes," Katie breathed.

"Oh, Punkin," Axel whispered, leaning forward to take Katie in his arms. "Of course I don't think – I don't think that. It was an accident. It was all just a horrible accident . . ."

Nothing but these words, from this particular person, could have eased the sharp pain in Katie's heart. She'd felt all morning as if the thing were going to break in two, but her father's words seemed to mend it again.

***

But then, the time came for Axel to leave. He held Katie tightly, and kissed her tenderly, but he still had to leave.

She watched him go with tears in her eyes. Even worse, she had to be at group in fifteen minutes.

She'd never had so much trouble peeling herself off the floor. She'd had quite a few of those days – too much wine, too much vodka (too much Mallory Kent) – but none like this one.

God, she would have killed for a drink. And there was nothing but diet ginger ale in the fridge.

She felt like throwing herself on her face, and crying until she was bone-dry. But you needed privacy for something like that.

And this wasn't a private place.

She squared her shoulders roughly, and set off towards the back of the room, where the group gathered in the mornings.

But she felt self-conscious about being the first one there. So she went out of the room, and down the corridor, pacing up and down a few times. She saw a couple of the group members go into the Community Room, but now she had a strange fear of joining them. She really didn't want to go.

What were they going to do? Cite her for bad behavior, after falling unconscious outside the office of a dead man?

Unless they thought she'd killed him, that was. Unless they thought the same thing Morgan thought.

She eventually made her way back to her room, probably a couple of minutes after group was supposed to start. She sat down at the edge of her bed, wishing she could stay there forever, until she hardened into a statue like the *Venus of Ille,* and was left alone for all eternity. With a look of curious malevolence on her face. With a mischievous expression that no one could quite understand.

Only God would understand that she'd been making fun of *herself.* Maybe that's what Mérimée's Venus had been doing. Making fun of herself for loving someone impossible.

Katie sat on the bed for a while, staring at the wall, her mind racing. She needed something to make her stop thinking. She needed to do something.

But what was there to do, in a place like this? There weren't even any books in the Community Room. Just a bunch of germ-covered magazines. And wouldn't you know it? Not a single National Geographic.

She thought of the garden, but to get to the door, she'd have to go through the Community Room. That's where they were having group.

She sighed, and stood up. She looked towards the door for a minute, wanting to leave, but not knowing where to go. If she just went wandering around the corridors, would someone stop her? Would it seem suspicious to be roaming around when she'd just been found outside a dead man's door?

She thought that it probably would. But she only had two choices: either go wandering, or go to group. She couldn't sit in this room any longer. She was starting to feel like the crazy person they were trying to make her out to be.

She decided to go out. Maybe someone would reprimand her, who the hell knew. She was sick of just sitting here.

She started slowly out of the room, as if she were afraid that she would step on a landmine with each footfall. She hated the thought of someone coming to tell her where she could go, and what she could do.

She wished she had a gun. She'd shoot everyone in the whole goddamned place, and then go waltzing out as if nothing had even happened.

She took a deep breath, and tried to clear her mind, as she stepped out into the dingy corridor. The walls and the floor were dirty. She wondered if anyone ever cleaned them. She thought, for a moment, that *she* would have been willing to clean them, if only to take her mind off of the restless buzzing in her brain. It was like a swarm of wasps. She could almost hear them.

And she fucking hated bees.

She walked on, down the West Corridor, far and away from the Community Room that lay on the South. She went slowly down the corridor, looking slowly to the left and the right, keeping an eye out for nurses and orderlies. But the place was completely quiet.

At this time of day, most of the patients were in group. The doors to their rooms were open, and they were all empty. All except one, as far as Katie could see.

The room had two beds, just like all the other rooms. There were two young women, one sitting on each bed, facing each other across a distance of only about a foot. They were looking very hard into each other's faces, but their expressions were blank.

Katie knew that she should leave them alone, but she was very interested in their strange behavior. And she still wanted something to take her mind off her own problems.

She stepped up to the doorway, and stood there for a few seconds, just watching the young women. They were very pale, with dark, stringy hair, and hollow eyes. They were identical twins.

Katie immediately thought of the girls that Officer Humphreys had mentioned. The ones from the bloody van.

Katie cleared her throat awkwardly, and knocked softly on the doorjamb.

Neither of the young women looked towards her. With their eyes still fixed on each other, they spoke the exact same words, at the exact same time.

"Are you the new girl?" they asked.

"Yes," Katie said slowly.

"They brought you against your will," they said, still in unison.

"Yes."

"They did that to us, too."

Katie stood there for a moment, wondering what to say. Wondering what to do. Were these the kind of people who might pick something up, and run to bash her over the head with it? She didn't know.

Suddenly, the young women rose up from their beds, and turned to face Katie. They looked so much like the twins from *The Shining*, she thought she was going to pass out.

"My name's Marion," one of them said.

"My name's Miriam," the other one said.

They stared at Katie with empty expressions, and Katie swallowed thickly.

"What did they say you did?" they asked together.

Katie's mouth was hanging open, and she was trying to think of what she should say, when someone touched her elbow. She cried out, and whirled around. She found herself standing face to face with Cora Halstead.

The doctor peered into the room, and watched the twins for a moment, her expression hard to read.

"Katie," she said slowly. "Come with me, please."

The twins stared at her with inscrutable faces. "Hello, Dr. Halstead," they said in unison.

"Hello, girls," Cora Halstead replied with a slight nod. Then she touched Katie's elbow, and pulled her gently away.

When they were walking away from the twins' room, Katie looked at her curiously, and asked, "Why did you do that?"

The other woman seemed hesitant to answer. She looked quickly towards Katie, and then looked away again.

"They're peculiar young women," she said simply. "Sometimes it's hard to know what to expect from them."

"Are you their doctor?"

"No."

She seemed to shiver, before she added, "Dr. Diederich takes care of them. They aren't very talkative, but he checks in on them, sits with them. He seems to see more in them than most people do."

Katie frowned, and asked, "Were you afraid they would do something to me?"

The other woman hesitated before she said, "You weren't supposed to be there, anyway. You were supposed to be in group. That's why I was looking for you."

Katie fought the urge to smile. "You go looking for everybody who misses group?"

Cora Halstead refused to look at her. She flushed a little, and took an abrupt turn to the left towards the Community Room. "Everyone's waiting for you," she said stiffly. "Hurry up."

Katie was still smiling as they walked into the Community Room. But then she stopped smiling, because she remembered that she had to sit next to all these people she hated. There was Eric Conley with his pasty skin and his sickeningly proud expression. There was Carmen Rodriguez, with her wild black hair and even wilder black eyes.

Katie wondered what Carmen had looked like in that gas station, when she slit her wrists in front of her boyfriend. Had she looked pathetic? Or just like a caged animal?

She saw Lamberto Esplanade, with his strange hat, and his strange mustache, and she realized that she didn't hate him. She just felt sorry for him. He was so far off the map, it was obvious there was no hope of him ever finding his way back.

She didn't hate Lydia Brock, either. Lydia was just – well, she was just sad. That was to say, Katie felt sad for her.

She didn't know what to think of Marcus Bickford. She remembered what Lydia had told her, about his father killing his sister, and then his mother shooting herself. He'd been in and out of institutions ever since.

Was that because the tragedy had unhinged him? Was he crazy enough to kill people?

Crazy enough to kill Dr. Damien?

Katie realized that anyone in the room could have killed the doctor. And there were people everywhere.

She took her seat in the small circle, and Dr. Halstead took hers. They looked at each other for a moment, and then glanced away, as if they'd never looked in the first place.

"All right," the doctor said, sounding very tired all of a sudden.

Ah-ha, Katie thought. *Back to her usual self.*

"Who wants to go first?" the doctor asked, pinching the bridge of her nose as if she were getting a migraine.

"I would like to discuss the murder of Dr. Damien," Lamberto said immediately.

"Of course you would, you fucking weirdo," Eric muttered.

"Eric," Dr. Halstead said warningly.

"There is a great mystery afoot," Lamberto declared, sitting up straight, and tugging at his lapels. "We must get to the bottom of it."

"I admire your enthusiasm, Lamberto," the doctor said. "But I'm afraid we'll have to leave this mystery to the police. Is that okay with you?"

Lamberto exhaled heavily, and slumped down in his seat. "I shall investigate on my own," he said in a defeated voice.

"Leave it to the police, Lamberto," Dr. Halstead repeated.

Lamberto didn't reply. His arms were crossed over his skinny chest, and his mustache was quivering over his lip. Katie wondered if he was going to cry.

Eric Conley looked at Katie, and jerked his thumb towards Lamberto. "Did you hear the whole story about this nut?" he asked.

"Eric!" Dr. Halstead exclaimed.

But Eric ignored her. "Well," he said to Katie, "this is what happened. The lunatic was making spaghetti, I guess. He had a habit of visiting his oldlady neighbor, Mrs. Rogers, every day at three. But everybody in the neighborhood knew that Mrs. Rogers was banging Mr. McClane."

Carmen Rodriguez snickered. Lydia Brock rolled her eyes.

"Anyway," Eric said, "when Detective Nutso called the old lady that day, she didn't answer. He went to look through her window, and saw she wasn't in her living room, where she usually was. So naturally he thought that there was a 'mystery afoot.' He left the gas burning on the stove, and went looking for Mrs. Rogers. He thought she'd been abducted. He called the police, and half an hour later, they found her naked in Mr. McClane's bed. By that time, though, Detective Nutso had burned down his parents' house!"

Eric rocked back in his chair, and roared with laughter.

Lamberto was staring blankly up at the ceiling. Katie wasn't sure if he was even listening to Eric.

"You really shouldn't be talking about people's pasts," Marcus said suddenly. "Because yours is a hell of a lot worse."

Eric looked at him angrily. "Mind your own business, nigger," he snapped.

"Eric!" Dr. Halstead cried. "If you don't knock it off, you're going to have to leave."

"After what you did to that girl," Marcus said to Eric, "how can you judge anybody else?" "Shut up!" Eric sad loudly.

"Why?" Marcus demanded. "Because you've got the hots for the new girl? Well, new girl, let me give you a heads-up."

He looked at Katie with a solemn expression, and said, "Sure, this guy went to Harvard. Thought he was hella diesel, too. But he was just a punk."

He glared at Eric, and said slowly, "He raped this one girl, you know. Nearly fucking killed her."

Eric shot up out of his seat, the veins in his neck popping out of his flesh. "That's a lie!" he shouted.

"Ain't no lie," Marcus said gravely, looking steadily into the other young man's face.

Eric didn't say anything. He just reached up, and grabbed at his hair, rocking back and forth like a psycho. He turned away from the group, and went to the window, where he sank down on his haunches, and started to scream. He ripped at his hair, and then pulled off his shirt, scraping the flesh of his chest and abdomen with his fingernails.

"Eric!" Dr. Halstead cried. "Eric, please . . ."

She went over to him, and knelt beside him, trying to calm him down. Katie wondered why he should deserve all her attention, all her energy. Why should he be the reason she was always so tired?

But then, she supposed that was the same thing as asking what the fuck she was doing in this place.

After a while, the doctor got Eric to calm down, and helped him to his feet. Then she led him out of the room. She glanced back at the group in apology.

Katie caught her eye, and held it for a moment, trying to convey some sort of message in her gaze. She wasn't even sure what she was trying to say. But she knew that she wanted to say *something*.

She looked away from the doctor, afraid that the other woman would see something in her gaze that she would rather hide. As she moved her head, though, she saw the orderly named Tim Reynolds. He was standing inside the door of the Community Room, his hands behind his back, surveying the patients calmly. He sensed Katie's eyes on him, and he looked towards her. He smiled grimly.

Katie didn't like the look of that smile. The orderly's eyes looked very dark, and very hollow.

She wanted more than anything to know if he was the man who'd been under the black hood last night.

Chapter 10

After group came lunch. Katie had been dreading it, but she was starving. She wanted to rip into that gluey food so badly, she knew she'd have to be careful not to take out pieces of the Styrofoam tray.

Fuck 'em all, she thought. Let them whisper about her behind her back. Let them judge her and hate her. What did she care? She was one of the only people in this place who *wasn't* a psycho.

She went up to the counter, and they passed her a tray of stiff-looking food. She nodded in thanks, and grabbed a plastic-wrapped spork. Then she hurried to the empty table she'd occupied at dinner the night before.

She was already inhaling her food, practically oblivious to the world around her, when she noticed movement out of the corner of her eye. She looked up quickly, wondering if someone was up to something. She wiped gooey chicken à la king from her chin, and found herself face-to-face with a little old woman.

"Hello," she said blankly.

"Hello," the old woman returned politely. She gestured towards the empty side of the table, and asked, "May I sit?"

Katie nodded.

The old woman sat down across from Katie. Katie watched her wonderingly, trying to figure out why she'd come over.

She was a very small woman, with short saltand-pepper hair, and olive-colored skin. She was wearing a white cotton shift and a pink housecoat.

"I noticed you were sitting alone yesterday," she said to Katie. "I thought you might like some company."

Katie nodded towards the old people's table, and asked, "Weren't you happier over there?"

The old woman sighed, and said, "Not really. All they do is complain. 'My knees hurt, my back hurts, I can't see as well as I used to.' Who the hell can?"

Katie smiled thinly, and went back to her lunch.

"My name's Elizabeth Parrish," the old woman said.

Katie opened her mouth to give her name, but the old woman just smiled, and waved her hand. "Already know it," she said. "Everybody knows *your* name, dear. Of course you know they're all talking about you?"

Katie looked surreptitiously around the cafeteria, scowling. "Well," she said, "I guess I sort of suspected it – but it would have been nicer not to hear it out loud."

"Ah, well," Elizabeth Parrish said. "That's the way it is with most things. But not hearing things doesn't make them any less true, does it?"

She looked into Katie's face with a wise expression, and Katie couldn't help smiling again.

"You know," the old woman said, "you don't look like the sort of girl who'd kill someone. But then, you can never really tell."

She peered inquisitively at Katie, and asked, "Did you kill your sister, dear?"

Katie looked steadily into her eyes, wondering if she should answer. The look in the old woman's eyes was so ingenuous, and the expression on her face was so benign, she didn't see what harm it could do. And besides, it was nice to talk to someone.

"No," she answered. "I didn't kill her."

"Hmmm," Elizabeth Parrish murmured, tapping her spork against the faux-wooden tabletop. "You appear to be telling the truth. I'm pretty good at deciding who's telling the truth."

She nodded resolutely, and set to work on her lunch. Katie's brows knitted together, and she stared at the old woman for a moment. But then she shrugged, and went back to her own food.

She was almost done, when she heard smacking footsteps behind her, as if someone were trying especially hard to make themselves heard. She sighed, and looked over her shoulder to see Carmen Rodriguez standing behind her.

"Goddamn it," she muttered.

"Hey there, newbie," Carmen said to Katie. She nodded to the old woman, and added, "I see you're sitting with Mrs. Parrish. Do you know what Mrs. Parrish did, newbie?"

Katie frowned. She didn't respond.

There was a small group of patients coming to stand around Carmen, obviously wondering what was going down. Eric Conley was among them. He was watching Katie with intense interest.

When Katie looked at him, all she could think of was him rocking back and forth on the floor of the Community Room, shirtless, scratching himself. She could see one of the scratches protruding from under his T-shirt, up towards his pale neck.

"Crazy old Mrs. Parrish," Carmen went on, her dark eyes burning with hate. "Crazy-ass old lady! But I guess you have to be crazy, if you're going to drown your own baby."

Katie looked sharply at the old woman. She just shrugged, and took a bite of chicken à la king. She dabbed her mouth daintily with a cheap napkin. "It's not as though you asked me," she said simply. "If you'd asked, I would have answered."

Katie was stunned. Granted, it shouldn't have been odd to hear something like this in an insane asylum, but for some reason she was stupefied. Maybe it was the way the old woman had asked her about her own innocence. Or maybe she was just tired of people screwing with her.

She looked back at Carmen, and made her face hard. "What are you telling *me* for?" she demanded. "It doesn't have anything to do with me."

"Then why are you sitting with her?" Carmen returned in a hostile tone.

"Four years in high school," Katie said, "and you're telling me you never sat next to a person who killed somebody?"

She paused, and sneered. "But wait," she said. "You probably didn't even get through all four years."

Eric Conley snickered, and hid his mouth behind his hand. Carmen's face twisted with rage, and she flew at Katie. She tried to wrap her hands around Katie's throat, and when Katie blocked her, she started scratching at Katie's face with her fingernails.

"Fight, fight, fight!" Eric shouted. Some of the other patients took up the chant, and started pumping their fists in the air.

"Fight, fight, fight!"

"Get off of me, you psycho!" Katie screamed. She managed to push Carmen away from her. Then she hauled back, and punched her in the face.

Carmen fell back on her ass, holding her nose, while blood dripped through her fingers. It slipped down to the floor in quick droplets, *one two three*. Eric tried to hold out a hand to Carmen, but she slapped him away. She struggled up to her feet, stepping in her own blood.

"You better watch out, bitch," she muttered to Katie, her entire body shaking with rage. "Maybe I'll come in your room at night, and cut that pretty throat."

She glared at Katie with a wrathful expression, and Katie knew that she was completely serious. She suddenly wished that there were locks on the patients' bedroom doors.

Carmen turned away, and stomped out of the cafeteria, leaving bloody footprints in her wake.

After she'd gone, her small group of cronies hung back for a few moments, looking at Katie wonderingly.

"Nice punch," Eric Conley said to her. Then he nodded, stuffed his hands in his jeans' pockets, and walked back to his own table.

Katie stood still for a moment, looking down at the mess of blood on the floor. Then she looked back at Elizabeth Parrish, and felt queasy, as if she were going to throw up her chicken à la king. She left her tray on the table, and went running out of the cafeteria.

***

The door to Dr. Halstead's office was open this time. But Katie lingered for a long moment behind the wall, breathing heavily, still raging after her encounter with Carmen.

She didn't want Cora Halstead to see her in this state. She didn't want to give the woman any reason to think that she actually *was* crazy. She'd stopped at the bathroom to check her face in the mirror, and was grateful that Carmen's fingernails hadn't left any visible marks on her skin. But she still had to compose herself.

The open door was throwing her off. She wished it was closed, so she could knock. That would make everything seem more normal.

What was she supposed to do? Just walk into the room? Should she announce herself somehow?

All these questions were making her tired. She didn't know how to answer any of them, so she took a deep breath, stepped around the wall, and walked quietly into the office.

Dr. Halstead was ready today. She wasn't distracted, wasn't thinking about anything except her upcoming appointment. She looked up at Katie as soon as she came into the room, and smiled brightly.

"Hi, Katie," she said. "Will you sit down?"

Katie didn't say anything. She just went to the desk, and sat down in front of it. Then she sighed, and looked out the window.

"You don't want to talk," the doctor observed. "I can understand that. This morning was difficult."

She peered sympathetically at Katie, and sighed. "I'm sorry if I was a little gruff earlier," she said. "After the twins. You were right – sometimes I think they're dangerous. Most of the patients know better than to get too close to them. But you didn't."

Dr. Halstead looked a lot different this afternoon. She didn't look tired at all. She looked ten years younger. No more beautiful, of course. She'd already been beautiful. But she seemed happy.

For some reason, that made Katie happy, and she began to let go of the angry adrenaline that was pumping through her veins.

"It's not that I don't want to talk," Katie explained slowly. "It's not that I don't want to talk to *you*. It's just – I'm just –"

She paused, and blew an exasperated breath through her lips. Then she blurted out: "I'm just afraid of what you're going to think."

Cora Halstead watched her carefully. "You're afraid of what *I'm* going to think?" she asked.

Katie nodded stiffly, feeling embarrassed. "But then," she said, "I guess I shouldn't have told you that. Is there any way you could forget that I said it?"

She smiled anxiously, and Cora Halstead returned the smile, but hers was calm and gentle. "If you're wondering," she said, "I don't think that you had anything at all to do with what happened to Dr.

Damien. You were just in the wrong place at the wrong time."

"Thanks," Katie said stiffly.

Dr. Halstead continued to watch her. "You have trouble trusting people," she remarked. "Don't you?"

Katie didn't know what to say. Of course she had trouble trusting people. Who didn't? She knew what the doctor was doing: fishing for a specific cause, a particular reason. To Katie's mind, it didn't seem as if there *were* any one reason. She had put her faith in people over the years, and they had always let her down.

Mallory Kent had asserted that Katie's bitterness and cynicism were directly linked to her mother's neglect. Katie thought that was ridiculous. Sure, her mother left when she was little. Lots of people's parents did that. It wasn't anything personal. Katie still loved her mother, and her mother loved her. If Katie was straight, and her father was the one who'd left, people would say her bad attitude was because of him. It was a very subjective business, the fingerpointing game.

"You could say that," Katie replied, a simple answer to the doctor's inquiry. "But then again, if I asked you how well *you* trusted people, what would you say?"

The doctor smiled again. A soft, light smile. Her way of saying "Touché."

"It's obvious that you don't want to talk about anything personal," Cora said. "I get that. So why don't we talk about something else?"

Katie eyed her warily. "Like what?" she asked.

"Well," Cora said slowly, with an almost sly smile playing over her mouth, "I already know you love literature. You're a writer. And I saw you eyeing my books when you came in here for the first time."

She nodded her head towards the bookshelves, continuing to smile.

Katie smiled back. "Okay," she said. "You've got me. I guess you like to read, too?"

"I didn't in college," Cora replied. "One too many books on psychiatry. But as the years went on, I fell in love with reading again."

She eyed Katie curiously, and then asked, "Who's your favorite writer?"

"I have three," Katie answered. "Oscar Wilde; Anton Chekhov; Guy de Maupassant." "Why?"

"Chekhov and Maupassant are easy to explain. They wrote simply: they got to the heart of the matter with as few words as possible. But the words were always the *right* words. As for Wilde – well, I guess I've always just been a little bit obsessed with him."

"Favorite book?"

"The Picture of Dorian Gray."

Cora grinned. "Somehow," she said, "I knew you were going to say that. Now – favorite short story?"

"Strangely enough," Katie returned, "not by any of my favorite authors. My favorite short story is 'The Venus of Ille' by Prosper Mérimée." "Why?"

Cora repeated.

"I've always had a soft spot for the combination of fiction and history. I think it takes a really good writer to put them together with conviction."

"I'll bet you could do it," Cora said with another soft smile.

Katie flushed pink, and looked away. "I've tried my hand at it," she said. "I've got the rough drafts to prove it. But I haven't nailed it yet."

"How do you know if you've nailed it?" Cora asked with interest.

"That's hard to say," Katie returned, biting her bottom lip, and looking down at the carpet with a thoughtful expression. "I suppose – well, I suppose you never really *do* know. You get the feeling that you have, but sometimes you're wrong."

"Tell me more about 'The Venus of Ille,'" Cora suggested. "I've never read it."

"I came across it when I was younger," Katie said. "In a copy of *The Bedside Book of Famous French Stories* that my father gave me. Maupassant was in there too, by the way. But there was just something about Mérimée's story. His Venus was just so – captivating. My father told me to read that story first, so I did."

"What was the story about?"

"It was about a statue of Venus that came to life. The owner's son had put his bride's wedding ring on its finger as a joke, but the statue had taken the oath as a real one. When it felt betrayed, it killed the young man who'd put the ring on its finger."

"Interesting stuff," Cora remarked.

"I think it was based on the Venus of Praxiteles," Katie returned. "The Greek sculptor. He received a commission from the city of Kos for a likeness of the goddess. He made two versions, one fully clothed, and the other half-nude. The people of Kos took the fully draped version, and rejected the other as obscene. But it's worth noting that today there's no idea what the draped version even looked like. It elicited no interest; people didn't care about it. It wasn't exciting enough. It didn't survive."

"What happened to the nude version?" Cora asked, looking genuinely interested.

"It was purchased by the citizens of Knidos," Katie replied. "They set it up in an open-air temple. It became a tourist attraction, and a patron of the Knidians. A man even went into the temple one night, and tried to have his way with the statue."

"Did he manage it?" Cora asked with an amused grin.

"I'd wager that he didn't," Katie answered. "Even if he'd escaped everyone's notice, he still would have had trouble getting the job done. At least – without a chisel of his own, that is."

Cora laughed out loud. Katie tried to hide her smile, though she was pleased that she'd amused the other woman.

"You're an interesting woman, Katie," Cora remarked. "Very interesting indeed."

Katie took a moment to savor that comment. Cora had phrased it in a strange way. She hadn't said, *You're an interesting person.* She'd said Katie was an interesting *woman,* which led Katie to believe that the doctor had some definite preference between women and men.

Or maybe she was just imagining things. Maybe she was seeing things where there was nothing at all to be seen.

Castles in the air, so to speak. Her own Cloud Cuckoo Land.

Chapter 11

Katie didn't know what to do with herself that afternoon. She was feeling somehow elated, as if she were walking on clouds, suspended somewhere between the floor and the ceiling. She knew it was her conversation with Dr. Halstead that had done it, and it scared her. She knew it was crazy to let herself develop feelings for the doctor.

What did they call that sort of thing? *Transference?* But, then again, would you still call it that if the person in question wasn't actually being institutionalized for psychiatric problems? What if they were just accused of killing their sister, got stuck in a hospital, and became attracted to their assigned doctor?

Katie knew she shouldn't even be thinking about it. It was a dangerous thing to think about. She should be focusing on the more important issue: How could she get *out* of this place?

No matter how hard she tried, though, she didn't think she'd be able to find an answer to that question. She would be incarcerated here for the foreseeable future.

For at least six years.

Despite all these damning details, Katie couldn't seem to get Cora Halstead out of her head. That was probably why she eventually found herself walking down the North Corridor, where all the doctors' offices were situated. She went past Abel Damien's door with a shiver. There was yellow tape stretched across the door, taped to either side of the jamb. POLICE LINE. DO NOT CROSS.

Everyone's seen that tape in movies, or maybe on *Law & Order*. But this was real.

For a single brief moment, it was almost too much for Katie to process. First, her half-sister falls down the stairs and cracks her head open. Everyone blames Katie, and she ends up in an asylum. But then comes another piece of shit on the crappy sundae. A doctor at the asylum is murdered horrendously, and Katie is found right outside his damned door.

Even though she knew that she'd had nothing to do with either incident, she was starting to see how it might be difficult to ignore the signs of her involvement. Even though she hadn't *been* involved, it sure did seem like she had.

Katie rubbed her temples, trying to stave off an oncoming headache. But she knew she didn't have a chance. It was barreling through the front of her skull like a freight train.

The sound of voices began to penetrate the dull, throbbing pain, and Katie looked around. The voices must have been coming from one of the offices.

She saw an open door on the left-hand. She hung back a little, and stayed near the wall, trying to peek into the room. She saw a corner of the desk. An arm of a chair. Heard the same voices.

Two male voices. She recognized one as that of Marcus Bickford. The other one she'd never heard before.

"I know things have been hard for you,

Marcus," the second man's voice said. "I know you're in pain. You don't want to let anyone in, and I understand that. But maybe you should think about it."

It wasn't difficult to infer who the voice belonged to. There were only five doctors here at Greystone. Three of them were male, and one of them was dead.

It wasn't Karl Diederich's voice speaking. So it must have been Dr. Wilkins.

"That's easy for you to say," Marcus replied. Katie tried to improve her view of the room by craning her neck, but all she could really see was the top of the desk. The door was only partially ajar.

Wilkins laughed. A very thin, very nervous laugh. It seemed incredibly out of place in a professional conversation between doctor and patient. "I can see why you'd think that," Wilkins said. "But please believe me, Marcus. This is just as hard for me as it is for you."

Suddenly, the doctor's pale hand appeared, reaching across the desk towards Marcus. The doctor laid his hand on Marcus's, and squeezed gently.

Katie could hear Marcus sigh. It wasn't a sigh of irritation, but one of frustration. He seemed annoyed, but not particularly with Wilkins. It was difficult to explain the mood that Katie inferred from that simple sigh.

Marcus leaned forward and pressed his forehead against Wilkins's hand. He let out a soft sob. Wilkins moved his hand to Marcus's head and stroked his hair. Marcus breathed deeply in and out, and began to calm down.

"Shhh," Wilkins said. "It's all right. But come on, sit up. The door's open, Marc."

"Then shut it," Marcus murmured.

"You know I can't," Wilkins returned. "I don't want to give Diederich any reason to think –"

Marcus nodded frantically against the doctor's hand, apparently alarmed by what he'd just said. Then he sat up, and Wilkins pulled his hand back. Katie could no longer see either of the men. Just the desk.

She stood there behind the wall, her eyebrows knitted in confusion, her lips puckered in an uncomprehending frown. At the least, this was a very strange doctor-patient relationship. At the most, it was a sort of sexual tension that both the men seemed to feel.

But hell, it wasn't as though Katie was judging. She'd just been flitting down the corridor like a bluebird, fantasizing about her own doctor.

Seeing the odd behavior of the two men put her own inexplicable feelings into context. They weren't real, there was no way they could be real. She was feeling helpless, and lost, and it seemed like she was going to feel this way for years to come. There was nothing and no one to make it better. Which explained why Katie had tried to drag someone in to make things seem less bleak, less hopeless. She had always been attracted to older women. It was only logical that the beautiful Dr. Halstead would have caught her eye.

What sad, lonely person wouldn't have started to fall for a pretty woman who smelled like rose water and lavender? Katie even took a moment to think about what kind of perfume that could be. She'd never smelled anything like it. She stopped walking for a moment, and stared blankly down the corridor, imagining Cora Halstead standing naked in her bedroom. She pictured her unstoppering a bottle of perfume, placing a few drops on the tips of her fingers, and daubing it gently around her throat.

Katie was seized by a sudden feeling of intense lust. There were butterflies in her stomach, and her loins were on fire. You could call it transference, if you wanted to, but the truth was that no woman had ever managed to turn her on this way without even being in view.

She felt a poignant longing to catch just a single, brief glimpse of Cora Halstead's face. Her office was just a little way down the corridor. Maybe her door would be open, and Katie could just peek inside . . .

She hadn't quite made it to Dr. Halstead's office, though, when the sound of more voices caught her ear. Coming from the right-hand this time. From Dr. Marina Salvador's office.

The door was nearly shut, but not quite. It looked like someone had flung it back in a hurry, probably thinking that it was shut, and not realizing that it wasn't.

The voices were female, this time. One, of course, was Dr. Salvador's. Katie was a little surprised to realize that the second was Dr. Halstead's.

Katie moved up beside the wall, and lowered her head towards the door. She had a sudden realization that what she was doing was wrong. Of course it was unethical to eavesdrop on the conversations of strangers. What had she been thinking, listening in on Marcus Bickford's private consultation with Dr. Wilkins? What if someone had caught her? What if someone caught her now? What would they say when they found her spying? Katie Throckmorton, the same girl who'd been found outside the dead doctor's office door. Presumably unconscious, they would say. Presumably being the key word.

She thought about these things, and obviously she realized the truth and the merit in them. But now that she knew Dr. Halstead was in the office, she couldn't seem to pull herself away. She wanted to listen to the sound of her voice. Wanted to listen to it when it was unreserved, and unaware that she was hearing it.

Katie wondered why Cora was in Dr. Salvador's office. The two women hadn't seemed to be on the best of terms in Cora's office while Detective Morgan was questioning Katie. Salvador had even seemed a little acidic. What could they possibly be talking about? Something to do with work, of course. Even if you didn't like a person you worked with, you were still obliged to consult with them from time to time.

Katie bent her head nearer to the crack in the door, and listened carefully.

"I don't like what's been going on here," Cora Halstead said. "And I know that things have been going on. We all know it."

"Of course we do," Marina Salvador returned. Her voice was nonchalant, almost bored. "But what are we supposed to do about it?"

"I don't know," Cora said, sounding desperate. "But we have to do *something*. God knows I hated Damien, but –"

"Shhh!" Salvador whispered violently. "Don't talk about that. If you had any common sense, you'd stop thinking about it altogether."

"But –"

"We don't know anything," Salvador interrupted. "Hopefully we never will."

Katie was intrigued. What could these two women know about what had happened to Damien? What could they know, unless one of them was involved? Or maybe both of them?

No. No, that couldn't be true. Dr. Halstead couldn't have had anything to do with it.

Katie leaned forward, trying to see inside the room, but the crack between the door and the jamb wasn't wide enough. If she wanted to see, she would have to open the door wider. She was afraid to do it, of course, but she was also desperate to see into the room. She reached out with a shaking hand, and gingerly touched a fingertip to the door. She applied the slightest amount of pressure, and nothing happened. She pushed a little harder. The door moved silently forward, about half an inch. Just enough to make the front of the room visible to her.

The two doctors were standing near the desk. Salvador behind it, Halstead beside it. Salvador looked enticing as always, in her short skirt and tight jacket. Cora, on the other hand, looked a little haggard, and a little drawn. Her neat skirt suit was impeccable as it had been when Katie saw her last, but there were dark shadows under her eyes, the kind that come from dark thoughts that are just too dark to think about. There had been a kind of light in her eyes, earlier in the day, but it was gone now. Her skin was pale. The corner of her mouth was twitching.

"Aren't you afraid other people might be in danger?" she persisted. "Aren't you afraid *we* might be in danger?"

Salvador laughed, apparently with genuine amusement. That devil-may-care expression never flickered from her face. "Hell no," she said. "Nothing's going to happen to us. Why would it? You're being paranoid."

"But –" Cora repeated.

Salvador didn't let her finish. She lunged forward like a tiger, and planted the palms of her hands against Cora's shoulders, thrusting her down against the desk. For a brief, wild moment, Katie thought of rushing into the room. She couldn't let another murder happen right in front of her. She couldn't let Cora Halstead die.

She was just reaching towards the door, about to throw it wide open, when she was taken by surprise. Marina Salvador's intentions immediately became clear, and it was obvious that she wasn't trying to kill the other doctor.

She was trying to fuck her.

Salvador pressed the front of her body against Cora's, pushing the other woman flat against the desk. Then she lowered her mouth to her neck, almost like a vampire, and kissed her hungrily. She unfastened the top buttons of her shirt, and reached down under her bra, squeezing teasingly. She thrust a hand up under Cora's well-ironed black skirt, and sought for her mark. Katie could pinpoint the exact moment she worked around the other doctor's underwear, and found the soft mouth beneath them. Cora Halstead arched her back, and threw her arms over her head, as Marina Salvador's mouth played over her chest.

As she watched, Katie felt incredibly guilty. She shouldn't be seeing this. She felt like she was watching some kind of surreal porno movie in the back room of a seedy massage parlor.

She looked away from the scene in front of her, her eyes stinging painfully. She ground the heels of her hands into them, and turned away from the door, hurrying down the corridor as quickly and quietly as she could.

***

She found Lydia Brock in their room, nestled in the chilly metal niche in front of the barred window. She had her sketchpad, and was doodling peacefully. Her expression was calm.

Katie walked into the room, and Lydia looked up at her. "Hi, Katie," she said with a bright smile.

Katie felt an inexplicable gratitude for her presence. She felt like she wasn't alone.

"Hey, Lydia," she replied. But her voice was off. She was a little breathless, and it was obvious that she'd been running. Running down the corridor. Running away from the sight of Cora Halstead having sex with Marina Salvador.

"Are you okay?" Lydia asked in concern, sitting upright in the uncomfortable niche. Rich people had lovely window seats with pastel cushions and expensive throw pillows. Lydia Brock had a wide bar of brown metal.

"Yeah," Katie answered haltingly, planting her hands against her hips, and heaving a sigh. "It's just been one of those days."

"Mm-hmm," Lydia murmured quietly. "I know what you mean. For me, *every* day is one of those days."

Katie looked at her sympathetically. She went to sit on the edge of her bed, so that she could talk more easily with Lydia.

"You look as if you've seen a ghost," Lydia said with an uncertain smile.

"Not quite," Katie replied. "Just a couple of weird things."

Lydia frowned. "Like what?"

Katie hesitated, and then said, "When we talked out in the garden, you seemed like you knew a lot about Marcus Bickford. Are you guys close?"

Lydia smiled softly. "To be honest," she said, "he's the only friend I have in this place. He's the only one who doesn't judge me."

"This is probably going to sound like a weird thing to say," Katie went on, "but do you know – well, do you know if Marcus and Dr. Wilkins have something going on?"

Lydia suddenly looked uncomfortable. She squirmed in front of the window, the late afternoon sunlight shining on the back of her neck. It was like a spotlight on someone being interrogated.

"I'm sorry," Katie said quickly. "I didn't mean to upset you. I wouldn't have even asked, if it hadn't been for something strange that Wilkins said about Diederich. Like he knew or something."

Lydia sighed heavily, and leaned forward so that she could lower her voice. "Okay," she said. "I know about Marcus and Wilkins. But Marcus made me swear not to tell anyone. You can't ever tell him that I told you."

"I won't," Katie promised. "I'm just trying to get a grip on what's going on in this place. Doctors are being killed, other doctors are sleeping with the patients, and on top of all that –"

She cut herself short, realizing that she hadn't planned on telling Lydia about Halstead and Salvador.

"What?" Lydia asked curiously.

"Well – it's nothing, really," Katie said hesitantly, rubbing the back of her neck uncomfortably. "When I was walking around just now, I saw Dr. Halstead and Dr. Salvador. In Salvador's office." She paused, swallowed thickly, and added, "Having sex."

Lydia sat bolt upright, looking shocked. "You're fucking joking!" she exclaimed.

This was the most animated Katie had ever seen her. She frowned, and looked at her curiously. "You seem pretty interested," she said.

Lydia sat back against the window, and pulled her knees up to her chest, looking embarrassed. "Sorry," she said. "I didn't mean to react like that. Before I came here, I used to love those stupid tabloid magazines – the ones that tell you who's sleeping with who, and who's cheating on who, even though most of it probably isn't even true. It gives me this weird high."

"Okay," Katie said slowly.

Lydia covered her face with her hands, and sighed. "Now you think I'm a freak," she said.

Katie leaned forward, and put a hand on Lydia's knee. "No," she said firmly. "I don't think that at all. I'm still just a little dazed, that's all. It was a weird thing to see."

Lydia dropped her hands, and looked suddenly thoughtful. Katie was pretty sure that the girl was bipolar.

"I like Dr. Halstead," she said. "But I don't like Salvador. Ever since I saw that boy going into her office —"

She paused.

"What boy?" Katie asked. "You've mentioned him before."

"He was just this sixteen-year-old kid," Lydia said. "His name was Jack. He had a major crush on Dr. Salvador. What sixteen-year-old boy wouldn't?"

She looked bitter for a moment, and then added, "But one day I saw him going into her office. She shut the door, but I was so curious, I risked pushing it open just a little. He wasn't her patient, after all, and I was wondering what he was doing in her office. Luckily they didn't notice me. I peeked into the room, and I saw her sit next to him on the couch. She started touching him, and he started crying. He was just a kid, and he had problems. But she just pushed him down on the couch, and started taking his clothes off.

I shouldn't have been watching, but she practically raped him."

"Do you think maybe she had something going on with Dr. Damien?" Katie asked. She didn't know what had made her ask that question. It had just popped into her head.

"I don't know," Lydia said. "Why? Do you think she might have had something to do with his death?"

"I'm not sure," Katie answered. "It was just something she said. Like she was involved."

"Hmmm," Lydia said. "Weird."

"Yeah," Katie replied with a sigh. "Pretty weird."

She didn't say anything else, but she was thinking about Cora Halstead's strange and possibly incriminating conversation with Salvador. She was really hoping that Cora didn't have anything to do with what had happened to Abel Damien.

Chapter 12

The rain was hammering steadily against the roof of the asylum, filling Katie's head with thoughts of dread. She used to love the sound of rain, but now it seemed cold and sad.

She pulled her thin, rough blanket more tightly around her. She looked over at Lydia, who lay asleep facing the wall. Her breathing was peaceful and regular.

Only Katie lay awake, tonight.

She threw off the useless blanket, her teeth chattering in the cold air. Her breath even went so far as to fan out in front of her face.

She'd left her shoes right next to the bed, and she swung her legs over the mattress to shove her feet into them. They were cold as an Eskimo's ass, but she gritted her teeth, and grabbed her black silk robe from the end of the bed.

Her father had asked if she'd wanted a new robe for the asylum. He thought it'd be cold. *And, damn it all, he was right,* she thought.

But she bit her lip, and slipped the robe over her shoulders. She didn't care. She didn't want some frumpy pink robe. No one thought she was worth much, at the moment, but the silk robe made her feel better. It made her feel like more than nothing.

Only a little, maybe. But that was better than nothing at all.

Clad in the asylum nightgown, the silk robe, and her slip-on sneakers, she meandered out into the corridor. She looked around warily for anyone who might be watching.

She should have known better. There was no one there at all.

The women's corridor was glowing with the dirty grey fluorescence that was cast by the plastic strips at the top of the wall, but she could see the light of the nurses' desk, burning in the hall that branched off to the right. So she crept to the left.

She walked down the women's corridor, looking briefly at each of the closed doors, and wondering if anyone was having nightmares behind any of them.

She hated nightmares. She was sick to death of them. But they seemed to like her just as much as ever.

She felt very tired, all of a sudden. Her limbs felt as if they were weighed down with lead. If she'd chosen, she thought that she could have gone back to her room, stretched out beneath the thin blanket, and fallen into a sleep like death.

If she'd chosen. But she didn't choose. They would have liked for her to choose that, but she refused.

She paused her steps for a moment, thinking hard. Was she becoming paranoid? Was she using the universal *THEY* to signify someone who didn't even exist?

No one really cared that she was there, after all. They thought she'd killed her sister, so they'd locked her up. It wasn't any more complicated than that.

Still, she couldn't force herself to go back to her room. The drowsiness was quickly being replaced with restlessness: an eerie, otherworldly restlessness that spoke of misery and defeat. She couldn't do anything other than continue on her way down the corridor.

She walked on. She began taking deep breaths, and exhaling them slowly. She was trying to calm herself down. This place gave her the creeps.

Breathe in, she thought. *One, two, three.*

Breathe out. One, two, three.

She was just taking another breath – she'd only counted to two – when she sensed movement at her left-hand, and someone grabbed hold of her arm. She wanted to scream, but the sound got stuck in her throat, like a baked bean in the sticky sauce at the bottom of the can.

"Do you know that the end is coming?" a male voice inquired huskily, puffing sour breath onto the side of her face. She grimaced, and turned her face away.

"You can't see me," the man said. "You don't know that I'm serious."

He tapped the side of her face, trying to make her open her eyes. She looked at him. The creepy Norman Bates guy.

Just my goddamn luck, she thought with an inward sigh.

"The end is coming," he repeated in an ominous voice. "Do you understand that?"

Katie looked steadily into his face. "I can't blame you for not knowing," she said, "but so far as ends go – mine's already come and gone. You and me are roomies, pal. What do you want to do? You want to strangle me? Tear my heart out? Go ahead, Norman. Save me at least six years of hell."

He looked curiously into her face. "My name's not Norman," he said.

"I suppose it isn't," Katie returned. "What is it, then?"

"Jacob. Jacob Barlow."

"Okay," Katie said, shaking her arm free of his grasp. "Nice to meet you, Jacob. For future reference, though – it's not polite to grab people's arms in the middle of the night. You might call it upsetting."

Jacob Barlow looked down at the floor, and ran his hands through his dark, wild hair. "I didn't mean to upset you," he murmured. "I just wanted you to know. The end is coming."

"We've already been through all that, Jake," Katie sighed, clapping Jacob Barlow on the shoulder. "Why don't you go and get some sleep?"

He frowned, and seemed to think for a moment. "Maybe," he muttered. "I can't remember the last time I slept . . ."

"Well, there you go," Katie said. "You just need some sleep, Jake. Go lie down for a while, man. And stop grabbing people."

"Okay," he murmured, running his hands through his hair again, and shuffling off down the corridor.

Katie shook her head. "Poor bastard," she muttered, setting off on her way again. She didn't know where she was going, but she hoped she'd get there soon.

At the end of the women's corridor, she came to the doctors' corridor. The North Corridor.

There was a light burning under one of the doors. She didn't even have to think about which door it was. She already knew.

It was Cora Halstead's office door.

What's she doing here at night? Katie wondered. She didn't wonder for long, though. She just started off towards the burning light.

When she got to the door, she stood there for a long while, her forehead pressed against the cold wood, her hand wrapped around the doorknob. She wanted to open it, but she knew she shouldn't.

She shouldn't even knock. That would be inappropriate, at this time of night.

She thought of saying something. A knock seemed too abrupt: too loud in the dark of the night. So she'd say something. But what to say?

She should probably say, *"Dr. Halstead."*

But that had never seemed right to her. Whenever she said the words – whenever she thought of the older woman that way – it never seemed like the *correct* thing.

But what was she supposed to say? She was at a loss.

She stood there for a while longer, grinding her forehead into the door. She felt like she might cry.

"Cora," she whispered finally.

There was nothing, at first. But then, there was the smallest noise of movement – like someone had thought that they heard something, but they weren't entirely sure.

"Cora," she repeated, a little more loudly.

There was the sound of definite footsteps, now. A moment later, the door swung open on slightly squeaky hinges, and Cora Halstead was revealed.

She stood in the doorway in a pair of flannel pajama pants, blue-and-white stripes. Her long-sleeved T-shirt was white. Her dark hair flowed down over her delicate shoulders in a way that Katie had never seen it do before. She always wore it pinned back, away from her face while she worked.

"Katie," she said. "Are you all right?"

She sounded genuinely concerned. It was as if a family member had come to her bedroom door in the middle of the night, upset about something. And she was concerned.

"Katie?" she repeated.

"I'm sorry," Katie said quickly. "I couldn't sleep, so I went for a walk – and I saw your light. I shouldn't have knocked."

"You didn't knock," Cora Halstead said with a soft smile.

"Oh," Katie said, with the slightest catch in her throat. "Sorry."

The psychiatrist didn't say anything more about it. She just pulled the door open wider, and ushered Katie into the room. "Will you come in?" she asked politely.

"If you're sure you don't mind," Katie said, feeling very self-conscious all of a sudden.

"I don't mind," the other woman replied simply.

So Katie stepped into the room. It was burning brightly, three lamps at once. There was the lamp on the desk, with a myriad of papers strewn in front of it. Then, there was the lamp on the table between the sofa and the armchair, in front of which sat the coffee table with the line of innocuous magazines. In the far corner of the room, there was a six-foot upright lamp, casting the remainder of the glow over the room. Katie had never seen that one turned on before.

"What are you doing here at night?" she asked suddenly.

For a moment, Cora Halstead was at a loss. She seemed like she wanted to answer, but she didn't know how.

"It's a long story," she said simply, though it was obvious from her tone of voice there was nothing simple about it.

"Okay," Katie said slowly. "Well, I'm sorry to have knocked – I really shouldn't have done that. I should just –"

"But you didn't knock," the other woman interrupted. "You seem to keep forgetting that."

Katie looked into her face, and saw the speculation there. For some reason, it made her angry.

"If you're just going to get all *psychological* on me," she said, a little sharply, "I'll leave you alone."

"I'm sorry," the other woman said, in a soft voice that made it sound like she really meant it. "I didn't mean anything by it. It's just a force of habit."

Katie stood for a moment, breathing a little quickly, and staring at the wall. But finally, she looked back to the other woman, and tried to smile. "No," she said. *"I'm* sorry. I shouldn't have snapped at you."

"It's all right," Cora Halstead returned. "Really. Won't you come and sit?"

Katie looked to the sofa, where it was obvious Cora Halstead had been lounging. There was a thick blanket thrown over it, and a glass of red wine on the low table in front of it, with a half-empty bottle set beside it.

The sight of the wine gave Katie a delicious chill. Oh, how she longed for a glass of the stuff! It would taste like the nectar of the gods, right about now.

Cora led Katie to the little corner where the sofa and the armchair were nestled. Katie thought she'd gesture to the armchair, so she could resume her own place on the sofa, but she took gentle hold of Katie's elbow, and pointed to the couch. "Have a seat," she said.

Her voice had grown a little hollow, and it was obvious that she'd started thinking about something else. Whatever she'd been thinking about before Katie came in, probably.

Katie sat down, almost gingerly, on the sofa, and the other woman sat down beside her. A little closer than Katie had thought she'd sit.

Cora Halstead reached for her wine glass, which was nearly empty. She poured a generous splash into the bottom, and sat back to take a sip. But then she started, and looked at Katie, as if she'd realized that she was being rude.

"Will you have a drink?" she asked.

Katie looked at her in disbelief. "Did you just," she asked wonderingly – "did you just ask me if I want a *drink?*"

Cora Halstead sat back a little farther, and pondered for a moment, swilling her wine around in her glass. "Yes," she said finally. "Yes – I think I did."

Katie didn't reply, so the other woman stood up, and went across the room to a high cabinet. The top was stuffed with books, but the bottom was a little storage area with two wooden doors. Cora opened the left door, and pulled out a second wine glass.

"Just in case I ever break the other one," she explained.

She carried the glass over to the sofa. She sat down beside Katie, and held the glass aloft, while she poured a deep splash into it.

"Here," she said, handing the glass to Katie.

"You're sure about this?" Katie asked doubtfully.

"I'm sure," Cora Halstead replied, looking into her eyes with a strange expression. But then she turned away suddenly, and took a sip from her own glass.

Katie took a drink, and nearly cried out with joy at the smooth taste of the wine running over her tongue. But she managed to keep quiet, and looked back at Cora.

"What are you doing here?" she asked again.

It was obvious that the woman still didn't want to answer. But she looked into Katie's face, sighed, and said, "A disagreement with my husband."

"Ah," Katie said softly, looking away from the other woman, and swirling the wine around in her glass.

Cora Halstead knew what she was thinking. It was written all over her face. *The older woman who has problems with her husband,* she was thinking. *The unhappy woman who mistakenly thinks she's attracted to a young girl.*

She watched Katie for a long moment, but then turned away, and fixed her eyes on the darkened window. She hadn't bothered to close the blinds, and the old square panes were covered in cold frost.

"We got married when we were young," she told Katie. She was still staring at the window, and her voice was flat. "His father was a friend of *my* father – we were both in medical school – blah blah blah. Dad talked me into it. He said Donald was the kind of man a woman could build a life with."

She fell silent for a moment. Then she drained her glass.

Katie thought for a second. "The first time I came in here," she said, gesturing towards the desk, "you were sitting there, and you'd just got off the phone with somebody. Was it your husband?" "Yes," Cora said quietly.

"That's why you were so upset?"

"Let's just say we don't have very healthy conversations anymore."

She leaned forward to refill her glass, and added, "Now we're stuck. Two professionals, afraid to get divorced because of the way it might affect our reputations. He's screwing other people. *I'm* screwing other people."

She swilled her wine around again, and downed nearly the whole glass in one swallow. "If you can call it that," she said softly. "I wouldn't even bother, if she wasn't so —"

Katie looked at her sharply. Of course she knew that she was talking about Dr. Salvador. But Cora didn't know that she knew that.

Cora fell silent, looking a little afraid. "I shouldn't have said that," she murmured.

Katie looked at her seriously. "I don't mind that you said it," she told her. "I only wonder – did you say it because you wanted me to hear it?"

Cora looked at her with a grave expression. "I suppose I might have," she said slowly. "But that doesn't make any sense."

"Why not?" Katie asked, her eyes boring into the other woman's. Their pupils were locked. Katie could see the shine in Cora's eyes.

"I'm sure you didn't want anyone to know that you were sleeping with Dr. Salvador," Katie said slowly.

Cora was dumbstruck, and Katie flushed bright pink.

"I shouldn't have looked," she explained. "But I saw you. In Salvador's office."

She paused, but Cora didn't say anything.

"In my defense," Katie added, "the door wasn't closed."

"Maybe it wasn't," Cora mumbled, looking as if she didn't disbelieve Katie. "Marina is something of an exhibitionist."

"Do you mind me knowing?" Katie asked. She hardly even knew why she'd asked. She just didn't want Cora to stop talking to her.

"I hardly know you, Katie," Cora said in a quiet voice. "And, more than that – you're my patient." "I didn't ask to be," Katie said simply.

"No," Cora said thoughtfully. "No – I suppose you didn't."

Neither of them said anything for what seemed like a very long time. But finally, Katie said:

"After everything you've heard, I don't even want to know what you think about me." She paused, and swallowed thickly. "But I didn't kill my sister," she added, in barely more than a whisper.

Cora watched her for a long moment. Finally, she said: "I don't believe you did."

Katie turned towards her in relief. She wanted to move near to her, but didn't know how. It turned out, though, that she didn't need to think about it.

Cora set her wine glass on the table. Then she took Katie's.

She leaned near to Katie, moving closer and closer until their shoulders were touching. She looked into Katie's face, and then closed her eyes, pressing her forehead against Katie's brow.

"Please tell me if I'm doing anything wrong," she whispered.

"If you think you are," Katie whispered back, "I'll leave."

"I *do* think I am," Cora breathed. "But I don't care."

She darted forward, and kissed Katie deeply. Katie was caught off guard for a moment, even though she'd known it was coming. She just sat there, paralyzed, as the older woman's mouth moved against hers. But then she realized what was happening, and she threw her arms around Cora. She kicked off her shoes, and lay back against the sofa, drawing the other woman down with her.

With the front of Cora's body pressed against her own, they lay still for a moment, breathing heavily. "You're sure?" Katie asked softly, laying her hand against the other woman's cheek.

"I don't know why," Cora replied, in barely more than a murmur. "But yes – I'm sure."

Katie fell back into her embrace. It was difficult to understand the way she felt – warm and light, as if the ground and the sofa were nowhere near, as if the ceiling were much closer. It was difficult to understand, so she didn't try. She just held Cora tightly, as her lips danced down over Katie's neck, and the soft lamplight shone against the frosty window panes.

Cora worked Katie's camisole up over her head, and dropped it on the floor. Then she lowered her head back down to her chest, kissing the curves of her breasts. She took one of the nipples into her mouth, and sucked it expertly.

She knows what she's doing, Katie thought, stretching herself out in ecstasy.

Cora pulled down her pajama pants, and tugged at her underwear, until every stitch of clothing was lying on the floor next to the camisole. Katie felt helplessly exposed, like a naïve young woman who didn't know if she could trust the person who was touching her body. The chilly air pressed against her skin, making her nipples stand up like hard bullets.

The doctor left a steady trail of kisses down her abdomen, and didn't hesitate for even a moment before burying her face between Katie's legs. Her tongue was like Mr. Miyagi's chamois cloth, touching all the right places, and leaving everything jubilant and sparkling in its wake.

Katie laid a hand on the back of the other woman's neck, and drew her up out of the trenches. She was a good little soldier, though.

"Let me see you," Katie begged, staring up into her face.

The lamplight shone like liquid sunshine over the doctor's skin, as she pulled her shirt over her head, and tossed it aside. She wasn't wearing a bra. Her breasts weren't as firm as some twenty-year-old's, but they were full and round, peeking down at Katie like playful kittens. Katie reached up with a moan, and took one of them in each hand.

Cora straddled Katie's waist, and Katie sat up to kiss her breasts. She licked the nipples, sucking hungrily, like a wolf cub who needed milk. Then she slipped her hand beneath the doctor's pants, and aimed a two-finger gun at her target. Cora arched her back, while Katie slid her hand in and out, and continued to suck fiercely at her warm breasts.

Katie couldn't remember the act of sex ever bringing her so much pleasure before. This wasn't even sex – it was like some black-magic ritual, making Katie's blood boil, and tickling her clit even after the doctor had taken her face away.

Chapter 13

Late in the night, when the world was enveloped in darkness, and the morning light was still a couple of hours away, Katie was lying asleep in Cora Halstead's arms. She slept peacefully, at first, but then she began to dream. A nightmare, of course.

She was dreaming of the red-faced demon. He was standing in front of her, just like always, just standing there staring at her. But this time, he opened his mouth to speak. Katie could see his lips moving, but no sound came out. Finally, he stopped talking, and started to smile. He gestured behind him towards an open doorway, and beckoned Katie nearer to it.

She walked forward with uncertain steps. She moved up to the doorway, and peeked inside the room.

It was Abel Damien's office. He was lying on the floor, completely skinned, in a pool of his own blood. He looked like something out of *Tales from the Crypt*.

On the wall behind his body, in dark red blood, were the words *Semper tecum. Always with you.*

Katie looked frantically at the demon, and he smiled gleefully.

Suddenly, Katie woke to the feeling of warm hands on her bare shoulders. She bolted upright, covered with sweat, shaking from head to toe.

Cora Halstead was beside her on the sofa, her hands still on her shoulders. "Are you all right?" she asked. "Were you having a nightmare?"

"It's no big deal," Katie muttered, passing a cold and clammy hand across her face. I have them all the time."

"Every night?"

"Usually."

Cora wrapped an arm around Katie's waist, and pulled her back down to the sofa. She held her tightly for a moment, her soft breasts pressed against Katie's back, her cheek touching Katie's shoulder.

It was a marvelous feeling – almost too good. Katie had learned a long time ago, if something seemed too good to be true, it usually was.

She untwined her naked limbs from Cora's, and fished her clothes off the floor. The lamp was still burning, and Cora's eyes were watching her hungrily. "I wish you didn't have to leave," she whispered. "I wish we were somewhere else."

"Probably not as much as I do," Katie replied in an empty voice. "Don't forget – I'm the one who has to go back out there."

Cora's eyes began to shine, and she pulled Katie towards her again. "I wish there was something I could do," she murmured, tucking a lock of Katie's hair behind her ear.

"You and me both," Katie said with a smile. But then she forgot her bitterness, and leaned down to kiss Cora. She felt her lips, her tongue. She could feel her breath passing into her mouth. Her heart, her soul felt like it was on fire. She was having trouble breathing. It was almost supernatural.

Suddenly, Cora pulled her lips away, and stared into Katie's face. "If I had a choice," she said, "I'd give all this up. Maybe we'd run away together."

She paused, bit her lip, and then smiled unhappily. "But no one really has a choice," she added. "Do they?"

"I guess not," Katie muttered. She knew that it was time for her to leave, but she didn't want to. She leaned down, laid her body against Cora's, and kissed her throat, breathing in the heady scent of rose water and lavender.

This was the first time she remembered her fear that Cora might have had something to do with Abel Damien's death. Earlier, she'd only remembered the way Marina Salvador had fucked her, pressing her flat against the desk, and reaching into her warmth like she owned it.

She hadn't remembered their conversation before that. She hadn't remembered the allusion to Dr. Damien.

Had Cora really had something to do with the man's death? Katie didn't know. She was still breathing in her scent, and feeling horrified, when she shot to her feet, and started tugging on her clothes. She went to the door.

Cora didn't say anything. Katie opened the door, darted out into the corridor, and hurried away towards her room.

She lay down on her bed, breathing heavily. The bathroom light was shining brightly, but she didn't care anymore. Lydia was snoring lightly. It was almost a peaceful sound.

Katie didn't know what to think. She didn't know what to make of what had just happened. She'd tasted Cora Halstead's skin; felt the other woman's heart against hers. But what did it matter? She was trapped in this prison, and there was nothing anyone could do about it.

She tried to go to sleep. Soon, she fell into a fitful doze, but it was penetrated by unpleasant dreams. She was walking along a narrow corridor, completely dark, with numerous doors to either side of her. All of the doors were halfway open, with bright light pouring through the cracks. The air was filled with the sound of sex. Behind every door, in the hidden light of every room, people were fucking.

Cora Halstead was in one of those rooms. With Marina Salvador.

She thought she could hear the sound of Cora's voice. At first, she wasn't sure where it was coming from. She stopped walking, and listened carefully. Cora's voice was coming from a room on the left-hand. She listened for another moment, and started towards the door she thought Cora was hiding behind. She approached it stealthily, moving carefully. She took hold of the doorknob, and pushed the door inward. There was the sharp sound of creaking hinges –

And then she snapped awake. She had a strange, eerie feeling that someone was watching her. She focused her bleary eyes towards the foot of the bed, and nearly cried out.

The red-faced demon was standing there. It was dimly illuminated in the glow cast from the bathroom light. It just stood there, watching Katie for what seemed like a long time.

"Who are you?" she whispered. "*What* are you?"

It stared at her for another long moment. Then, without a sound, it turned away, and walked out of the room.

Katie sat frozen for a moment, staring after the demon. Then she threw herself against the mattress, and pulled the blanket over her head. She shut her eyes, and whispered frantically to herself.

"It's not real. Get a grip, Katie, it's not real . . ."

Her eyes flew open when she heard the sound of screaming. She threw the blanket off, and looked over at Lydia, expecting her to still be asleep. But this time, the young woman was sitting at the edge of her bed, looking towards the open doorway.

"Do you hear it?" Katie asked softly. Lydia didn't answer. She just nodded.

Katie put her feet on the floor, and stood up slowly. She walked just as slowly towards the doorway, and stood staring out into the dark corridor.

"Don't go out there!" Lydia hissed.

Katie looked back at Lydia, whose face was perfectly visible in the glow of the bathroom light. She looked terribly afraid. Afraid, yes – but not surprised. It was as though this had happened before. Well, it *had* happened before, but she'd been asleep that time. So had it happened before that?

"What's going on?" Katie demanded.

"Quiet!" Lydia begged. "Shut the door."

Katie complied, and walked towards Lydia's bed. The young woman was shaking like a leaf, and there was cold sweat on her brow.

"If someone's being hurt," Katie said firmly, "we have to go and see what's going on."

"No, we don't!" Lydia replied, in a voice that was just as firm. "There's nothing we can do."

"What are you talking about?" Katie asked in confusion. "Do you think – do you think someone else is being killed?"

"I don't know," Lydia breathed. "I don't know what they do back there."

"Back where?"

"In Dr. Diederich's office."

Katie was extremely perplexed. Dr. Diederich's office? What did Dr. Diederich have to do with anything?

Katie knelt down in front of Lydia, and put her hands on her knees. "Listen, Lydia," she said urgently. "You have to tell me what you meant by that. What about Dr. Diederich's office? Does he have something to do with all this? Did he kill Dr. Damien?"

Lydia stared into her face with a horrified expression. Katie could feel the young woman's legs trembling beneath her hands.

"I don't know," she said in that same breathless voice. "I don't – I don't know, Katie. I don't know what they do back there."

"You keep saying they. Who is *they?*"

"Dr. Diederich and – well, Dr. Damien."

"Dr. Damien is dead, Lydia."

"I know that!" Lydia cried, leaping off the bed, and hurrying to the barred window. She huddled down in the metal niche in front of the window, and drew her knees up to her chin. "I know that," she repeated, more quietly this time. "But that's what I meant by *they*. The Dr. Dees used to go around at night, with clipboards in their hands, glancing in at people's doors. I saw them a few times. They'd lean their heads together, and whisper so that you couldn't hear them. And then – later – I'd hear the screaming."

Katie stared at her in bewilderment. She had no idea what she was talking about, and she didn't have time to try to make sense of it. All the time they'd been talking, the screaming hadn't stopped.

Lydia put her hands over her ears, and rocked back and forth, singing softly to herself.

Katie marched over to her, and pulled her hands away from her ears. Lydia fought against her with more strength that Katie would have thought she possessed.

"No!" she cried. "No! Leave me alone! I don't want to know!"

Katie held onto her arms. "Lydia!" she said desperately. "Please tell me what's going on. Tell me . . ."

The screaming grew louder. Katie let go of Lydia, and raced away towards the door. Barefoot, she pelted down the women's corridor, towards the South Corridor, where the noise was coming from. She squinted her eyes, saw the nurses' station. It was dark. There was no one there.

A bright light burned at the end of the corridor. That must have been where the screaming was coming from.

Katie took an indecisive step in the direction of the light. She could turn back now. She didn't have to go on. She didn't have to do what she'd done last time.

A high-pitched scream went up. It was obvious that the voice was male, but whatever was happening to him had just made him scream like a woman.

Katie looked desperately towards the nurses' station. Why was it dark? There was supposed to be someone there 24-7.

She looked back towards the light. The screaming had stopped now. There was a flash of darkness against the light, and it was clear that someone had just hurried into the corridor. A dark hooded figure, maybe?

Katie didn't know, because whoever it was seemed to go in the opposite direction. She wasn't sure, at first, but she waited with bated breath for someone to start running towards her, and no one came. The dingy fluorescent squares on the walls, like creepy nightlights all along the corridor, showed her that no one was coming. Whoever it was had run to the left, not to the right. But the bright light at the end of the corridor was still burning.

Katie stood stock-still, as if she were rooted to the spot. She wanted to know what lay beyond the light, but at the same time, she was wary of going forward. What if they caught her again? It was obvious that something terrible had just happened. How would it look, if she was the first person to view the scene – for the second time?

She hung back, not knowing what to do. Why was the nurses' station dark? Why wasn't there anyone here to help her?

Everything was quiet, but it was an eerie quiet, as if everyone in the asylum were awake in their beds, listening with straining ears for the next sound. Katie knew that she and Lydia couldn't have been the only ones who'd heard what had just happened.

"Help!" Katie called out. Her voice came more softly than she'd meant for it to, more like a screeching whisper than a plea for assistance. "Help!" she called again, a little louder this time. "Can't anyone hear what's going on? Something's wrong! Someone come! Nurse – nurse!" But no one came.

Katie knew that she could have turned around and gone back to her room. Then, whatever had happened would have nothing to do with her. She would lie awake all night, staring at the ceiling. The next day, she'd find out what had happened. Someone else would figure it out for her.

For some reason, though, she felt a strange connection to whatever was going on. Almost as if she'd had a part in it, even though she knew that she hadn't.

But wait. What if she *did* have a part in it? This was the second time this had happened, and no one else could seem to hear it. No one else would come.

Was that because they couldn't hear it? Had she already killed someone? Was all this just a figment of her imagination, a defense mechanism to protect her from the truth?

Did that mean she'd actually killed Lockwood?

Wait, wait – this was impossible. She was being ridiculous. She was terrified, and it was making her think these ridiculous things. She hadn't been the only one who'd heard the screaming, after all. Lydia had heard it, too.

She had a sudden paralyzing thought, and her muscles tensed. *Had* Lydia heard the sound? Or had Katie only imagined that she did?

All this was just too surreal to actually be happening. A dark nurses' station, and screaming that only she could hear? What could that possibly mean?

Was she imagining all this? Had she already killed someone?

Had she killed Dr. Damien? Had she killed Lockwood?

She shook her head as if she were trying to wake herself from a daze, and shuffled forward down the corridor. The light was still burning. She had to know what lay beyond it.

She went on down the lengthy corridor, listening to the sound of her bare feet against the cold tiles. A soft *smack smack smack*.

She came abreast with the wall just beyond the doorway that housed the light. She paused, and took a deep breath. Then she stepped forward, and looked through the doorway. The room beyond was a small storage closet that held various cleaning supplies.

The scene was as horrific as she'd imagined. The victim was Eric Conley, son of District Attorney

Daniel Conley. Katie wondered what the DA would have thought if he could have seen his son now.

Eric was lying stomach-down on an old ironing board. His head was turned towards the doorway, and his right cheek was pressed against the faded blue cushion of the ironing board. His throat was slit wide open, and blood was dripping down onto the dingy tiles.

It was obvious that he'd been beaten. His back, and the backs of his thighs, were covered in large bruises. To complete the picture, there was a broomstick shoved deep into his rectum.

On the pale wall behind him, there were a few words scrawled in blood.

Dalla sua pace mia dipende.

Katie was horrified. She was distraught, and she was shaken. But she had the presence of mind to know that she should leave. She turned away from the storage closet, and stepped out into the corridor.

In doing so, she walked right into someone. Someone very tall, and very hard. Hard as a rock. His muscles must have been like iron.

She looked up, trying to find a face. Finally, her eyes adjusted to the dim light sifting out into the corridor from the storage closet, and she made out the identity of the person she'd crashed into.

It was Tim Reynolds.

Chapter 14

Half an hour later, Katie was sitting alone in a small room off the South Corridor of the asylum. At Tim Reynolds's behest, people had magically appeared, and more orderlies had come to escort Katie into this particular room.

She couldn't begin to understand why they'd come when *he* called. She'd called like a madwoman for someone to come. But no one had.

She sat alone in the room, at a small metal table, seated on a small metal chair. She couldn't help thinking that it looked remarkably like an interrogation room. Was this intentional? Were they messing with her? What was going on?

She sat silently, sipping at a paper cup filled with lukewarm water. Tim Reynolds had asked her if she'd wanted anything, and she'd just glared at him. He'd brought her water. Now she was sipping it.

She wished it was vodka. She wished she had a couple pills of Nembutal.

Could that have been what made her see things that might not have been exactly what she thought they were? Withdrawal from the pills? She didn't know. She didn't think so. Nothing like that had ever happened to her before.

She stayed silent. She wanted to cry out for someone to come and speak to her, but she didn't want to make it seem as if she were desperate or paranoid.

She felt like Golyadkin in Dostoyevksy's *The*

Double. She didn't know what was going on, and she felt like she was perfectly normal, but something very strange was obviously going on. She wondered if she'd see her doppelgänger walking down the corridor past the doorway of this strange interrogation room. Maybe it would turn towards her, and smile an evil smile. Or maybe it wouldn't look at her at all. It was hard to guess.

She put her elbows on the table, and dropped her head in her hands. She hadn't had time to put on her robe before she left her room. She was wearing a pair of silk pajama pants, and a black camisole made of satin. The same ones Cora Halstead had stripped off her earlier in the evening. Mallory Kent had purchased both of these articles.

She was shivering from the cold, and wishing she had a blanket. Wishing she had that frumpy pink robe her father had offered to buy for her.

Wishing she were any place other than this.

After what seemed like a very long time, the door to the room creaked open, and someone walked in. Detective Morgan.

Katie let out a heavy sigh, and stared down at the shiny metal tabletop in despair.

She looked up. Morgan was just the same as last time. Beige trench coat, short and stocky, looking like a cross between Sheriff Tupper and Columbo. Gun at the holster that he was too obvious to make known.

"Good evening, Miss Throckmorton," he said genially. "But then, it's not really evening anymore, is it? More towards morning, actually."

Katie watched him blankly as he sat down in the chair across from her.

"Are you here to accuse me of murder again?" she asked.

He looked at her with a perfectly innocent expression.

"Well," he said, "that depends. Is there anything you want to admit to?"

Katie stared at him. "No," she said slowly.

"Hmmm," the detective murmured thoughtfully, looking off at the wall with an empty expression. "That's a different matter, then."

He kept staring at the wall for about a minute, clearly thinking about something. But then he looked back at Katie, and smiled innocuously.

"How are you, Miss Throckmorton?" he asked kindly.

Kate stared at him for a moment.

"I'm sure you don't really care," she said. "So why don't we skip that part?"

"Fair enough," Morgan conceded, shoving his hands into the pockets of his trench coat, and blowing a thoughtful breath through his lips. "Fair enough. Now, Miss Throckmorton. What's been going on here tonight?"

He looked up at her with that familiar, innocent expression. But Katie knew that it was a lie. He'd do anything to get her out of this place, and stick her in some maximum-security prison where carbon copies of old Martha Jane shoved wooden spoons up her ass.

"I couldn't really tell you," she said slowly. "I heard screams. I came out into the corridor, and found the nurses' station dark. I came down the corridor, and saw Eric Conley dead. That's about it."

"The nurses' station dark, you said?" Morgan repeated thoughtfully. "That's funny. It looks all right now."

Katie wasn't at all surprised. Anything she said, they'd make it seem like the opposite.

"Sure it does," she muttered.

"What was that, Miss Throckmorton?"

Katie didn't reply. She just glared at him.

There was a knock at the door. Katie looked desperately towards the sound.

The door swung inward, and two people appeared. Karl Diederich was the first. Katie's father was the second.

"Daddy!" Katie cried, jumping to her feet, and racing across the room.

"Oh, my girl," he murmured regretfully, taking Katie in his arms, and holding her tight. "What is all this . . .?"

"I think I'm going crazy, Daddy," Katie sobbed. "I don't know what's happening . . ."

Axel Throckmorton held his daughter tight, and sighed with a lack of comprehension. "My poor baby," he whispered, kissing the top of Katie's head.

Detective Morgan got out of his chair, and stood watching the father and daughter. He was remarkably unsympathetic.

"Mr. Throckmorton," he said politely. "I'm glad you could come so quickly. I'm sure you never could have imagined something so strange, but . . ."

"What are you talking about?" Axel spat. "Of course I couldn't have imagined it. Who could have?"

He glared at Morgan, and smiled thinly. "Unless you mean to say that *you* could have," he said in a sharp voice.

"Ah," Morgan said softly. "I see how it is. You have a lot in common with your daughter, I think? But that's no matter. It is what it is. Let's move on."

"Move on to what?" Axel demanded.

"To what's happened tonight," Morgan replied promptly. It was obvious that he wasn't shaken. He laid a gentle hand on the butt of his pistol, and smiled genially.

Dr. Diederich stood behind Axel Throckmorton, surveying the scene quietly, keenly observant but not making any overt attempt to interfere with the situation. He was just watching and waiting.

Katie stepped away from her father, and stood as tall and straight as she could. "I already told you what happened," she stated in a peremptory voice. "If you don't have anything more specific to ask me, then I have nothing more to say."

She stared at the detective, and her lip curled up. "Although," she added, "you might want to ask Tim Reynolds a few questions."

"Who's Tim Reynolds?"

"The orderly who appeared out of nowhere next to Eric Conley's dead body."

"Ah," Morgan said. "The orderly. Yes – he spoke with me. Said he found *you* in front of the closet."

"Of course he did," Katie snapped. She wasn't daunted in the least.

Morgan watched Katie for a moment, his expression impossible to read. Then he nodded, and flashed a strange smile. It was almost as if he were impressed by Katie's firm stance.

"All right then, Miss Throckmorton," he said. "You'll hear no arguments from me. You're free to go."

"I don't suppose you're going to question Tim Reynolds?"

"I assure you I'll do everything I can, Miss Throckmorton. The District Attorney's son was just killed, after all."

Katie glared at him, but thought it best not to say anything more. She turned to leave, and her father moved to follow her, but Morgan called out, "Will you indulge me in a few minutes' conversation, Mr. Throckmorton?"

Axel looked back with an acidic expression. "Of course," he said stiffly.

He looked at Katie, and tried to smile reassuringly. "You go on to bed, Punkin," he said. "Try to sleep as best you can."

Katie nodded uncertainly, casting a doubtful look at Detective Morgan. The little man just nodded politely, and flashed another smile. "Goodnight, Miss Throckmorton," he said.

Katie didn't reply. She stepped out of the room, shivering a little as she passed by Dr. Diederich. There was just something creepy about the man, and it had nothing at all to do with Lydia Brock's comments about nefarious goings-on earlier in the evening.

After Katie had left the room, Dr. Diederich turned towards the detective, and made him a slight bow of respect. "Naturally," he said, "I looked in to ascertain whether I can be of any use to you, Detective Morgan. It goes without saying that, as the warden of this hospital, I am entirely at your service."

The detective looked at him curiously. Perhaps the doctor seemed a little too obsequious for his taste.

"That's good to know, doctor," he said simply. "I appreciate the sentiment, of course."

Diederich seemed conscious of the fact that his offer of service hadn't made the impression he'd intended. He bowed again, more uncertainly this time, and withdrew from the room.

Morgan took a few quick steps to the door, and snapped it shut, still wearing that same meaningless, sterile smile. He pulled out a chair for Axel Throckmorton, and then pranced round to the other side of the table, taking his own seat with almost supernatural grace.

"Now, Mr. Throckmorton," he said, in a polite but concise tone of voice, "I just want to speak with you for a moment or two. I hope you don't feel too put out? It's only, you know, considering the circumstances – your daughter being involved and all . . ."

"She wasn't involved," Axel snapped.

"You're her father," Morgan said with another smile. "Of course you'd say that. Keep in mind, now, I'm not accusing her of anything. But you have to admit this whole business is rather strange. Two people have been killed since Miss Throckmorton arrived here, and she was first on the scene on both occasions."

He peered carefully at Axel, and went on, "Now, Mr. Throckmorton, if you were an uninvolved third party – what would you make of something like that?"

Axel was silent for a long moment. He seemed to be thinking furiously. It was obvious that he wanted to argue with the detective, to blatantly deny that his daughter had had anything to do with all this. But then he thought a little more, and it seemed as though he hit on the idea that it wouldn't hurt to try and curry favor with the detective. It might not help – but it wouldn't hurt.

Axel sighed despondently. "I suppose I'd think it was suspicious," he admitted. "I'm not trying to deny that the whole thing is strange. And I know you won't take my word for it, detective, because I'm her father – but I can promise you that Katie had nothing to do with this."

Morgan stared at him for a moment, and for the first time, he looked almost sympathetic. It was as though he could feel the other man's fatherly anguish, and it touched some inner part of him, some part that wasn't often touched.

"You love your daughter, sir," he said in a grave voice. "I can respect that. You must believe that I respect that."

He was quiet for a minute, staring down at the shining metal tabletop, obviously thinking hard about something.

"But you must understand," he went on, "it's my job to investigate these murders. I'll follow every lead I have, you can rely on that. And I regret that your daughter is one of those leads."

Axel stared at him for a moment. The two men were like a pair of Old West gunslingers in front of a dusty saloon. The only problem was, Axel didn't have a gun.

"Of course I can't argue with you," Axel said carefully. "And I don't intend to. But you must know, detective, that I'll advocate my daughter's innocence until my dying breath."

Morgan showed a thin smile. "Who said anything about dying?" he asked curiously.

"I only want to make it clear how much I believe in her," Axel said firmly, staring straight into the other man's face.

"Yes," Morgan said slowly. "I can see that. You love her very much, sir. I can see that."

He paused, and thought for a moment.

"Tell me, sir," he said finally. "What was Miss Throckmorton like when she was younger?"

Axel peered suspiciously at Morgan. It was obvious he thought the other man was trying to trick him into revealing something.

Morgan held up his hands in defense, and grinned. "Please don't be so suspicious, Mr. Throckmorton," he begged. "I'm not trying to bamboozle you. I just want to get a better idea of who your daughter really is."

He paused, and was so bold as to add, "Perhaps knowing her better would make me readier to think along the same lines as you."

Axel thought about this for a moment. It was clear that he doubted the other man's intentions, but it was also clear that he wanted more than anything to sponge the blot from his daughter's name. So he said:

"Katie was a good little girl. I lived with her mother for about six years after she was born, but then we started to drift apart, and we got divorced. Most kids go to live with their mothers, but Katie stayed with me. Her mother agreed it was the more stable option. Linda's never been what you'd call – reliable."

"Do you resent her for that?" Morgan asked curiously.

Axel looked surprised. "What?" he asked. "No. Well – I suppose any man would. I loved her, but we couldn't live together. I can accept that. I just wish she'd been there for Katie."

"She wasn't?" Morgan asked.

Axel knitted his brows, looking suspicious again. "I can't say that she was," he said slowly. "But we've always got on all right without her."

"You and your daughter?"

Axel smiled with a look of tender nostalgia. "Yes," he murmured.

"And Miss Throckmorton wasn't a problem child?"

Axel looked shocked. "No," he replied. "She was always a good little girl. She's still a good girl."

"The night of your younger daughter's death," Morgan said in a softer voice, "the night they picked Miss Throckmorton up – she was drunk as a skunk and high as a kite. Is that your definition of a good girl, Mr. Throckmorton?"

Axel looked at him darkly. "It's not a crime," he muttered. "She didn't do anything wrong."

"So far as the drugs she took," Morgan went on, "they weren't her own prescription, so as to it being illegal, well, we'll leave that alone for now. My real question, Mr. Throckmorton, is whether it's possible that you don't know your daughter as well as you think you do?"

"I know her better than anyone," Axel protested indignantly.

It was obvious to Morgan that he wasn't going to get any farther with Axel. So he sighed, and shrugged his shoulders. "All right, Mr. Throckmorton," he said wearily. "You can go."

Axel glared at him, rose from his seat, and went out of the room like a breath of icy wind.

Detective Morgan remained in his chair for a while, looking at the bright overhead lights, and thinking. There was something really foul going on in this place. Now he just had to figure out what it was.

He hadn't asked Katie Throckmorton about the words on the wall of the storage closet. There was no need. He had an Italian cop with him who'd translated the bloody message.

Dalla sua pace la mia dipende, the words read.

On her peace my peace depends.

"It's an old-fashioned way to say it, though," Battistelli informed Morgan. "Nobody nowadays would say it like that."

"How would they say it?" Morgan asked.

"Sua pace la mia dipende," Battistelli answered.

"Do you have any idea why someone would write it this way?"

"I don't know," Battistelli said with a shrug. "Maybe they were quoting from some old book."

Morgan stood as if rooted to the spot. Some old book?

Now, who would be likely to quote from some old book? A literature major with a minor in Roman studies? After all – after they stopped speaking Latin in Rome, they started speaking Italian.

Morgan thought about it for a while, but the whole thing just looked too clean. Too easy.

He decided he'd need to do a little more thinking.

Chapter 15

Back in their bedroom, Katie found Lydia Brock lying curled up beneath her blanket. It looked like she was shivering, and it sounded like she was crying.

Katie went to her own bed, and thrust her icy feet under the blanket. The whole time she'd sat in the interrogation room, she'd been barefoot.

She settled her head on the pillow, and sighed with exhaustion. But she knew she wouldn't get much sleep tonight. Or, if she did, it would be plagued by nightmares.

A particular nightmare about a boy with a broom shoved up his ass. She had to admit, she'd never had *that* dream before. She wasn't looking forward to it, either, so she planned to stay awake for as long as possible.

The bathroom light was shining over both of the beds. Katie could see Lydia's thin body beneath the blanket, racked with sobs.

"Lydia?" she said softly.

The young woman didn't answer.

"Lydia?"

The blanket stopped moving, and it seemed as if Lydia were trying to take a few deep breaths. "I'm okay," she murmured. "I'm fine." It sounded like she was trying to convince herself.

"Eric Conley is dead," Katie said. "I found him. Then the police came, and that's – that's what took so long."

She drew a long breath, and exhaled slowly.

"Eric's dead?" Lydia asked in disbelief. "That's strange to hear."

"Why?"

"I don't know," Lydia said uncertainly. "There was just something about him. Something superhuman . . . something almost god-like."

"Like Percy Jackson, you mean?" Katie asked with a soft laugh. She knew it was inappropriate, but she was trying to lift Lydia's spirits.

Lydia laughed a little, too. It wasn't any use crying over spilled milk – and Eric had been an asshole.

Hmmm, Katie thought. *Maybe a bad way to put it, considering where they found the broom.*

"I don't understand why people keep dying," Lydia said with a catch in her throat. She still hadn't thrown the blanket off, and she looked like a ghost underneath it, a ghost with no mouth talking about dead people.

Katie shivered again.

"I don't know, Lydia," she said softly. "I'd say I wish I knew – but I'm not really sure if I want to." "I know what you mean," Lydia whispered. "It's been going on for so long. They take people back there, and sometimes they never come back . . ."

Katie's breath stopped. Her muscles froze. It was a long moment before she could speak.

"Lydia," she said slowly. "Are you saying that Dr. Damien wasn't the first person to die?" "Yes," Lydia breathed.

"How – how many?"

"I don't know. Maybe a dozen. Maybe more."

Katie's breath caught again. "And you're saying – you're saying Dr. Diederich killed them?"

"Dr. Diederich," Lydia whispered. "And Damien."

"How do you know?"

"They took them back there," Lydia muttered, almost breathless, "and they didn't come back. One night, while the Dr. Dees were walking around with their clipboards, I followed them down the corridor. I saw them go to old Mr. Parker's room. They led him down to Dr. Diederich's office. They went in, and they didn't come out. I sat there for hours, until the sun came up. But they didn't come out. I went back to my room so I wouldn't get in trouble, but I looked for Mr. Parker at breakfast. He wasn't there. He never came back."

She paused, and took a shuddering breath. "And he wasn't the only one."

Katie was silent for a long moment. She lay staring at Lydia's back, thinking furiously. What was going on here? Had Diederich and Damien – the "Dr. Dees" – had they really been killing people?

And if they had, who'd killed Damien? Dr. Diederich? If that was the case, had he killed Eric Conley, too?

What the hell was going on?

Katie was still thinking madly, and staring at Lydia without really seeing her, when suddenly Lydia threw off her blanket. She looked over at Katie, and saw Katie's eyes on her. It seemed as if she saw some sort of look in them that wasn't really there, because in an instant, she'd bounded from her bed, and thrown herself on top of Katie.

Katie was shocked. She'd been lost in her own thoughts, and she hadn't been paying attention to Lydia. She had no idea what was happening.

"Oh, Katie," Lydia murmured, running a hand through Katie's hair, and leaning down to kiss her motionless mouth. "I have to tell you — I have to tell you how I feel, because I think you might feel the same. I'm attracted to you. I have feelings for you."

She dropped her head down to Katie's chest, and let out a sound that was half a laugh, and half a sob. Katie felt sorry for her, but at the same time, the feeling of Lydia's tears against her skin disgusted her. She wished she'd get off her.

"Lydia," Katie said slowly, "I think you're confused."

Lydia raised her head off Katie's chest with the motion of a snail. It was obvious she was afraid to look into her face. It was obvious that she'd just made a fool of herself.

"Then you don't," she said softly, clutching tightly at Katie's arm, "you don't care about me at all?"

Katie tried to push her away so she could sit up. "Listen, Lydia," she said urgently. "That's not what I said. It's not that I don't care about you, I just —"

Lydia leapt up to her feet, and started pacing frantically back and forth, tearing at her hair. "I should have known," she whispered quickly, with a touch of madness in her voice. "I should have known that you were just the same as everyone else. I should have known. Who could care about me, anyway . . .?"

She bounded across the room in two strides, and disappeared through the doorway.

"Lydia!" Katie cried. "Lydia, wait!"

She hurried to the door, and looked up and down the corridor. But Lydia was nowhere to be seen. Katie had no idea how she'd managed to disappear so fast, but the fact of the matter was, she had no idea where she'd gone. And considering the fact that she'd already found a dead body and been interrogated by a suspicious detective, she didn't think it was a good idea for her to leave the room.

She left the door open, and tiptoed back to her bed. Then she lay down, pulled the covers up to her chin, and stared up at the ceiling.

It was as if there were a whole parade of ghosts stenciled across the expanse of white paint. They marched like circus performers, beating drums, blowing trumpets, and heralding the approach of some supreme evil.

Katie shuddered, feeling a deep sensation of cold that shot through to her very bones. She turned away from the open door, and shut her eyes.

***

At group the next morning, everyone was quiet and sullen. Eric Conley's chair stood empty, and everybody kept glancing at it uneasily, as if some bloody apparition was going to appear in the place where Eric usually sat.

But Lydia wasn't there, either. She'd never come back to the room last night.

It was a while before Dr. Halstead said anything. It was obvious that she was tormented by her own thoughts.

Suddenly she looked up, and glanced around the circle. Her eyes lingered on Katie for a long moment, and she glanced away with a fierce blush across her pale cheeks.

"Where's Lydia?" she asked.

Everyone looked at Lydia's chair, and noticed that it was empty. They'd been so busy thinking about Eric, they hadn't even noticed Lydia wasn't there.

Katie thought about telling Dr. Halstead what had happened between her and Lydia (in private, of course), but then she decided that was a bad idea. The doctor would want to know why she hadn't told someone Lydia was missing. She'd want to know why Katie hadn't done something.

Well, Katie thought bitterly, *because every time I decide to* do *something, I end up finding a dead body. And when I go for help, there's no one at the fucking nurses' station.*

All this was perfectly true, and for a moment Katie savored the act of feeling sorry for herself. But still, she felt badly about not paying more attention to Lydia's disappearance. Who knows what could have happened to her? Two people had already turned up dead. What if Lydia was the third?

Katie tried to shake these thoughts away, even going so far as to shake her head wildly. She didn't notice that she was doing it, at first. But soon she realized that everyone was looking at her.

"All you all right, Katie?" Dr. Halstead asked in a disconcerted tone.

"Yes," Katie replied quickly. "I'm fine. It was just – it was just a long night."

Everyone was silent for a moment. And then – of course – it was Carmen Rodriguez who spoke first.

"Everyone's been saying that you found him," she said in an accusing voice. "That you found the body – again."

Lamberto and Marcus looked hard at Katie, and waited for her to answer. Even the doctor was looking at her with what seemed to be a suspicious expression.

"No one's accusing you of anything, Katie," she said (though her voice was a little accusatory). "But maybe it would make everyone feel better if you explained what happened last night."

Katie stared at her in disbelief. Was the woman really talking to her like that, after everything that had happened between them the night before? Didn't it matter to her at all?

I guess not, Katie thought. It was as if her stomach and chest were filled with scalding acid, burning her from the inside, thickening her heartbeat and making her eyes cross with rage.

Fine, then. If it didn't matter to Cora, then it didn't matter to Katie, either. It was no big deal. What's a little fuck between doctor and patient, after all?

Katie looked at Marcus Bickford, and realized that *he* could answer that question just as well as she could. The thought made her laugh out loud. She knew that she looked crazy, but she didn't care.

"What's the matter, Marcus?" she asked. She looked hard at the young man who was glaring at her.

He was looking at her as if she were some person who was about to be hanged, and she hated it.

"What's the matter?" she repeated. "Are you so busy judging me that you forgot about yourself? If everyone here knew you've been screwing Dr. Wilkins, they might glare at you, too."

Marcus was horrified. He couldn't believe Katie knew about that. He couldn't believe that now everyone else knew, too.

Lamberto and Carmen looked at him wonderingly. Then Carmen started to laugh.

But Dr. Halstead was looking at Marcus with sympathy. She looked at Katie with an expression of condemnation, obviously trying to make her feel guilty for what she'd just done.

Fuck you, Katie thought. And that's exactly what the doctor read in her expression.

Cora Halstead looked away quickly, and said, "Listen, now. That's enough of that. Stop laughing, Carmen. It's none of your business . . ."

But Carmen continued to roar with laughter. She threw herself back in her seat, and slapped her thighs with raucous amusement. Marcus leapt out of his seat with tears in his eyes, and raced out of the Community Room.

He's pretty fast, Katie thought. *He'd be good at cross-country.*

When the young man was gone, Carmen looked back at Katie, and glared at her like a tiger from behind the bars of a cage. "So, newbie," she drawled slowly. "You gonna tell us why you keep finding these bodies? Wanna admit to anything, baby-killer?"

Katie glared back at her; and she thought for a moment. She was stuck here for the foreseeable future. Not even good behavior could get her out.

So why be good?

She leapt out of her seat, and jumped across the circle towards Carmen, thrusting her body against the other young woman's, and wrapping a hand around her throat. Carmen looked terrified. Lamberto giggled with supreme amusement.

"Katie," Dr. Halstead said warningly. "Let her go."

Katie glanced at her with a perfectly composed expression. She was sitting on Carmen's lap, and she had her chest pressed against the other woman's. She was gripping her throat as if she were squeezing a grape. Carmen was choking like a kitten drowning in a burlap sack.

"What's the matter, Cora?" Katie asked with a grin. "Are you fucking her, too?"

The doctor looked at her with an injured expression, but Katie didn't feel an ounce of guilt.

She squeezed Carmen's throat a little harder, reveling in the sound of her babyish blubbering. Then she laughed, and let her go. She slapped her right cheek, and leaned down to kiss her neck. "Adios, *señorita,*" she murmured in her ear, rising up off her lap, and laughing again.

She strutted out of the room. Everyone was staring at her. She did a quick pirouette, and blew them all a kiss. "Here's Johnny!" she cried in delight.

Then she sighed, and went out of the room.

Chapter 16

Soon it'll be time for lunch, Katie thought as she went along down the corridor, picking her way towards her room, but not really wanting to go there. *Soon it'll be time for lunch,* she thought, *but I'm not going.*

She went into her room, and slammed the door shut. She flung herself on her bed, and looked over at Lydia's bed with narrowed eyes.

She wouldn't go to lunch, and she wouldn't go to her appointment with Dr. Halstead, either. She couldn't trust her. Nothing she said would be confidential.

Not that I want to say anything, anyway, she thought bitterly. *The bitch has made her position clear.*

She was lying still, and her eyes were fluttering shut, when she heard a strange sound from down the corridor. It was like a half-hearted scream.

Goddamn it, she thought angrily. *Haven't I heard enough screaming?*

She got off the bed, and walked carefully towards the door. The sound repeated itself, but it was much quieter this time, like a stifled moan.

She opened the door, and peered out into the corridor. It was empty. Everyone was probably at lunch.

She stuck her head through the doorway and listened carefully. There it was again. A low cry, then a loud moan.

What the fuck?

Katie stepped out into the corridor, and turned left, towards the noise. She started down the corridor, listening carefully. The sounds persisted, and even seemed to grow louder as she went on.

Finally, she came to the door that she thought the noises were hiding behind. It was firmly closed, but obviously not locked. Patients' doors couldn't be locked.

Katie was fairly sure that this was the twins' room. Marion and Miriam. The creepy girls from *The Shining.*

She grasped the doorknob in her cold fingers, holding her breath. Should she open it? What business was it of hers?

Then she heard another sound. It was the loudest she'd heard so far. A barely strangled cry.

She turned the knob slowly, and pushed the door open just a little. She put her eye to the crack, but couldn't see anything. So she pushed the door just a little farther.

The twins came into sight, then. They were in between the two beds. One of them (Katie didn't know which) was standing up, and the other one was kneeling down. It almost looked, for a moment, like the kneeling one was kissing the other one's arm.

Katie was disgusted, and was just about to turn away, when she noticed that blood was dripping down from the standing twin's arm. She looked more closely at the kneeling twin, and saw that she was holding a fat razor in her right hand. She took her mouth away from her sister's arm, revealing a long, straight gash. But she had sucked it clean, and it had ceased to drip blood. So she made a new gash with the razor, and lowered her mouth to suck at the second wound. Her mouth worked like that of a vampire, with an easy and effortless motion. The standing twin cried out in ecstasy, laying her hand on her sister's head, her eyes shut tight.

Katie was huddled down in front of the crack in the door, watching all this with a strange fascination, when she felt a hand on her shoulder. She couldn't help it. She cried out in alarm.

The twins looked up calmly, and turned towards the door. It didn't even look like Katie's cry had startled them. They were just standing there, staring at the partially open door. The twin who'd been cut was dripping blood down onto her white cotton shift.

Katie looked back, and for some reason, wasn't at all surprised to see Cora Halstead standing behind her. "Are you following me or something?" she demanded, though her voice was shaking from the scene she'd just witnessed.

"You were late for your appointment," Cora snapped. "What's going on in there?"

"Have a look for yourself," Katie suggested, stepping aside. Her voice was still shaking.

Cora pushed open the door, and drew an audible breath.

"Hello, Dr. Halstead," the twins said in unison.

"We must apologize," one of them said. "If we'd known you were coming, we would have cleaned ourselves up a bit."

Almost against her will, Katie peeked through the doorway. The twins were standing side-by-side between the beds, one with her arm smeared with blood, the other with her face covered in the thick red liquid.

Katie fought to swallow her bile. She thought she was going to throw up.

"I thought Dr. Diederich talked to you about this," Cora said firmly. "This isn't healthy behavior, girls. Don't you understand that?"

"We're afraid not," the twins said in unison. The sound of their voices was almost unbearably creepy.

"This won't be tolerated anymore," Cora said firmly. "We're going to have to put you someplace where you can be watched."

"We don't mind if people watch," one of the girls said.

Cora didn't seem to know what to say to that. She remained silent, but moved forward to take the razor from the girl who held it. "Please give that to me," she said quietly, holding out her hand.

The girl obviously took her too literally. She leaned forward with a perfectly blank expression, but then slashed the razor across Cora's hand, opening a wide gash that immediately began to drip onto the floor.

Katie looked through the doorway. The girl's eyes were shining like those of a demon. She was staring at the wound on Cora's hand.

"I can clean that for you, if you like," she said, in an almost polite tone of voice.

"That's it," Cora said in a trembling voice, backing out of the room, and coming through the doorway to the place where Katie was standing. "I'm sending someone to collect you," she said to the twins. "And put that razor down!"

With her unbloodied hand, she took hold of Katie's arm, and dragged her away from the door.

"Where are we going?" Katie asked. "We need to take care of your hand."

Cora looked down at the floor, and realized that she was trailing blood behind her. So she darted into an empty patient's room, went into the bathroom, and took a wad of paper towels to wrap around her hand. Then she took hold of Katie again, and they set off on their way.

Katie had to admit it. She would have never admitted it out loud – but she sort of liked the way Cora was pulling her around. The other woman was flushed and flustered, the thin curls of hair that had sprung out of her bun were damp with sweat, and her face was deathly pale. She was breathing hard. Katie could hear it. She imagined Cora taking hold of her right this moment, kissing her ferociously, sucking at her tongue. The thought sent a delicious shiver down her spine.

They stopped at the nurses' station, where Cora ordered in an authoritative voice for a pair of orderlies to be sent to the Holloway twins' room. "And tell them to be careful," she added. "One of the girls has a razor."

The nurse nodded efficiently, and picked up the phone to make a call.

Cora sighed in exhaustion, tightened the paper towels around her hand with a wince, and dragged

Katie along behind her, this time in what seemed to be the direction of her office. They went down the South Corridor, turned up the West Corridor, turned onto the North Corridor, then took a sharp left into Cora's office.

The doctor slammed the door shut. Then she locked it.

"Why did you lock the door?" Katie asked slowly.

Cora shook her head in frustration, as though she wasn't even aware that she'd done it. "Unlock it if you want," she muttered.

She went to her desk, opened one of the drawers with a key, and took out a first aid kit. She popped open the white plastic box, and started fishing around in it with her one good hand. In the process, she knocked the whole thing onto the floor. Stuff went spilling everywhere.

"Goddamn it!" she cried, dropping down into her chair, and covering her face with her hand.

Katie immediately went to work. She shot forward, and looked through the debris on the floor. There was the gauze, and there was the rolled bandage. There was the antiseptic. Medical tape, too.

She gathered these items off the floor, and knelt down in front of Cora, taking gentle hold of her wounded hand. Cora lowered her hand from her face, and watched Katie with wide eyes, her breath sounding as if it were caught in her chest.

Katie removed the paper towels from the wound, and set them on the floor. Then she opened the antiseptic.

"This is going to sting," she warned the doctor.

"I was fairly sure of it," Cora breathed. Her eyes were fixed on Katie's face.

Katie splashed some alcohol onto a square of gauze, and then pressed it to Cora's palm. Despite how angry the doctor had made her that morning, she took no pleasure in causing her pain. She grimaced as she wiped the blood gently from Cora's palm, making sure that she saturated the wound with alcohol.

It was a terrible wound. It looked like it might have needed stitches. But Katie certainly wasn't qualified for *that,* so she just finished cleaning the wound, then pressed a couple of clean gauze squares to it, and wrapped the gauze with the rolled bandage. She put a couple pieces of medical tape on the bandage, then sat back on her haunches.

All this time, Cora hadn't even made a sound of discomfort. She was still staring into Katie's face.

"Thank you," she whispered. "That would have been hard to do by myself."

"You don't have to do everything by yourself, you know," Katie said, almost in a scolding tone.

Cora sighed, but the sigh gave halfway over to a sob, and she covered her face again. Katie moved up to her, and put her hands on either side of her head. "Shhh," she said. "Look at me."

Cora lowered her hands reluctantly, and looked at Katie with shining eyes.

"Are you okay?" Katie asked urgently.

Cora took a deep breath, and nodded. "I'm fine," she murmured.

"Then kiss me," Katie begged.

Cora didn't even take a whole two seconds to think about it. She leaned forward, and dragged Katie up onto her lap. Katie straddled her waist, and pressed herself against the other woman's body. She buried her face in her neck, and breathed her in slowly. She kissed her neck tenderly.

She sought the doctor's lips with her own, and kissed her deeply, passionately. She could feel her breath in her mouth. She could feel the slick life of her warm tongue.

She took her mouth away for a moment, then kissed the tip of Cora's nose, then her forehead. She unbuttoned her pants, and slipped a hand beneath her underwear. She played with the warm lips for a moment, savoring the feeling of them between her fingers. Then she slid in two fingers with a quick, sharp motion. There was thick liquid running around her fingers like wine from Bacchus's fountain. The doctor was incredibly turned on.

She thrust her fingers in and out, using her thumb to work the clit. She thrust her face into the doctor's neck, sucking at her tender flesh, licking it passionately.

Cora was stifling her cries. Both her arms were circled tightly around Katie's back. There were tears staining her beautiful face.

Katie kissed her mouth sweetly, then slipped down to the floor, where she worked down the doctor's pants, and left them hanging round her ankles. Next she got rid of the underwear. She didn't even bother to separate the pussy with her fingers; she just dove in with her face, dividing everything with her mouth, and darting her tongue through the opening like a viper. She licked the clit as if it were a magic apple from the Hanging Gardens of Babylon. She licked it slowly, gently, and then enveloped it with her mouth, sucking hard. Cora arched her back, and put her hand on the back of Katie's neck, squeezing gently.

Katie took her mouth away, and tenderly kissed the insides of Cora's thighs. Then she stood up, and dragged the other woman up to her feet. She put her foot on the shorn trousers, so that Cora could slip out of them, then whisked her away to the couch. She pulled her down beside her, and wrapped her tightly in her arms, kissing her lips passionately.

A few minutes later, they lay still, with Katie's back pressed to the couch cushions, and Cora's back pressed to Katie's chest. Katie was still holding her close, with her face buried in her fragrant hair, breathing in the luxurious scent of flowers and sweat.

She thought that Cora fell asleep for a short while. So she stayed still, making her breathing slow, lying with Cora's hands enveloped in hers. She could feel her soft skin, the fine bones of her fingers.

After a short time, Cora woke up, and rolled over to bury her face in Katie's chest. Katie stroked her hair softly, kissing her face.

"Why are you so good to me?" Cora asked in a strained voice. "I don't deserve it."

"You weren't very nice this morning," Katie agreed. "But I guess I forgive you."

Cora took a shuddering breath, and pressed herself closer to Katie.

"Hey," Katie said quickly. "I'm sorry. I'm not mad. Just let me hold you . . ."

Cora laid her cheek against Katie's chest, and heaved a deep sigh. "I don't know what to do anymore," she whispered. "I don't even know what's going on."

Katie thought for a few minutes before she spoke. Should she bring it up?

"Lydia told me something about Dr. Diederich," she said finally. "Something about him and Dr. Damien."

Cora looked into Katie's face with a terrified expression.

"You know about it?" Katie asked. She wasn't exactly surprised.

"Yes," Cora breathed. "I know about it."

Katie laid a hand against the side of her face, and looked desperately into her eyes. "Tell me what's going on, Cora," she begged.

"It's not that I don't want to," Cora said quickly. "I'd tell you everything – but I can't get you out of this place . . ."

She tore herself away from Katie, and leapt to her feet, tearing at her hair. Her bare legs glistened in the dying light from the windows.

"I don't want him to hurt you," she muttered in a desperate voice, flying to her desk, and fumbling in her pants' pocket for the key to the drawer. She unlocked it, pulled it open, and drew out a long skeleton key.

She looked at Katie with a momentous expression. "This key will open every door in the building," she said gravely. "Every single door. If you find yourself trapped, or –"

She swallowed thickly, and put a hand to her mouth.

Katie got to her feet, and went to stand beside the doctor. She took the skeleton key, and slipped it into her pocket. "Thank you," she said.

Cora looked pointedly into her face, seeming as if she were regaining some of her composure. "How are you doing?" she asked seriously. "Are you all right?"

She put her hand behind Katie's neck, and squeezed gently. There was a look of deep compassion in her eyes.

"I'm okay," Katie said in a shaky voice.

"I wish I could get you out of this place," Cora murmured, leaning forward to lay her mouth against Katie's. She kissed her desperately, frantically. It was like she was trying to tell her something.

"I wish you could, too," Katie murmured, pressing her forehead against the doctor's.

The sun was falling outside the windows. Night was coming.

Chapter 17

As it turned out, Cora's husband was waiting for her at home. Apparently, they were supposed to spend the evening going over their divorce papers.

"Sounds like fun," Katie said, trying to smile.

"Loads of it," Cora returned with a wry grin. She furrowed her brow, and pressed herself against Katie, kissing her hungrily. "I'll be back in the morning," she whispered.

"Okay," Katie said. There was a slight catch in her voice. It wasn't that she was afraid of being left alone, but – well, hell, she *was* afraid of being left alone. She didn't want Cora to go.

But she wasn't about to admit it.

"Are you all right?" Cora asked with concern.

"Yes," Katie replied in a firm voice. "I'm fine."

Cora looked into her face for a long moment, but then kissed her cheek, and touched her face. "All right, then," she said. "Time to go."

The corridor was nearly dark. The dirty little fluorescent squares hadn't snapped on yet.

They slipped out into the corridor like a pair of naughty schoolgirls. Cora went left, towards the staff exit, and Katie went right, towards her room.

She went into her room, and stood in front of the barred windows for a while, looking out into the darkening evening. This is where Lydia liked to sit. Where could she have gone? Katie remembered her telling her that there were places she liked to hide, especially at mealtimes, when she didn't want the orderlies to be able to find her.

Was she hiding in one of those places right now? Katie didn't know. There was no way to find out. All she could do was wait for Lydia to come back.

She went to her bed, and put on her pajamas. But she had a strange feeling while she was standing there naked. It was as if someone were watching her. She could feel cold, hard eyes fixed on her. It was very unnerving.

"You're just being paranoid, Katie," she whispered to herself, pulling back the covers, and sliding into the cold bed. She bunched the pillow under her head, and clutched it tightly.

She'd left the bathroom light on. Just in case Lydia came back.

***

She woke in the middle of the night, thinking that she'd heard the sound of scuffing shoes against the hard, cold floor. She sat upright in bed, blinking in the harsh light from the bathroom, and trying to let her eyes adjust to being awake.

She looked over at the second bed. "Lydia?" she murmured.

But it seemed as though the bed was empty. So she cast a quick look around the room, and saw nothing. Yet there was a strange mass at the left corner of her vision.

She looked towards the bathroom, and sucked in a sharp breath.

Lydia Brock was dangling from the bathroom ceiling. There was a leather belt cinched around her neck, but it was obvious that she hadn't killed herself. Her breasts had been cut off, and her eyes had been gouged out. The front of her body was nothing but four bloody holes with blotches of pale skin in between.

Behind the hanging body, there was a line of crimson words painted across the wall.

L'ultima prova dell'amor mio.

Katie shoved her pillow against her face. She threw herself prostrate over the mattress, and screamed wildly. Then she lost consciousness.

***

She woke sometime later. She had no idea how much time had passed, but she glanced at the clock, and saw that it was two in the morning.

She was lying on her stomach, having had her face pressed into the pillow. She turned over onto her back with a grunt, feeling exhausted from this simple motion, and staring up at the lighted ceiling with a blank expression. She closed her eyes, and prepared herself to look back at the bathroom.

When I look, she thought, *there won't be anything there. I was just imagining things. It was only a nightmare.*

She opened her eyes slowly, and turned her head to the left. Lydia was hanging there, dead and mutilated.

Katie thrust her head over the side of the bed, and vomited onto the floor. There wasn't much in it except bile, since she hadn't had anything to eat since breakfast the morning before. But it tasted foul, like something dead and decayed.

She wiped her mouth, and stumbled out of bed, trying hard not to look back towards the bathroom doorway. She tripped out of the room, moving on weak legs. She went through the open doorway, and started towards the South Corridor. She hoped to God there would be someone at the nurses' station tonight.

Suddenly, she stopped dead in her tracks. The sound of a woman's scream was splitting the air like a Christmas nutcracker.

She didn't even need to look. She knew there wouldn't be anyone at the nurses' station. There was no point in even walking that far.

She had come to a halt near the end of the West Corridor. The screaming was coming from back in the direction of the North Corridor.

From Dr. Diederich's office, maybe?

Katie had a sudden thought. She'd just remembered something that Officer Humphreys had said, the morning he brought her to Greystone.

"The doctor favors Italian cigars," Humphreys had said. *"There are no German cigars, really, so he settles for what is at least European."*

Katie thought of the words in Italian that had been left at two of the murder scenes. First, Eric Conley's – and then Lydia's.

Dalla sua pace la mia dipende, the first message had read. *On her peace my peace depends.*

Behind Lydia's body had been the words *L'ultima prova dell'amor mio. The final proof of my love.*

Katie realized, all of a sudden, where these quotes were coming from. They were from the opera *Don Giovanni*. She remembered, because she'd gone with her father a couple of years back to see a production of the opera in New York City.

If Diederich was so fond of Italian cigars, maybe he knew a little of the Italian language, too. Maybe he liked *Don Giovanni*.

As for the first message on the wall, which had been found with Dr. Damien's body – well, that could mean anything. Like Katie had said, anyone with access to Google Translate could have written it.

Maybe Karl Diederich had written it. Lydia had said that he and Damien were working together on some sort of shady project. The two Dr. Dees. Maybe Damien had crossed Diederich, and Diederich had killed him. It at least made sense.

But why would Diederich have killed Eric Conley and Lydia Brock? What reason could he have had?

Katie heard the screaming again, and she looked in the direction of the sound, blinking slowly.

Goddamn it, Katie, she thought. *You've already found three dead bodies. You really want to go looking for another?*

Well, the truth was that she didn't really *want* to – but she was standing alone in the middle of the corridor, there was a dead body in her room, and there was no one to turn to for help. What did she really have to do, other than pretend to be Nancy Drew?

"Oh, fuck you, Nancy Drew," she sighed, turning back towards the North Corridor.

She didn't even bother taking slow steps. She wasn't hesitant, wasn't careful. She knew exactly where she was going. She was going to Dr. Diederich's office.

She walked purposefully down the corridor, firm in her resolve, and hardly caring what happened. If she walked in on Dr. Diederich doing something – well, doing something *evil,* what did she really have planned? Nothing, that's what. But she was going, anyway.

The woman's screaming pierced through the silence of the hospital. When Katie reached the North Corridor, though, another sound cropped up underneath the screaming, mingling with it, grating on her ears. It sounded like sobbing.

She paused at the intersection between the West and North Corridors, squinting into the expanse of otherworldly blue-grey light. She saw a masculine form huddled up against the wall. A tall, thin man.

Son of a bitch, Katie thought. *I'm about to die, aren't I?*

But then she realized that the man was turned towards the wall, facing away from the corridor. And the sound of sobbing was coming from *him.*

There was something very familiar about the man. She crept up slowly behind him, and said in a quiet voice, "Hello?"

He spun around in terror, gazing at Katie with a tear-stained face. It was the Norman Bates guy. Jacob Barlow.

But Katie was beginning to understand that this man was nothing like Norman Bates. He was just some poor messed-up guy who didn't know what to do with himself.

"Hey, Jake," she said kindly. "Are you okay, buddy?"

He had to take a few deep breaths before he could make himself speak. "I'm okay," he answered softly. "I just – I just hate it when they scream. I go to look for help, but there's never anyone there . . ."

He started to sob again, and covered his face with his hands. Katie went up to him and laid a hand on his shoulder. "Hey, now," she said. "It's all right, Jake. I'm here with you. You'll be all right."

Jacob Barlow dropped his hands, and looked at Katie wonderingly. "You'll stay with me?" he asked.

"Sure I will," she replied. "We'll figure it all out together. Okay?"

"Okay," he said with a nod, though he still sounded uncertain.

It almost felt good to have been thrust into a position where she had to take some measure of control. The sight of Lydia's dead body had shaken her to the core, and she needed to distract herself.

She was just wondering what she should do, when there came a sound of scuffling feet from behind her, and she whirled around. It was Lamberto Esplanade, still wearing his suit and tie, even his grey bowler hat. Katie wondered if he slept in those clothes. "Good evening," he said politely to Katie and Jacob. "Have you come to take part in the investigation?"

"We want to know who's screaming," Jacob replied simply.

"Ah," Lamberto said seriously. "Yes, of course. That is my desire, as well. The whole thing is most mysterious – most mysterious indeed. I have inquired about the screaming, and no one ever seems to have any information about it. After the death of Dr. Damien, however, I decided that action must be taken. I would have been on the scene, the night of Eric Conley's death, but a particular nurse claimed that I was unruly, and that I required a sedative." He paused, looking thoughtful. "I do not remember being unruly," he remarked. "It may be that she was lying. It is sometimes difficult for me to remember."

The screaming had stopped for a few minutes, but now it started up again, louder than ever. Their heads all swiveled towards the sound, which seemed to be coming from a little way down the corridor.

"We must get to the bottom of this," Lamberto said resolutely.

He tugged at his lapels, and marched off down the corridor. Jacob looked questioningly at Katie, and asked, "Do you think it's the end? I've been saying for years now that the end was coming."

"I don't know, Jake," Katie replied, patting the guy's arm. "I really couldn't tell you." But she smiled reassuringly, and together, she and Jacob started off after Lamberto.

Sure enough, the screaming seemed to be coming from Dr. Diederich's office door. Lamberto stopped in front of it, and Katie and Jacob stepped up alongside him. They all listened for a minute.

Everything went quiet for a few seconds, but then the screaming started again. They were so close, now, they could hear a few words mixed in.

"Damn you!" a woman's voice cried. "Damn you to hell, you devil!"

Neither Lamberto nor Jacob moved, so Katie laid her hand on the doorknob. But then she paused. She remembered the demon that sometimes visited her at night.

"Damn you to hell, you devil!" the woman had screamed.

But no – that made no sense. The demon couldn't be in Diederich's office. It had been coming to Katie for years now. What would Karl Diederich have been doing in her bedroom when she was fifteen years old?

She scratched her head with her left hand, her right hand still poised on the doorknob. She jiggled it a bit. Of course it was locked.

"What are we going to do?" Jacob Barlow asked curiously. He seemed to have forgotten his fear for the moment, and was merely interested in the mystery. Katie was Nancy Drew, and Jacob and Lamberto were two of the Hardy boys.

"I don't know," Katie replied absently.

"We must get to the bottom of this!" Lamberto repeated. "Stand back! I shall pick the lock."

He got down on his knees, and searched in his pockets. "Confound it all," he muttered. "I don't have a paperclip."

He looked up at Katie. "Miss Throckmorton," he said in a chivalrous voice. "Is there any chance that you are in possession of a bobby pin?"

Katie shook her head slowly, not really listening. She put a hand on her hip, thinking carefully – and in so doing, she touched the skeleton key in her pocket that Cora Halstead had given her. When she'd gone into her room earlier in the evening, she hadn't taken the key out of her pocket. It was still there.

She took the key out of her pocket, and looked at it for a moment.

"What's that?" Jacob inquired in that same curious voice.

"It's a key that will open any door in the building," Katie answered.

"Then it'll open *that* door?" he asked.

"Yes."

"You should open it, then."

Katie looked sideways into his face, and smiled at the innocent look she saw there. "Okay, Jake," she said. "I think I will."

"What a miraculous circumstance," Lamberto remarked in a wondering voice. "I wonder, Miss Throckmorton – where did you get that key?"

"From a friend," Katie murmured. She lowered the key into the lock, but paused before she turned it. She looked at Lamberto, then at Jacob. "You guys ready?" she asked.

"10-4, Roger," Jacob answered seriously.

"Full steam ahead, Miss Throckmorton," Lamberto said brightly.

"All righty, then," Katie said quietly. She held her breath, and turned the key in the lock. It made a loud *click*. The screaming had stopped for the moment, and she hoped Diederich wouldn't hear the key.

She waited for a minute, but no one came to the door. So she took a deep breath, and then pushed the door open.

The office was lit dimly with a single lamp. The room was sparsely furnished. The largest piece of furniture was the desk: a dark and heavy article, incredibly ornate, with intricate flowers and spirals carved in the legs, and more carvings in a thick panel that ran below the writing surface. It looked like an antique. An expensive antique.

Other than the desk, a chair behind it, and two chairs in front of it, there was no other furniture. Just the small lamp on top of the desk. That lamp cast the only light in the room.

But there were just as many bookshelves, and just as many books, as there were in Cora Halstead's office. There were numerous medical volumes, books on psychology, psychiatry. Yet there were numerous titles on other types of science: chemistry, biology, even mathematics. Katie also noticed that there were a lot of books about the Holocaust. Books about the Third Reich, books about Adolf Hitler, books about Josef Mengele. Auschwitz, Dachau, Treblinka.

The room smelled strongly of smoke, and the air was thick with it. Katie looked at the desk, and saw a stubbed-out cigar lying in a crystal ashtray.

She was startled when the screaming suddenly started up again. Obviously, it wasn't coming from anywhere in the office itself. She looked around quickly, and spotted a dark, heavy door that must have led into some hidden room. She crossed over to it, and almost touched the knob. But she was more afraid, this time.

Then the screaming stopped again. She could hear a man's voice speaking quietly. She couldn't hear what he said.

"Are you going to open that door, too?"

The sound of Jacob Barlow's voice almost made her cry out in alarm. She put a hand to her heart, and looked back at Jacob. "Do you think I should, Jake?" she asked seriously.

"Someone needs help," he said simply. "We have to help them."

"A gentleman never ignores a lady in distress," Lamberto remarked. "And I am not ashamed to say that I consider myself a gentleman. For that reason, there is no other recourse. The door must be opened." Katie looked at the young man for a moment. She felt as if she were trapped in an episode of the *Twilight Zone* with a Hispanic replica of Sherlock Holmes.

"Logical enough," she finally muttered, reaching for the knob again. But her heart was racing, and her hands were sweating. A trickle of perspiration ran down her temple from underneath her hair. "Though I have to admit," she whispered, "I think you're both a little braver than me."

"Do you want me to do it?" Lamberto asked politely, holding out his hand for the key.

She shook her head. "It's okay," she said. "I've got it."

She inserted the key in the lock, and turned it carefully. Another heavy *click*. But no one seemed to hear it this time, either.

Katie huddled down behind the wall, and Jacob and Lamberto followed her lead. She turned the doorknob cautiously, and let the door swing open just the slightest bit. Then she put her right eye to the crack between the door and the jamb. Lamberto put his head over hers. Jacob put his head over Lamberto's; and this is what they saw.

It was a very large room, much larger than the office itself. It had a darkish vibe, with no windows anywhere, and three bright white fluorescent orbs hanging from the high, vaulted ceiling. It was a strange room. It looked like a room in Victor Frankenstein's castle.

There were numerous shelves along the walls, and they were filled with various-colored liquids in dirty-looking beakers of different shapes and sizes. There were also larger jars, holding what looked like human body parts. Katie could have sworn she saw a pair of eyeballs floating in hazy liquid. And there, a whole man's hand.

Beneath the nearest fluorescent orb, on a long, dark table, there was a woman lying on her back. Katie squinted at her face, and was horrified to realize that she recognized her. Mrs. Parrish, the woman who'd sat with her at lunch.

Dr. Diederich was standing beside her, the dirty-looking fluorescent light flowing over his pale hair, his sharp eyes gleaming. He was looking down at Mrs. Parrish with a merciless expression.

"We have been at this for a long time now," he said impatiently, holding up a syringe filled with dark serum. "If I have to, I will keep at it all night long."

He paused, and showed a cruel smile. "I have nowhere else to be, you know."

"I'll never give you what you want," Mrs. Parrish murmured, though her voice was choked with pain. "I'll never talk about it."

"Never talk about the daughter you killed?" Diederich inquired. "Never mention Elaina's name, you mean? Why not, Mrs. Parrish? Don't you want to remember her?"

"No!" the old woman cried. "That's the whole point, you evil . . . you horrible man . . ."

She was bound to the table with stiff restraints. Her limbs were shaking. She turned her face away from the doctor, miserable tears running down her cheeks.

"It's a strange thing, Mrs. Parrish," Diederich said. "You may call me evil. Perhaps I am. But you, a woman who has killed her own child . . . you have a certain element of character, a lack of weakness for what is usually called 'blood ties.' This would be a good trait in a soldier, yes? A good characteristic? I think so. There are many useful traits that we can harvest from many different people, Mrs. Parrish. And yet, in order to harvest them properly, we must make you remember."

She turned her face towards him with a stubborn expression. "I won't!" she screamed.

"Very well," Diederich said with a sigh. "Then you must feel the pain."

He pressed the needle of the syringe into her neck, and emptied the serum into her vein. She was very still for a moment. Then her eyes began to bulge; the veins stood out in her throat; and she started screaming.

Katie watched in horror. She didn't know what to think, and she didn't know what to do.

"How can we help her?" Jacob asked desperately.

"I don't know," Katie murmured in a helpless voice. She didn't like feeling helpless; but this was a damned mess.

"We must do something," Lamberto announced purposefully.

He leapt up to his feet, and pushed the door to the strange laboratory open wide.

"Wait, Lamberto!" Katie whispered urgently.

But it was too late. Lamberto Esplanade had already barreled into the room, and he was wrestling with Dr. Diederich. It was obvious that the young man was no match for the doctor.

Jacob saw this right away, and he raced in to try and help Lamberto. Jacob was a tall, wiry man, and Katie certainly wouldn't have opted to tussle with him in a dark back alley. But Dr. Diederich was taller, and more muscular, and he had a strange steadfastness of purpose that Katie had never seen in anyone before. *A cool cucumber,* as Katie's mother would have said.

The doctor struck Lamberto across the head, and he fell to the floor, lying still and straight like a plank of wood. Diederich fought with Jacob, tooth and nail it looked like, for a couple minutes. Katie couldn't help thinking that, if she rushed in and tried to help, things might be a lot easier for Jacob. But she couldn't find the courage to try. She thought of it a few times – but it just looked too daunting.

When the doctor finally threw Jacob down to the floor, and injected him with the rest of the serum in the syringe, Katie felt ashamed of herself. She might have been able to help him. She might have been able to keep all this from happening.

But she just stayed there, huddling behind the wall. If she was going to be such a damned coward, it would have been better to run, to get out of there before the doctor noticed her presence. But after Jacob fell to the floor, she couldn't shake that feeling of guilt. She couldn't bring herself to run.

She went into the laboratory too late. She didn't even really know why she went in there. Maybe to assuage her guilt? Probably.

Either way, she went into the room, and looked down at Jacob and Lamberto lying on the floor. Diederich was looking down at them, too, and he didn't notice her. So she took her opportunity to lunge at him.

First, she wrested the syringe out of his hand. He was so taken aback, it was like taking candy from a baby. She pried it out of his fingers, and threw it across the floor. Then she pushed him down.

He got the wind knocked out of him pretty good, and he lay there wheezing, still not really understanding what was happening. He hadn't suspected that there was anyone with the two men. Now he knew otherwise.

Katie knew she didn't have much time to work with. Soon, he'd regain his composure, and recall his full strength. If she was going to do something, she had to do it now.

She looked all around, and saw a tray of instruments lying on a metal tray next to the table on which Mrs. Parrish was lying. The old woman had stopped screaming, and she was lying there twitching, her eyes blinking erratically, the cords still standing out in her skinny neck.

There was a shining silver scalpel on the tray. Katie snatched it up, and lunged towards Diederich. She was aiming for his throat. Jacob Barlow was lying off to the side, moaning and twitching. Lamberto still hadn't moved.

Katie jumped at the doctor, and stabbed him in the neck with the scalpel. But her aim might have been off.

Damn you, Katrina, Mallory Kent used to say to her. *You never hit the clit properly. What the hell else do you have to do, other than to hit my fucking clit properly? Put all of your worthless fingers to good use!*

Katie hesitated above Diederich's still form, swallowing thickly, breathing shallowly. Had she hit a vein? Had she nicked an artery? She couldn't tell. There was blood, there was a lot of blood . . .

She pulled the scalpel out of his neck, holding it high in the air, probably looking like a crazy Indian who wanted to scalp somebody. Diederich grabbed at his neck, sucking in mouthfuls of air, choking on his spit. Choking on blood? She couldn't tell.

He'd seen her face. He wasn't dead. Should she kill him? How should she kill him?

She hit him in the neck with the scalpel again. She dragged it across the front of his throat, trying to slit it like an envelope. Trying to make all the blood spill out.

A lot of blood came out, but not as much as she'd hoped for. How could she kill him? She didn't know. She didn't know what the fuck she was doing. It was like a stupid teenager trying to kill herself. She kept trying, but the fucker kept breathing . . .

She looked down at him, and saw him blinking up at her. Blinking angrily, she thought. Blinking maniacally.

She pulled her arm back, and punched him in the face. Then she leapt to her feet, and ran out of the room.

She raced into the office, and towards the second door. She hurried out into the grey, dingy light of the corridor – and something struck her across the head. She fell senseless to the floor.

Chapter 18

She woke up in her room. She sat up frantically, and looked to the left, towards the bathroom.

The bathroom was empty. Lydia was gone.

Katie ran her hands through her hair, breathing quickly, not understanding what had happened. She closed her eyes, and tried to think. She tried to think . . .

She threw off the covers, and let her brain race furiously. How had she gotten here?

She'd thrust a scalpel into Dr. Diederich's neck. He'd been bleeding. But there wasn't any blood on her.

Wait . . .

There was a small, strange spot of red down on the cuff of her pajama pants. From Diederich? Probably. But she couldn't say for sure. She wasn't even entirely sure what she was remembering. Had she killed him? Had he chased her? What had happened?

She touched her pocket, feeling for the skeleton key. But it was gone.

She leaned forward, clutching her head in her hands, feeling like a sad collegian who'd just had too much vodka. What could she remember? What was the truth of it all?

She stared straight ahead of her, fixing her eyes on the bright spot of plain white wall. It was plain, yes, and it was bright, but it was real. What else was real? What could she remember?

She'd stabbed Diederich in the neck. Stabbed him, yes – but she hadn't killed him.

He'd been bleeding. Where was he now?

Where was Lydia's body?

She had to find out what was going on here. She leapt to her feet, and ran out of the room. She raced away down the West Corridor, making towards Cora Halstead's office. She didn't care anymore if anyone found out about her and Cora. Well, Cora probably cared – but Katie didn't have the time or the energy to care. She needed answers, and she needed help. She had no one else to turn to.

There were a few women walking slowly up and down the corridor, a couple of them looking bored, a couple of them looking incredibly insane, whispering to themselves and staring at nameless faces on the ceiling. One of the bored-looking women – short and thin, with stringy hair and a greasy face – looked at Katie with a malignant smile.

"Where's the fire?" she asked curiously, still smiling.

"Mind your own business," Katie snapped.

"Testy, testy!" the woman returned. "Well, have it your own way."

She looked carefully into Katie's face, and added, "But I might have been able to help you, you know."

Katie stared at her for a moment, feeling a little surprised. But then she shook herself, and hurried off down the corridor.

Cora's office door was closed. Katie knocked urgently, and Cora's voice called out, "Come back later, please."

But Katie couldn't come back later. She had a feeling that, the longer she waited, the more people they'd find dead.

Against her better judgment, she pushed her way into the room. When she entered, two people looked up at her with cross expressions. There was Cora Halstead behind the desk. In front of the desk, in one of the two chairs, was Karl Diederich.

Katie's breath caught in her throat. Just last night, she'd seen this nut torturing Mrs. Parrish. He'd left Jacob Barlow and Lamberto Esplanade lying on the floor. Then Katie stuck a scalpel in his neck . . .

She looked at Diederich's neck, at the places where she'd hit him with the blade. But there was nothing there. The skin was perfectly white and smooth.

Katie shook her head in confusion, staring at the doctor's neck. He noted the direction of her eyes, and he smiled. A little malignantly, she thought.

What was going on here? Had last night actually happened? Were Jacob, Lamberto, and Mrs. Parrish asleep in their rooms, oblivious to all of this? Had Katie just imagined everything?

Her head felt like it was spinning. She'd felt so sure of herself when she barged into the room, but now she had no idea what she was doing. She coughed softly, and put a hand to her mouth. Then she looked pointedly at Cora.

"Hello, Katie," Cora said brusquely. "Didn't you hear what I said?"

"I heard you," Katie said in a stiff voice, looking uncomfortably at Diederich. "But I need to speak with you." She hesitated; thought for a moment; then added, "It's important."

Cora looked anxiously at Diederich. He nodded solemnly, then rose from his chair, and crossed to the door. He smiled eerily at Katie. "Miss Throckmorton," he said with a slight bow.

Katie had no idea what he was thinking. She looked more closely at his neck, but she still couldn't make anything out. The skin was clear and unblemished.

What the hell was this?

Katie didn't reply to Diederich's greeting. She just stared levelly into his face, and waited for him to leave.

He smiled again: a soft, mocking smile. The door closed softly behind him, and Katie turned to look at Cora.

"What was that?" she demanded. "What's going on?"

"What do you mean?" Cora returned. She pretended to look as if she didn't know what Katie was talking about, but it was obvious that she did. Who was she trying to fool?

"Are you being serious right now?" Katie asked in a low voice, stepping forward towards the desk.

"I don't know what you mean," Cora said absently, looking away from Katie, and shuffling a few papers on the desk.

Katie couldn't believe what was happening. She couldn't reconcile the woman in front of her with the woman she'd fucked the day before.

Was it really all in her imagination? If last night had only been in her imagination – then maybe she'd never slept with Cora after all . . .

All these thoughts were getting to be too much for her. She felt like a sane person trapped in a crazy person's dream.

But wasn't that probably how all crazy people felt? *Was* she actually crazy? She didn't know.

She went closer to the desk, laid her palms flat on its surface, and leaned down close to Cora. "What's going on?" she whispered. "Are you afraid to tell me? Did he threaten you?"

Cora tried to take a breath, but it caught it her chest, and she gave a thick, messy cough. "I don't know what you're talking about," she said in a soft voice, looking straight into Katie's eyes. "I think you should go back to your room now. Take a little rest. It'll be time for group soon."

"I need your help," Katie said desperately, staring into Cora's face with a pleading expression. "I went to Diederich's office last night. I heard screaming again. Lydia Brock is dead, but now her body's gone. Jacob Barlow and Lamberto Esplanade were with me last night, but I don't know what happened to them . . ."

Her words trailed off with a note of despondence, and she looked at Cora with that same desperate expression.

Cora stared at her blankly. She'd never even gotten out of her chair.

"I'm sorry, Katie," she said. "I still don't know what you're talking about. If there's an official complaint you'd like to make, of course I can make a note of it . . ."

Katie didn't understand. Was this a joke? No, of course it wasn't a joke. There was some meaning in it. Was Cora afraid of something? Afraid of Diederich? *Had* he threatened her? What was going on?

Katie furrowed her brows, and examined Cora's face carefully. She didn't recognize anything she saw there.

"Lydia Brock is dead," she repeated. "Didn't you hear me?"

For a moment, Cora looked anxious. But she quickly composed herself, and said, "I think you're imagining things, Katie. I'm sure Lydia is fine." She paused, and looked carefully into Katie's face. "You probably just dreamed it," she added.

"What do you know about my dreams?" Katie demanded. She didn't like it when people talked about dreams; especially *her* dreams. They were filled with evil things, with demons who had red faces.

She wished she'd never told Cora about her nightmares. She wished Cora had never held her like that, the night Katie woke up terrified in her office.

"You don't know anything about me," Katie said in a low voice. She felt betrayed.

Cora   smiled uncomfortably. "Everybody dreams, Katie," she said lightly. "There's no harm in it."

"Lydia's dead," Katie said for the third time. "You don't have to believe me. Whatever it is you're playing at – I hope it catches up with you soon."

The doctor didn't say anything. Katie looked back at her once, but she was still wearing that same blank, uncomprehending expression.

It was like looking at the face of a ghost.

***

Katie didn't go to group that day. She skipped lunch, and she didn't go to her appointment with Cora Halstead, either.

What she wanted most was to know what had happened to Jacob and Lamberto. So she ventured into the East Corridor for the first time.

She came to the end of the South Corridor, and prepared to turn left into the men's wing. What would happen when she went down the corridor? Would anyone care? Was it really a wise thing to do?

She didn't know, but she was going, anyway. She turned left, and started down the East Corridor – where the first light of morning shone through, when the women's corridor was still bathed in shadow in the wake of the dirty fluorescent lights.

Just like in the women's corridor, there were a few men passing up and down, some whose eyes were fixed and intent on some purpose, some who looked as if they were lost in space. A couple of them glanced curiously at Katie, obviously wondering what she was doing there. She wasn't a man, and she wasn't a doctor. What business did she have to be there? Well – she was still trying to figure that part out.

A tall figure down the hall caught her eye, and she looked to see Tim Reynolds standing outside one of the rooms, scribbling on a clipboard, his face pinched with concentration. Tim Reynolds – the tall, thin orderly who'd come to collect Katie on her first morning in the asylum. Tim Reynolds, who'd found her outside Dr. Damien's office on the morning after his death. Tim Reynolds, who'd been first on the scene – after Katie, that was – the night Eric Conley was murdered.

Well, it *appeared* that he'd arrived after Katie that night. But what if he'd been there before? What if that was the reason he'd come so quickly – because he'd already been there? It made sense. He was tall and thin, just like the man under the black hood. He'd been in all the right places at all the right times.

But then, she had to consider everything that had happened with Dr. Diederich. If she wasn't crazy – and she didn't think she was – she had to take into account the fact that he'd been torturing an old woman in a secret room next to his office. He'd attacked Lamberto Esplanade and Jacob Barlow, and he may have been responsible for knocking Katie unconscious. If he hadn't hit her, who could have done it? Who could have brought her to her room afterward?

But then – where had the wound on his neck gone? She'd stabbed him viciously with a scalpel. Where was the evidence of that? Washed away, it had looked like, as if wounds could be made invisible with soap and water.

Katie looked carefully at Tim Reynolds. He scribbled away on his clipboard, looking up now and then to speak with someone on the other side of the doorway. Katie took a few steps towards him. He hadn't noticed her yet, but it was only a matter of time.

Tim Reynolds kept scribbling, kept talking to the person on the other side of the doorway, while Katie continued to inch closer. Soon, it was as though the young orderly felt someone's eyes on him, and he glanced around, looking uncomfortable. It was only a moment or two before he saw Katie. His eyes fell on her face, and he frowned sternly. He couldn't have looked more displeased.

He said a few words to whoever it was he'd been talking to, then tucked his clipboard under his arm, and started towards Katie down the corridor. He was glaring at her as if she were some sort of sticky bug attached to the bottom of his boot.

"Miss Throckmorton," he said bitterly. "What are you doing here?"

"I'm taking a walk," Katie said shortly. "How about you, Tim? What have you been up to lately?"

Her tone was pointed, and it was obvious that she was accusing him of something. He couldn't have been more pissed about it.

"Look," he said snappishly, "I'm just trying to do my job here. I don't know what it is you think you're playing at, but –"

"I'm not playing at anything, Tim," Katie interrupted. "I'm just trying to stay alive."

The young orderly frowned, looking confused. It was clear he didn't know whether or not he should believe Katie.

"Listen," he said, "I've spent too much time around crazy people to let them rattle me. And I'm not going to let *you* rattle me. So why don't you just get the hell out of here?"

"Out of this asylum?" Katie asked with a crooked grin. "I'd be glad to, if you'd be kind enough to give me the key."

"I meant out of this hallway," Reynolds said in a low voice. "And you'd better listen to me, little girl. I know you have something to do with all the nasty shit that's been going on around here. You'd better stay the hell away from me – or I'll make sure you end up in a real prison, where you belong."

Katie didn't reply. She just glared at him.

He stared her down for a moment or two, but then he shivered, and walked away. He curved to the right, and marched away towards the South Corridor.

Katie looked after him for a moment, thinking hard. But she couldn't come to any definite conclusions, so she set off on her way again, farther down the East Corridor.

Most of the doors were standing open at this time of day. Katie looked in a few of them, hoping against all hope that she'd catch a glimpse of Jacob or Lamberto. But she didn't see either of them. She saw a few sleeping men, their backs turned towards the doors, their faces averted in the direction of the barred windows. She saw a few pacing men, their steps quick and furious, their expressions taut and anxious.

But she didn't see Jacob or Lamberto. The closest she came was a door with glaring red letters painted across it. The letters formed words which read: *FUCK YOU SHERLOCK.*

It wasn't hard to discern that this must have been the door that led to Lamberto Esplanade's room. Someone had obviously been making fun of his strange tendency to act like Sherlock Holmes. Eric Conley, maybe?

Katie didn't know. She just stared at the red letters for a moment, wondering why someone didn't paint over them.

There were any number of explanations. Maybe there wasn't any leftover paint; maybe no one ever had the spare time. Maybe the simple fact was that nobody cared. Yeah – that made the most sense.

Katie moved closer to the painted door, and listened carefully. The door was closed, but she was hoping to hear some indication of Lamberto's presence. Maybe his voice; maybe just some sort of movement. But she heard nothing, at first.

It was a minute or two before she heard anything. Eventually, a few soft sounds drifted into her ears. A wet smack; a stifled moan.

The doors to the patient's rooms didn't have locks. Even if someone had wanted to, they couldn't have kept Katie from looking into the room. So she stepped forward, and laid a hand on the doorknob. She turned it silently, and pushed the door inward.

The occupants of the room didn't notice her spying. They went on with the same thing they'd been doing before; and this is what they were doing.

Marcus Bickford was standing at the end of one of the beds. He must have been Lamberto's roommate. At the moment, though, that was the least interesting thing about him.

Marcus was standing there, and his jeans were dropped down around his ankles. His boxers were down, too, and his cock was sticking out like a flag pole. Dark, hard and long. Sort of like Dostoyevsky's *Crime and Punishment.*

Marcus stood there, naked below the waist, his hands grasping his own muscular thighs. He was perturbed and excited, no doubt on account of the fact that someone was sucking his cock.

Katie was shocked – but not surprised – to see that it was Dr. Wilkins's mouth attached to Marcus's dick. The doctor was kneeling down in front of the young man, and his lips were fastened firmly around his penis. His right hand circled the shaft around the base, and he moved his head up and down, leaving a trail of spit and cum in his wake. The most intriguing part was, he didn't even look grossed out by the semen that was flooding his mouth. He let go of Marcus's penis for a moment, looked to the right, and spit out the cum. Then he went back to sucking, and Marcus threw his head back in rapture.

Katie had had enough of being a voyeur. She tossed the door open, and stepped into the room. At the sound of the door hitting the wall, both of the men looked over in shock. Marcus's cock began to droop. Dr. Wilkins shot to his feet, looking as if he were standing in front of a Nazi firing squad.

"Before you ask," she said to them, "I don't give a fuck that you were just sucking his dick. It's the least of my problems."

She looked at Marcus, and asked, "When was the last time you saw Lamberto?"

Marcus hurried to pull up his pants, and Dr. Wilkins wiped his mouth self-consciously. "I don't know," Marcus replied distractedly, when he'd finished cinching his belt. "Sometime yesterday?"

"You didn't see him this morning?"

Marcus thought for a moment. "No," he said slowly.

"Did you say anything to anyone?"

Marcus put a hand on his hip, and bit his bottom lip. He was obviously still feeling flustered.

"Look," Katie said, "I'm sorry I walked in on you guys like that. It was a shitty thing to do. But I have good reason to believe that Lamberto might be in trouble."

The fog cleared from Marcus's face, and he knitted his dark brows. "What do you mean?" he asked.

"Something happened last night," Katie said quietly, looking at Dr. Wilkins, and wondering if she should be saying any of this in front of him.

"I can see there's something you don't want me to hear," the doctor said, not looking as upset as Marcus about Katie walking in on them. It was strange, because Katie would have thought it'd be the other way around. Wilkins was so meek and mild, she couldn't believe he hadn't run from the room screaming already.

"But you know," Wilkins added, "I might be able to help. I can tell from the look on your face that you're scared. As far as I know, there's only one person in this place who scares people. Is this about Dr. Diederich?"

Katie was surprised. "Yes," she answered uncertainly.

She could see Marcus shiver.

"What do you know about him?" Katie asked the doctor, looking warily from him to Marcus.

"I know about his experiments," Wilkins replied, starting to look uneasy. "Poor Marc knows even more than I do."

Katie looked at Marcus. "What does that mean?" she asked.

"He's taken me a couple of times," Marcus replied in a strangled voice, looking to the doctor for support. Wilkins smiled gently, and reached over to press the young man's hand. "Him and Dr. Damien. They injected me with something – something that burned like fire. They said they'd keep doing it if I didn't tell them what they wanted to know."

"What did they want to know?" Katie asked quickly.

Marcus hung his head, and let go of the doctor's hand. "They wanted to know how it felt to be gay," he answered in a quiet voice.

Katie thought of what she'd seen the night before. Diederich had injected Mrs. Parrish with the same serum Marcus must have been talking about. Up until now, Katie hadn't really given what he'd said a great deal of thought. She'd been so upset about being knocked out, and then waking up in her room with no idea how she'd gotten there, she hadn't taken the time to analyze the conversation between Diederich and Mrs. Parrish. She'd been so worried about Lamberto and Jacob, she hadn't thought of anything else. She'd felt responsible for what had happened to them, because she hadn't helped them. She could have acted sooner, but she didn't.

She thought for a long moment. *"I'll never give you what you want,"* Mrs. Parrish had said. *"I'll never talk about it."*

Diederich had wanted her to talk about her daughter. The daughter she killed. But why? What had he said?

"There are many useful traits that we can harvest from many different people, Mrs. Parrish."

Useful traits? How could you harvest someone's personal characteristics?

Wait – what had he said next?

"In order to harvest them properly, we must make you remember."

Katie took a step towards Marcus, looking a little frantic. "He said – he said he wanted to know how it *felt* to be gay?"

"Yeah," Marcus muttered. "Him and Damien kept asking me all sorts of questions, and they took a bunch of notes. While I was talking, they kept drawing my blood. I think they took too much, the first time, because I passed out. I woke up the next morning in my bed."

Katie tried to work it all out. There was a ghastly picture forming in her mind – but it was still vague, still without edges and corners. The puzzle was still missing a lot of pieces.

"If you see Lamberto," she said softly, "will you tell me right away?"

Marcus nodded seriously. He cast a desperate look towards Dr. Wilkins.

"Isn't there anything you can do, Sam?" he asked.

Wilkins frowned. "You have to believe me when I say," he declared gravely to Marcus, "I did everything I could after they took you the first time. I threatened them; I even punched Damien in the face. But none of it did any good."

"You punched Damien in the face?" Marcus asked wonderingly.

"Yeah," Wilkins said with a sigh.

"For me?"

The doctor cast a deep look into the young man's face, and it was full of meaning. "Of course I did it for you," he said quietly.

Katie didn't have the patience for such a saccharine moment. "Did you kill him, too?" she asked snappishly.

Wilkins looked at her in confusion. "What?"

"You said you punched Damien in the face," Katie went on, rolling her eyes. "Did you kill him, too?"

"No!" Wilkins exclaimed. "Of course I didn't. Besides – even if I'd tried, I probably wouldn't have gotten far. After I punched him, he hit me back, and broke my glasses. He was six inches taller than me, and fifty pounds heavier. He would've killed *me.*"

Katie scrutinized the doctor for a moment, and had to admit that he did look pretty pathetic. It was hard to imagine him killing anyone.

"All right," she said. "I believe you. But listen – I have no idea what's going to happen. I don't know how I got to my room this morning, and I don't know where Lamberto is. Him, or Jacob Barlow, or Mrs.

Parrish. All I know is, one second I was fighting with Diederich, and then I got knocked out as I was running away from him."

"What exactly happened last night?" Wilkins asked.

Katie took a deep breath, and began to tell him the whole sordid story.

***

By the time dinner came, she was starving. She hadn't eaten since the day before.

She went into the cafeteria, hardly caring if someone came and tried to start a fight with her. She went through the line, got a tray with a greasy chicken sandwich and fries, and sat down at that same empty table.

She picked up the sandwich, and took a bite. Not that different from a McChicken. And a hell of a lot cheaper.

She wondered if she'd ever use money again. She was consigned to this hellhole for the next six years, at least. But would she even live that long? People were dropping like flies, and they all seemed to be centered around her.

Why was that?

She took another bite of the sandwich, chewed thoughtfully, swallowed thickly. What the hell had Cora been playing at? *Was* she trying to make a fool of Katie? Was she in league with Diederich, and playing for information? Had she slept with Katie like a cheap whore trying to get coke from a pimp?

Katie shivered horribly, and the sharp sensation of cold cut through to her bones. A momentary fear of complete and total insanity returned to her. She had no idea what to expect from herself or anyone else. She took a third bite of her sandwich, and choked on it.

While she was coughing, and trying to get the piece of greasy grey chicken out of her throat, someone sat down across from her. With a red face and watery eyes, she looked up, halfheartedly expecting to see Mrs. Parrish.

But it wasn't Mrs. Parrish. It was that short, thin woman from the hallway this morning. The one with the malignant smile.

"Hey," she said brightly. She was still smiling. And she still looked evil.

Katie didn't answer. She threw down her sandwich impatiently, wiping her greasy fingers on her jeans. Hundred-dollar jeans that Mallory Kent had bought her. For the moment, the greasy stripes filled her with glee. It was like she'd gotten one over on that damned old vampire.

"Found anything out yet?" the thin woman asked with a faint note of excitement.

Katie propped her elbows up on the table, and looked at the other woman carefully. "Who are you, exactly?" she asked.

"Midge Hampton," the woman answered matter-of-factly. "Resident know-it-all, snoop, and kiss-ass. Nice to meet you."

She smiled politely, and took a bite of her sandwich.

"Look," Katie said wearily. "I don't mean to be rude, but I don't know what it is you want from me."

Midge Hampton looked at her with one raised eyebrow, chewing with a blank expression. "I want to help you," she said simply.

"Help me what?"

The woman continued to stare at her, not even blinking. "I want to help you get out of here alive," she said, as if this were the most obvious thing in the world.

Katie decided it was time to stop playing dumb. It was clear that this woman knew something about what was going on. How much did she know? And the more important question was – was she sane enough to *really* know anything?

"You should stop trying to figure things out," Midge Hampton pronounced in a crystal-clear voice. "It's a good way to get yourself killed."

Katie wasn't sure if she could trust this woman, but the truth was, it comforted her to hear someone else talking about what was going on. This woman knew that *something* was going on, that much was obvious. For the moment, it made Katie forget her fear of being nuts.

"How much have *you* figured out?" she asked the woman.

"Enough," Midge Hampton answered. "The only difference is, I keep my mouth shut about it."

At that moment, Marcus Bickford appeared next to the table. Apparently, he'd made his way over from the weird kids' table. He looked shamefacedly at Katie, but didn't say anything. The memory of their last encounter must have still been fresh in his mind.

"Thought I saw you over here, Midge," he said, taking a seat next to the woman. "Don't wanna sit with us no more, huh?"

"Is baby boy feeling insecure?" Midge asked, a little cruelly. "Well, it's not my job to fix that. Anyway – I just wanted to talk to this young lady here."

Marcus looked back at Katie. "Yeah," he said slowly. "Yeah – me and Katie already had a little talk earlier today."

"Is that so?" Midge asked curiously.

"Yeah," Marcus repeated. "Seems like things in this place just keep getting weirder and weirder."

Katie stared at him for a moment, feeling sorry for him. She thought about his family. About his mother and sister.

But thinking of *that* made her think of Lydia. Lydia was the one who'd told her the story in the first place.

Where had Lydia's body gone? What had they done with it?

Who had killed her?

Katie shook herself, and took a deep breath. This wasn't the time for thoughts like those. They weren't productive right now. She had to be productive.

"Whatever's going on around here," she said quietly, "we have to figure it out. And fast. Marcus, I didn't tell you – but Lydia is dead."

The young man's face froze, and he dropped a French fry that he'd been raising to his mouth. "What?" he spluttered.

"I'm sorry," Katie said. "But she's gone. When I woke up last night – before I heard Mrs. Parrish screaming – I saw Lydia. In the bathroom." She swallowed thickly, and added, "Someone had murdered her."

"God almighty," Midge said with a sigh. "Poor little thing."

Katie was still pretty upset, but she suddenly realized that she was still hungry, too. She hadn't eaten since the day before, and more than half of her dinner was still on the tray. So she picked up her sandwich to take another bite.

But it tasted strange, this time. Not like chicken.

She began to cough, and she tried to spit the food out, but the sharp cough forced her to swallow it. Next moment, she felt her throat starting to close.

She pulled the top bun off the sandwich, and saw a raw shrimp lying on top of the chicken patty. Half-eaten. Half was on the sandwich; the other half had gone down Katie's throat.

She was deathly allergic to shellfish. Lockwood had tried to kill her with shrimp once. But who'd done it this time?

Marcus and Midge were looking at her in alarm. Marcus said her name, and Midge reached across the table to lay a hand on her arm, speaking words Katie couldn't hear. She was too busy coughing and choking.

Marcus yelled something, then ran around the table. He slid his arms under Katie's armpits, presumably to begin the Heimlich maneuver. At that moment, though, Katie's head began to feel as if it were on fire, and she tried desperately to draw a breath. But she couldn't. So she passed out.

Chapter 19

She came around the same way she had that morning, not knowing how she'd gotten wherever it was she'd gotten to, and not knowing how long she'd been there.

The only difference was, that morning, she'd known exactly where she was. She'd known that she was in her room. But now – now she was lying on some hard surface, the place was dark, and she was bound. She strained her eyes, trying desperately to make out anything in the nonexistent light. But it was no use. She couldn't see.

She felt pretty messed up after choking on that shrimp. Her throat was tight and sore, and her head was pounding.

It seemed like ages before she heard a noise of any kind. For a very long time, everything was perfectly silent. It was as if she'd been locked in a tomb.

Maybe that was it. Maybe they'd put her in a coffin, and buried her somewhere. But no – if they'd done that, why were her wrists and ankles bound? And besides, the air felt too open to be the air of a small coffin. She was in a room somewhere. That much was for certain.

Suddenly, she heard a noise off to her right. A slight scuffling, and then a whispering voice. She couldn't make out what the voice was saying, at first, but when she strained her ears she began to hear.

"It's an interesting thing," a female voice said quietly. "What he's doing."

"Interesting my foot," another female voice – a remarkably similar voice – said in slight irritation. "I dislike being someone's guinea pig. I am what I am, and that's my own business. I'd rather be asleep in my bed."

"Who is that?" Katie asked loudly. "Who the hell is that?"

The voices fell quiet. It was a few seconds before anyone said anything.

"We don't remember your name," one of the voices said.

"But we remember *you,*" the second voice said.

Suddenly, a door opened, and a bright rectangle of light flooded the front of the room. Katie strained her neck to lift her head as far as it would go. The rectangle of light revealed her location. She saw the end of the table she was lying on, and she felt like an idiot for not realizing it was the same table Mrs. Parrish had lain on the night before. It was the same room.

Karl Diederich was standing in the doorway, looking into the room. He glanced at Katie first, but then looked off to the side, where there were two young women chained to the wall. Marion and Miriam Holloway. The twins who liked to suck each other's blood.

Katie shivered, and fixed her eyes on Diederich. He came into the room, and flipped a switch that turned on the three fluorescent bulbs on the ceiling.

The place was suddenly flooded with light. Katie blinked her eyes, looking all around, grimacing at the sight of the strange jars on the shelves along the walls. Eyes, ears, and all sorts of nastiness floated in those jars.

She noticed more, now, than she'd noticed last night. There was a narrow cot pressed up against the wall, as well as a small desk, and a comfortable-looking armchair at the end of the room. On one side of the chair was a low table, and on the other side was a stone pedestal, with a marble bust of Venus set on top of it.

Katie was immediately reminded of the Venus of Ille – the story she'd told Cora Halstead about.

That's ironic, she thought. *Now if only it would come to life, and strangle that fucking maniac.*

Diederich came into the room, and shut the door behind him. He made his way towards the armchair, and took a seat. There was an ashtray and a box of cigars lying on the little table beside him. He took out one of the cigars, and lit it with a match from his pocket.

"You like Italian cigars, Doctor?" Katie inquired in a dry, scratchy voice. She needed water. Her throat was parched.

"Ah," Diederich said with a cruel smile, puffing at his cigar. "I suspect dear Officer Humphreys told you that. He's really a very pleasant man – rather intelligent for an ordinary cop."

Katie didn't reply. She was looking from the doctor to the twins, and wondering what was about to happen.

"Ah," Diederich repeated. "You're wondering why the girls are here tonight. Well, I plan to do a little experiment on them. We've done it before, haven't we, girls?"

The twins glared at him. They were huddled close to each other, their pale, skinny arms linked together.

"These girls are really very admirable psychopaths," Diederich went on, still puffing at his cigar. "I don't suppose you know what brought them here, Miss Throckmorton?"

Katie didn't want to answer, but she knew that the doctor had something nefarious in mind, and she thought it would be best if she delayed whatever he was planning for as long as possible.

"No," she said simply. "I have no idea."

"Well," Diederich said, looking proudly at the girls, "they killed their entire family. They had a mother and a father, of course, as well as a younger brother. Didn't you, girls?"

The twins lost their menacing look, and began to smile malignantly.

"They are very proud of themselves, as you can see," Diederich added. "But anyway. Officer Humphreys found them in their parents' van, with no one else around. They were both covered in blood. Everything was covered in blood."

He glanced at the twins again, and smiled. "Do you want to tell her what you did, girls? I know how you like to tell the story."

The young women maintained their evil smiles, and sat forward on their haunches, staring at Katie eagerly. "We killed them," one of the twins whispered. "We killed them all!"

"Well, to be fair, Marion," the second twin said, "I killed two of them. *You* only killed one."

"Ah, yes," Marion returned, not seeming deterred in the least, "but we drained them dry together! Isn't that right, Miriam?"

"Fair enough," Miriam muttered. "I still cut an extra throat, though."

Marion sighed, and rolled her eyes. Then she looked back at Katie, still wearing that excited expression. "We slit their throats," she said quickly, "and then we drank their blood! Every single drop! I've never had so much at one time before. It changed my life."

Obviously, Katie didn't know what to say to that. Luckily for her, Marion didn't need any encouragement to go on with her story. She was full of enthusiasm.

"There was blood everywhere," she murmured, her eyes gleaming with hell-fire. "It got on everything. It seemed like there was more blood than air. When we finished drinking, we threw the bodies over a cliff. The wolves must have got them, because no one ever found them."

"Not that it mattered much," Miriam added in a bored voice. "We've still been stuck here all these years."

"Oh, my poor dears," Diederich murmured, sounding truly sympathetic. "What a trying life for such exceptional girls! But I do my best to make it better, don't I?"

The girls smiled a little, apparently against their will. They seemed drawn to the doctor, and repelled by him, simultaneously.

"What lovely smiles you have," Diederich observed. "I've always thought that, you know."

He looked sharply at Katie. "You'd do well to keep that in mind, Miss Throckmorton," he said. "A simple smile can transform your entire day. Why not try one now? You look so glum, you're making *me* depressed."

The twins snickered, and rattled their chains a little.

Katie looked at the three of them, and though she wanted to keep them talking, she couldn't think of what to say. She was disgusted by all of them. She wished they would drop dead on the spot, even if it meant she'd be trapped in that room for all eternity.

Suddenly, a knock sounded on the door, and Diederich went to answer it. Katie took a moment to wonder who it could be. Not Damien, obviously. He'd never set foot in that room again. He occupied a different one – though it was probably remarkably similar – down in hell.

Diederich pulled the door open, and ushered his visitor inside. When Katie saw who it was, her breath caught in her throat, and her eyes burned.

It was Cora Halstead.

***

The door closed behind Cora with a heavy *click,* and everyone took a moment to look around at each other. Cora nodded politely to Diederich, and glanced wordlessly at the twins. Then she looked at Katie.

Her face was completely blank. There was no emotion in it at all. It was like she was staring down at a dead mouse in a trap.

"Miss Throckmorton will be joining us tonight," Diederich said simply. "I put a little extra something in her supper to ensure her safe delivery."

He glanced curiously at Katie, and added, "Do you know exactly what a shellfish allergy is, Miss Throckmorton? It's an abnormal response by the body's immune system to proteins in certain marine animals. Like shrimp, for example."

He showed that cruel smile again, and stared at Katie, obviously waiting for her to answer.

"Very informative," she muttered.

Diederich looked away from her with a chuckle, and fixed his attention on Cora.

"It was very kind of you to come, Dr. Halstead," Diederich said courteously. "I was hoping you would."

Cora nodded, and came farther into the room. "What would you like me to do?" she asked the other doctor.

"Well," Diederich said, "I intend to get as much information as I can out of Miss Throckmorton. She's a curious case. I'm very interested to know whether or not she actually killed her sister – because, if she did, she may possess some useful traits that I'd like to collect."

He paused, and looked back at Katie with a thoughtful expression. "And then there are the other murders," he added softly. "I have no idea who has been killing people in this hospital – and the truth is that you are my prime suspect, Miss Throckmorton. You were first on the scene for two of the murders, and the third body was found in your bedroom. Don't you find that at all strange?"

Katie looked at him in disbelief. Was he really pretending that he'd had nothing to do with the murders?

"Why are you looking at me like that?" he asked curiously. "Did you think *I* was the murderer?"

He laughed quietly. "I'm afraid I can't take responsibility, Miss Throckmorton," he said. "No – someone else will have to do that. Abel Damien was my partner, and I had no reason to kill him. He was a great help to me. As for Eric Conley – well, he was a troublesome boy, but he was also useful to me." He grinned evilly. "I performed more than one experiment on the boy. He was an interesting study, what with all that animal-like hostility."

"I don't believe you," Katie declared in a stalwart tone. "I know what you've done. I don't know why you killed Damien and Eric – but why did you have to kill Lydia? She might've had a life someday."

"Ha!" Diederich laughed. "I seriously doubt that, Miss Throckmorton. Lydia Brock was a hopeless case – a worthless human being, in every sense of the phrase. If she ever got out of this place, she would have just tried to kill herself again."

He laughed again, and added, "Not that I'm the one who killed her! I'm only saying that it wasn't much of a loss."

Katie glared at him, but didn't say anything.

"Ah, Miss Throckmorton," Diederich went on, with a soft *tut-tut.* "I believe you are in possession of many secrets – many dark and deep secrets! I think you try very hard to fool the rest of the world, but be assured that you cannot fool *me.*"

All the while he spoke, Cora Halstead stood just a little behind him, watching Katie surreptitiously. Katie was nearly livid with the feeling of betrayal; but still, when she looked at Cora, she couldn't bring herself to hate her. She remembered the feeling of her breath on her skin, and she could still taste her kiss. She could still smell rose water and lavender.

Looking at Cora was starting to make Katie lose her composure, so she looked away, and glared at Diederich again. "What did you do with her body?" she demanded.

"Lydia Brock's body, you mean?" Diederich inquired, starting to sound bored with the conversation. "I found it when I brought you back to your room. After I knocked you out. I had to keep you round for a while, though, while I saw to this."

He gestured to his throat, and smiled a smile that made his teeth appear strangely sharp.

"I cut you," Katie murmured. "How did you hide it?"

"With a certain serum I invented," Diederich replied. "It has wonderful regenerative properties. Just a single injection, and even a severe wound will heal in a matter of minutes."

"That's impossible."

"Ah! But it's not. My work may be difficult, Miss Throckmorton, and rather grisly at times – but it's all very much worth the effort."

Katie ignored this comment for now, and repeated, "What did you do with Lydia?"

"She has been disposed of," Diederich said curtly. "I didn't want that detective sniffing round here again. I've had quite enough of him."

"What about Jacob and Lamberto?" she persisted. "What did you do to them?"

He smiled that same, cruel smile. "They saw too much," he said simply. "And neither of them were of any use to me. A delusional young man who thought he was a detective, and a pitiable fellow who was scarcely brave enough to confront his own shadow on a sunny afternoon." He sighed, and looked down at his hands, picking at a hangnail on his right index finger. Then he looked up, and pointed towards the jars of body parts on the shelves.

"Though their personalities were useless to me," he added, "some of their body parts proved to be choice specimens. I have a deep interest in dissection. I believe it helps a physician to better understand his patients."

Katie swallowed down her bile, fighting the urge to be sick. "You killed them," she muttered.

"Not to worry," Diederich said with a grin. "You'll be joining them shortly."

Katie's breath caught, and she swallowed again. Her courage was beginning to wane.

"But first," Diederich said, starting up with a sudden look of resolve, and glancing over at Cora, "we have work to do. Come, Dr. Halstead. Let's begin."

The twins rattled their chains against the wall, and let out a few excited shrieks. Katie started nearly out of her skin, having forgotten that they were there.

"Quiet, girls," Diederich commanded. At the sound of his voice, the twins fell silent immediately, and sank back to lean against each other's shoulders.

"Now, Miss Throckmorton," Diederich said smoothly, stepping up beside the table, and fingering the instruments on the metal tray. "I think it's only fair that I explain what I'm going to do to you. I will ask you certain questions; and if you answer those questions candidly, I will simply draw your blood, and try to extract your personality from it." He smiled that sharp smile, and added, "Though you don't have to worry about waiting around for the whole tedious process. By the time I get to work on your blood, you'll be quite dead."

Katie swallowed hard, but tried to hide her fear. She cast a cutting look into Diederich's face, and said, "You're insane. What you're talking about is impossible."

She looked desperately at Cora, but the woman didn't even seem to be paying attention to her. She was standing off to the side, staring blankly at the opposite wall. Her expression was indecipherable.

"On the contrary," Diederich said. "It's entirely possible. I have been working on the method for the past twenty years – and two years ago I perfected it. I invented a device that isolates certain elements in the blood, elements that no one ever knew existed before. Not cells or plasma, not proteins or hormones. Something that becomes solid when isolated, and can then be boiled down into a solution that I combine with certain chemicals. The result is a variety of serums that, when ingested, can impart characteristics that were derived from the person who gave the blood. That's what Damien and I were working on for the past two years."

"I still say you're nuts," Katie muttered, not really caring what the doctor thought anymore. She didn't care about placating him. It was obvious he was going to kill her, and it was obvious that Cora wasn't going to help her.

Diederich laughed lightly. "Well," he said, "your reaction is understandable. Most people would doubt my research. It's of no consequence to me, however. I need nothing but my own resolve."

His eyes gleamed as he spoke these words, and he looked maniacal. Like Carrie's mother before she locked her in the closet, preparing to launch into some sort of sermon that was meant to explain what she believed in. It looked like Katie was about to find out what Karl Diederich believed in.

"I hail from Germany," he said. "I came to this country when I was young, but my adoptive parents were loyal to our true land. They were stalwart supporters of the Aryan ideal." He paused, and grinned. "It might interest you to know that Josef Mengele was my biological father."

"Josef Mengele?" Katie repeated dubiously. "Your father was one of the SS doctors at Auschwitz?

The man who killed countless Jews with his sick experiments?"

Diederich nodded enthusiastically. He looked very proud to be the son of the Angel of Death.

"Mengele only had one son," Katie said doubtfully.

"No," Diederich answered. "Josef had another son in the '70s, while he was living in Sao Paolo, only a few years before he died. And that son was me."

He thought for a moment, looking wistful. Then he said, "He spent a lot of time with me during the first years of my life. He died when I was only six, but I never forgot him. I wasn't like Rolf Mengele – I didn't want to disown my father for his wartime activities. I kept all of his personal notebooks, and I used them in my own research when I got older. Perhaps you noticed the beautiful desk out in my office?" he inquired.

Katie didn't answer. But of course she remembered the ornate, antique-looking desk from the doctor's office.

"Well," Diederich went on, "that desk belonged to Josef. I took it for my own after his death."

He paused, and sighed, a half-sad and halfhappy sigh. "Because I was illegitimate, however," he added, "I used the name of my adoptive parents. The ones who brought me to Germany after Josef's death. Their name was Diederich."

The doctor smiled pleasantly, obviously thinking fondly of these horrid memories.

"Now," he said, "I go on with my father's honorable research. I go on with his work – as well as the work of other pioneers like Aribert Heim and Carl Vaernet. My work with twins –" (he grinned over at the Holloway women) "– is meant to further Josef's own experiments."

He frowned, and added, "You girls should feel fortunate that my experiments are very different from his. I still intend to prove, and to nourish, the supremacy of heredity over environment – but I don't plan on sewing you together, or infecting one of you with typhus to see if the healthy one's blood will cure the sick one. All that's been done before. My work is different."

At the mention of typhus and being sewn together, the demonic twins shivered a little. But they soon got over it, and then began rattling their chains again.

"Carl Vaernet," Katie murmured. "He used hormone therapy to try to reverse homosexuality."

"Yes," Diederich confirmed. "I still believe it can be done – though not in the way he tried to do it. I have my own methods."

"And you've been testing them on Marcus Bickford."

The doctor grinned, and nodded.

Katie looked pointedly at Cora, but the other woman refused to meet her eyes.

"Ah, yes," Diederich said. "You're looking at Dr. Halstead. Someday, when my research is complete, I will be able to cure her unfortunate condition. Her strange attraction to her own sex. It's unnatural, and is a weakness in human nature." He frowned, and added,

"I only hope that your own unnatural tendencies won't taint the samples I take from you."

Katie might have been indignant, had she been listening properly. But she was thinking about something else. She was thinking of the dark and empty nurses' station, and feeling sure that Diederich had something to do with it.

"Is that why the nurses are never at their station at night?" she asked the doctor. "Because you tell them to stay away, in case any of the patients come asking questions?"

"I pay them extra for the service," Diederich explained. "The same way I paid the cook to put that shrimp on your sandwich. I tell the nurses when I plan to perform an experiment; and they stay out of the way."

Katie glared at him in disgust. He noticed her expression, and smiled lightly.

"It's my aim to improve human nature," he went on, "and to increase its strength and resilience. I believe that someday we'll achieve the ideal Hitler strove for all those years ago. With a little time, and a little patience, it can be a reality."

"I suppose you're going to start gassing Jews, then?" Katie asked bitterly.

"Not just Jews," Diederich replied candidly. "And not *particularly* Jews. All the weakest links in the chain will have to be eradicated. Survival of the fittest, and all that. Darwin had many good points. The ideal will be achieved by a combination of many great men's methods. And I will be the conduit."

His eyes shone in a frightful way. He looked like a treasure hunter who'd just caught sight of the golden gleam of El Dorado.

"You really are insane," Katie murmured quietly. For the first time, she was feeling truly terrified. She knew she was in the hands of a madman, and she knew she was going to die.

"You are welcome to your opinion, of course," Diederich said in a level tone. He arranged his instruments on the tray, and inspected them carefully. There were various metal tools – many of them very sharp-looking – as well as several syringes. One of the syringes was attached to an empty vial, and one was filled with that same dark serum that Katie had seen him inject Mrs. Parrish with.

Mrs. Parrish. Katie had forgotten all about her.

"What did you do with Mrs. Parrish?" she asked.

"Never fear," Diederich said, smiling brightly into her face. "I still have need of the old woman. I sedated her, and she's been asleep in her room all day."

For some reason, Katie was relieved to hear that. That day in the cafeteria, when she heard what the old woman had done to her child, she'd been disgusted. But there was something about her – a part of the woman that seemed to hate what she'd done, a part that seemed to long for something better. Katie was glad she wasn't dead.

It was as though Diederich could read her thoughts. "I see you're comforted by Mrs. Parrish's fate," he observed. "I regret to inform you, however, that the same fate won't be your own. You're too much trouble – and I'll have to get rid of you. But I hope you won't hold it against me."

He smiled again, and put his hands into the pockets of his white coat. Then he adopted a blank expression, making it clear that it was time for business.

"Now I will begin my questioning," he said. "It's imperative that you answer me with complete honesty. In order to isolate the particular element I'm looking for, you must allow yourself to feel the emotions related to the questions at hand. You must remember, and you must feel. Then, and only then, will your blood be of use to me."

He looked at her carefully, his hands still shoved deep into his pockets.

"Do you understand?" he asked.

Katie didn't know what to say. She looked all around in a last desperate attempt to escape; but she was bound tightly, and there was no way out. She hung her head in despair.

Suddenly, Cora cleared her throat, and touched Diederich's elbow. "I have a bit of a headache," she said. "If you don't need me at the moment, do you mind if I sit? It'll pass soon."

Diederich looked over at her, and thought for a moment. Then he nodded. "Go ahead," he said. "I'll call you if I need you."

Cora nodded, and fixed her eyes on Katie for a moment. Her expression was still impossible to read, but there was something in her eyes – something that Katie couldn't put her finger on. Katie frowned, and watched her in confusion.

Cora walked to the end of the room, and sat down in Diederich's armchair. The twins rattled their chains, and leered at her. She looked at them in disgust.

"All right, then," Diederich said. "First, I'm going to ask you about your sister."

He peered curiously into Katie's face. "Did you kill her, Miss Throckmorton?"

"No," Katie murmured.

The doctor knitted his brows, and looked at her disbelievingly. "Then what happened?" he asked.

"You're going to kill me, anyway," Katie said in an acidic tone. "I don't have to answer your questions."

"Did you forget what I told you?" the doctor asked politely. "You're going to die either way – but it's up to you how much it hurts."

He picked up the syringe filled with the dark serum, and looked down at Katie with a serious expression. "It's entirely up to you, Miss Throckmorton. Are you going to answer my questions?"

Katie stared as hard as she could into his face, but she couldn't keep back the tear that fell from her eye. She was afraid, and she couldn't deny it.

"No," she whispered. "I won't help you."

"Fine," Diederich said with a sigh. "Have it your own way, Miss Throckmorton. You'll soon change your mind."

He lowered the syringe towards Katie's neck, preparing to inject her with the serum. Katie closed her eyes, not wanting to watch as the cursed needle entered her skin.

But suddenly she heard the twins' chains start clanking madly, and her eyes flew open. She saw Cora Halstead racing across the room, with the heavy bust of Venus clutched in her hands.

Diederich spun towards her, but she was too quick. He raised the syringe defensively, but she used the Venus to knock it out of his hand. Then she hit him over the head with the marble statue.

The crazy doctor fell to the floor like a sack of stones, thoroughly unconscious. Cora stood for a moment, staring down at him and breathing heavily, while the twins continued to rattle their chains. But eventually, as if the sound of the chains were just invading her consciousness, she sprang into action. She rummaged through the instruments on the metal tray, and found an empty syringe. Then she took a vial of clear liquid from the side of the tray, and filled the syringe.

She hurried over to the twins, and fought to inject them with the drug. But they were wild as tigers, more like beasts than people, and she had a hard time of it. Finally, though, she managed to stab both of them with the needle. Almost immediately, they slumped against each other, and were silent.

Cora stood for a few seconds, still breathing heavily, looking down at the unconscious twins. Her hands were shaking. The syringe dropped from her twitching fingers, and clattered against the floor.

It was a long moment before Katie could bring herself to speak. But finally, she coughed through the dryness in her sore throat, and whispered, "Cora?" The other woman stood stock still, her arms rigid, her back stiff. Then, she slowly turned around. Her face was stained with tears. She started to shake again.

Katie stared into her face. Even if she'd tried to look away, she couldn't have.

Cora took a deep breath, and crossed the space that separated them with two long strides. She started working desperately at the straps holding Katie down.

When she'd gotten the straps undone, she sank weakly against the table, breathing shallowly, now. She tried to take a deep breath, but it caught in her chest, and she heaved against the table.

"Cora," Katie murmured.

The other woman straightened up a bit, and looked at her with an uncertain expression. "I'm sorry, Katie," she whispered. "I'm sorry for what I put you through. The morning after you caught him with Mrs. Parrish, Diederich came to me – and he made me swear to help him. If I didn't, he promised to kill you. I didn't know he planned to do that, anyway. So I – I lied to you. I pretended I didn't know what you were talking about. I'm so sorry, Katie . . ."

Katie stared at her for a moment, unable to comprehend. After a few moments, the other woman's words began to register, and she let out a thick sob. She hated it, but she had to lean forward on the table so she wouldn't choke. Tears streamed from her eyes, and her chest was on fire.

"I'm so sorry," Cora repeated, leaning forward to take Katie in her arms. "I'm so sorry. Please, baby . . ."

Katie fell against her, and threw her arms around her. She buried her face in her neck, and breathed her in like a drug. She immediately felt calmer, and sank motionless against Cora's breast.

Cora tipped Katie's face up towards her own, and kissed her deeply, tenderly. She tucked a lock of hair behind her ear, and pressed their foreheads together. They both breathed deeply, trying to calm themselves.

Katie was just opening her eyes to look at Cora, when she saw something that made her cry out. Cora turned around to see what was wrong, but it was too late. There was a black hooded figure standing behind her, holding the bust of Venus over his head. He must have slipped into the room while they weren't paying attention.

Katie tried to jump off the table and push Cora out of the way, but the hooded figure was too quick. He brought the Venus crashing down, and struck Cora over the head with it. So she fell, just like Diederich had fallen.

"Cora!" Katie screamed, trying to drop to her knees to check on the other woman. But she never made it that far. The hooded figure held a damp rag in his hand, and he clamped it over Katie's face.

She swooned, and fell to the floor beside Cora.

Chapter 20

She woke up in Karl Diederich's office. The door to the experiment room was closed, and she couldn't see anyone at all. No one but the black hooded figure.

"Where is she?" she demanded. "Where's Cora?"

The black figure turned the hollow of its hood to face her, and stood motionless for a long moment. It didn't speak.

"What are you waiting for?" Katie demanded. "Why don't you say something?"

The air was silent. There was no sound, either from the office or from Diederich's grisly experiment room. It was as if everyone was dead.

Oh, God, Katie thought desperately. *Please don't let Cora be dead.*

"Say something!" she shouted at the hooded figure, who was still staring at her.

The figure stood still for another moment, but then reached up for its hood. It paused for a moment – and then lowered the hood.

Katie sucked in a startled breath. She could never have guessed who'd be standing in front of her. It was the demon with the red face.

She stumbled backwards, nearly tripping over herself and falling to the floor. But she steadied herself in time, and leaned her back against the wall, staring at the demon in disbelief.

"Who are you?" she whispered.

The demon reached up, took hold of its face, and pulled it off.

Wait – no. It was only a mask. If Katie hadn't been so terrified of the demon – if she hadn't lived in its shadow for so many years – she might have realized that it was only a mask. But her adult eyes saw with the eyes of a child; the eyes that had first seen the demon.

When the mask was gone, she was even more shocked. It was the last person in the world she would have expected.

"Hi, Punkin," her father said.

She tried to draw breath, but she choked on her spit, and leaned forward in her seat, coughing violently.

Axel Throckmorton was the mysterious hooded figure. She'd thought it was Karl Diederich – she'd thought it was Tim Reynolds. But it wasn't either of them. It was her own father.

Even worse – he was the demon, too. He was the one who'd tormented her all these years.

She leapt out of her seat, and started pacing madly, tearing at her hair. Finally, she stopped near to the door of the experiment room, and turned to look at Axel with wide eyes.

"Daddy?" she whispered uncertainly.

It was starting to make sense now. *Semper tecum* – always with you. Those same words were written in *The Venus of Ille,* one of Axel's favorite short stories. Katie's favorite, too. It was written differently in the story, though. *Sempr' ab ti.* Always with thee.

Axel hadn't bothered to change the Italian words, though. He'd kept them the same as in *Don Giovanni* – the opera he'd gone to see with Katie in New York City.

"Hi, sweetie," he said softly.

"Daddy," she repeated, starting to feel a little sick. "Please tell me that you didn't . . ."

"That I didn't kill those people?" Axel said brightly. "I'm sorry, Punkin – but I did."

Katie stared at him with wide eyes. He looked so strange, standing there in that cloak and hood, she didn't know what to think.

"Why?" she whispered. Her throat had been parched for a long while now, but she'd never gotten a drink of water. She was starting to feel like a goldfish left out in the desert sun.

"Well," Axel said seriously, taking a seat in the chair behind Karl Diederich's desk, "it's like this, Punkin. When you got sent here, I couldn't believe it. I really thought Marty Walsh would do more for us. But he didn't – and here you are. So I've been trying to help."

Katie swallowed thickly, feeling as if she were about to throw up. "Why did you kill them, Daddy?" she whispered.

He smiled thinly, and gestured to one of the chairs in front of the desk. "Why don't you sit back down, sweetie?" he suggested.

"I don't want to sit down," Katie said firmly. She didn't want to get any closer to him – didn't want to get any closer to her own father – than she already was.

"Okay, Punkin," Axel said. "That's all right."

"Why did you *do* it, Daddy?" Katie demanded.

Axel sat back in Diederich's chair, and thought carefully. "Well," he said slowly, "it's like this. That Dr. Damien was a sicko – and I'm sure you agree. He was doing all sorts of heinous experiments. I know it, because I got in here just a little while after you came.

When I came to visit you, I stole a passkey from some stupid orderly. This place is so Stone-Age, they didn't even think to deactivate the passkey after it was stolen. I trailed one of the doctors to the back door, and hid while they entered the code to the security system. There's no nurse stationed at the back door, so no one saw me."

He sat back in his chair, twiddling his thumbs on the desk, and looking very proud of himself.

"Why did you kill Damien?" Katie asked. "Because of the experiments?"

Axel lowered his head, and his brows knitted together, as if he were thinking very hard about something. "The first night I came in," he said, "I followed him to this very room. I stayed out in the hallway, while he and Diederich talked about their experiments. They had some weird thing planned for a gay boy. They said they would draw his blood, and take some of his semen too, trying to figure out how to reverse homosexuality."

Marcus Bickford, Katie thought.

Axel hung his head, and sighed. "I guess it was because of you, sweetie," he said. "I know you don't like men – but I've never been ashamed of that. I know all about Mallory Kent, whatever. When I heard those men talking about gay people, like they were something that needed to be fixed . . ."

He dropped his head again, and took a deep breath. "I knew I needed to do something," he said firmly. "I knew I needed to take care of things. Dr. Diederich, though – he was way too careful. He was always looking around; and he always had a syringe in his pocket. But Damien, he was different. He was cocky. So I got him."

He smiled brightly, and added, "The man never took the time to notice what was going on around him. He was too full of himself. I took advantage of that, and I snuck into his office. I injected him with a sedative I'd stolen from his office, and I tied his hands together, so he couldn't get at me. When he woke up, I went to work on him."

His eyes shone like flaming embers of a wild fire, and he smiled at Katie. "I did it all for you, Punkin," he said. "I wanted to let you know how much I love you."

"If that's what you were trying to do," Katie said stiffly, with tears starting up in her eyes, "why didn't you just get me out of here?"

Axel hesitated, and bit his lip. "Well," he said, "I guess that's the complicated part. After everything that happened with Lockwood, I got to thinking. I haven't been well for a long time. I've known it; but I didn't know what to do about it. I know that Lockwood took after me. She did bad things – very bad things."

He sighed, paused a moment, and then went on: "The night she died, I knew it wasn't your fault. I knew it must have been something she did, even before you told me what happened. I never doubted what you told me for a second. I knew it was Lockwood – not you."

Katie was stunned. She didn't know what to say. She racked her brains for a long moment, and finally blurted out: "Why did you do it to me, Daddy? Why have you been doing it all these years?"

"What, Punkin?" he asked with a baffled expression.

"Wearing that mask," Katie whispered, her voice so low her own ears could barely hear it.

Axel looked down at the red demon mask, which he'd tossed onto the desk. "The answer's simple," he murmured. "I couldn't show you who I really was, during the day – so I showed you at night. I wanted you to know me. I wanted to tell you who I was, so many times, but I was afraid you wouldn't love me anymore." He hung his head, and looked so depressed, Katie almost felt sorry for him.

"So I wore the mask," he added, brushing a tear from his eye. "And I came to see you in the shadows."

He fell silent, and neither of them said anything for a long moment. Everything was absolutely silent. There was nothing but the ticking of a clock on the wall.

"You've told me why you killed Damien," Katie said quietly. "But what about Eric Conley? What about Lydia?"

Axel looked up, and the pain in his expression eased somewhat. He began to look a little maniacal. Katie had never seen that expression on his face before, and it terrified her.

"Eric Conley was a disgusting rapist," he announced. "I didn't like the way he looked at you."

Katie frowned. "How do you know how he looked at me?"

"I hid in a storage closet one day while you were in group. I saw the way he looked at you. I didn't want him to hurt you – so I killed him. And I defiled him, the same way he defiled that girl."

"And Lydia?" Katie asked breathlessly.

He smiled. "I was in your room the night she kissed you. I saw that you didn't want it – and I didn't want her to bother you anymore."

He thought for a moment, and sat back in the chair, pursing his lips. "I would have killed Carmen Rodriguez," he added, "but I never got the chance. I wanted to kill her for the way she treated you."

Katie didn't know what to say. So she didn't say anything at all. Her father was quiet, too, and the ticking of the clock became apparent again.

The sound of a voice from out in the corridor took them both by surprise. Their heads swiveled towards the door, which Katie was sure her father had locked.

"Is anyone in there?" the voice asked. Katie couldn't place the voice at first, and she thought desperately. It was a male voice, gruff and quick.

Detective Morgan.

She looked quickly at her father, blinking back tears. Her hands were shaking.

"Where's Cora, Daddy?" she asked.

"Katie!" another voice called out. From behind the door to the experiment room. Cora's voice.

Katie flew to the door, and turned the knob frantically, but it was locked. That skeleton key would have come in pretty handy right about now.

She struck her fist against the door. "Cora!" she cried. "Are you all right?"

"I'm all right," the other woman's voice replied. "What about you? What's going on?"

Katie looked back at her father, not knowing what to say.

Axel was staring at the office door. "How could he have known?" he whispered. "How did he know I was here?"

He thought for a while longer, and everything was silent again. But finally, Detective Morgan called out.

"Who's in there?" he demanded. "Miss Throckmorton, are you in there?"

"I'm here," Katie replied, her voice much steadier than she'd thought it would be. Her feelings of shock and despair were beginning to ebb. She needed to get Cora out of that room.

"Let her out, Daddy," she said in a firm voice. "Let her out right now."

Axel looked at her blankly, and asked in a threadbare voice, "What did you say, Punkin?"

"I told you to let her out," Katie said slowly. "Open that door, Daddy."

Axel frowned, and his brows knitted together. "Why do you care?" he asked moodily. "What is she to you?"

Katie hesitated for a long moment, unsure what she should say. She wondered if she should say anything at all. She looked her father straight in the eye, and said, "I love her, Daddy."

Axel continued to frown, and said, "She's old enough to be your mother."

"That doesn't matter to me," Katie replied. "And it shouldn't matter to you. You said yourself you did all this for me. Why would you want to hurt someone I love?"

Axel got out of his chair, and started across the room, holding his hands out to Katie. She moved away from him, watching him warily.

"Please, sweetie," he begged. "Just listen. Now that you know my secret – now that you know who I really am – we can be together! We can get out of this place, just you and me. And someday – well, someday you'll find somebody who's right for you. And I'll be happy for you." He jerked his thumb towards the door of the experiment room, and said, "But it's not her. She's just like all the rest of them."

He peered desperately into Katie's face, and said, "She'd lock me up if she could, just like everybody else. She doesn't love you, baby. You're just some game to her. A game to play when she gets tired of her own life."

Katie narrowed her eyes, and frowned. "It doesn't matter what you say, Daddy. I'm not going to change my mind."

His face fell. "Then – then you're not coming with me?" he murmured.

"No, Daddy."

He fell back a little, and his shoulders sagged, as if all the strength and resolution had gone out of him. He just stood there in his black cloak, looking like a little boy who wanted to dress up like Batman.

His copper-colored hair was gleaming in the light from the lamp. Katie watched it sadly, remembering how much she'd always loved his hair. It was like Edward Cullen's hair.

"Your hair looks pretty, Daddy," she whispered, her hands shaking by her sides. She couldn't believe what was happening. She couldn't believe what had already happened.

Detective Morgan began to pound on the office door. "If someone doesn't open up," he hollered, "I'm breaking this door down!"

A mad look flashed in Axel's eyes. He hurried towards Katie, and grabbed her arm. Then he jerked her towards the office door. He thrust her behind it, while he yanked it open, and launched himself at the detective. Morgan had his gun at the ready, and he fired. But he must have missed. Axel knocked the gun out of Morgan's hand, then pulled a knife from his belt, and stabbed the detective in the neck. "Daddy!" Katie cried. "Stop!"

At the sound of the gunshot, Cora began to scream.

"Katie!" she called. "Katie – are you okay?"

"I'm all right!" Katie shouted. "I'll come back for you!"

"No, you won't," Axel hissed, reached around the door with a bloody hand to take hold of Katie's arm. He dragged her through the doorway, and made her run with him down the corridor, towards the doctors' exit.

The corridor was bright with that dingy grey light. Katie looked down towards the junction that turned into the West Corridor, and saw a group of uniformed officers hurtling towards them. They must have started off when they heard the shot. But everything had happened so quickly, they had only covered half of the distance. The asylum was enormous, and the corridors were long.

"Hurry, Katie!" Axel shouted, pulling his daughter along behind him.

"And what if I don't?" she returned breathlessly.

"Then I'll use my last dying breath to kill your Cora Halstead," Axel snapped. "I might not make it – but I'll damned sure try."

Katie quickened her pace, and kept stride with her father easily. They came to the end of the corridor, and she saw the bright red EXIT sign above a metal door. Axel swiped the stolen passkey through the reader, and the door clicked open. He threw it back against the wall, and dragged Katie through the open exit.

"Come on, Punkin!" he shouted. "We have to hurry! We have to get into the trees!"

Katie stopped dead in her tracks, and her father, who was clutching her hand, was yanked backwards. "Katie!" he cried. "What are you doing? We have to hurry!"

"No, Daddy," she said softly.

He knitted his brows in confusion, and stared into her face. "What are you talking about?" he asked, his voice sounding very high and childlike.

"I can't come with you, Daddy," she said. "But if you hurry, you can still get away."

He looked at her with a pained expression. "I can't go without you," he said. "I came to get you. I came to do the right thing."

He looked so lost and hopeless, Katie's heart broke for him. "I know that's what you think, Daddy," she said. "But it's not the right thing – not for me."

He watched her steadily for a long moment. Finally, he asked, "Do you hate me, Punkin?"

"No, Daddy," Katie answered, running forward to throw her arms around him. She felt his arms around her, and she buried her face in his shoulder. "I love you," she whispered.

"I love you too, Punkin," he murmured, kissing the top of her head.

As they stood there in the middle of the doctors' parking lot, a shout rang out from back towards the exit.

"Put your hands up where we can see them!" the voice commanded. "Both of you!"

It seemed that the officers had finally caught up with them. Katie glanced back over her shoulder, and saw them crowded in the doorway, their dark uniforms mingling with the shadows of the night.

Axel let out a heavy sigh. "I'm sorry, Punkin," he said. "I was trying to save you."

Katie looked back at him with a strained smile, and fought back a sob. "I know, Daddy," she whispered. "I know you were."

"Put your hands up!" the voice repeated sternly.

Katie turned towards the building, and slowly raised her hands in the air. But Axel didn't. He turned on his heel, and dashed off across the gravel, moving faster than a jackrabbit on cocaine.

But one of the cops had a good aim, because even with the shadows and the black cloak Axel was wearing, he hit his mark. Axel didn't make a sound, but he fell down on his face in the gravel. The hit must have been severe.

"Daddy!" Katie cried. She turned and ran towards him, risking being shot herself. She found her father still lying face-down, and she turned him over carefully, looking down into his pale face, which was dimly illuminated in the glow from one of the parking lot lamps. There was blood trickling from the corner of his mouth.

She dragged his head onto her knee, and held him tightly, unwilling to accept the situation for what it really was. Her father wasn't a crazy killer. He wasn't the demon with the red face. He was just Daddy . . .

She leaned down, tears streaming from her eyes, and pressed her forehead against Axel's. Her sobs were heavy and painful. She knew he was dying, and she didn't know what to do.

"Please don't die, Daddy," she whispered. "Please don't leave me. You're the only one who's never left me."

He stared up into her face, and coughed thickly, more blood spewing from his mouth. He reached up with a shaking hand, and laid it against her face.

"It's okay, Punkin," he said in a weak voice. "It's probably better this way. Please don't cry . . ."

Katie pressed her head against his chest, and cried hard. She couldn't accept it. She didn't want to lose him.

"Please, Punkin," he said. "Will you say something to make me smile?"

She raised her head, and looked into his face. She sniffled, and tried to smile. "Well," she said, making her voice as steady as she could, "at least I can be happy with the fact that Queen Regina will be fucked. What'll she do without your paycheck? I hope she ends up in the soup kitchen."

Axel laughed, and squeezed her hand. "I hate to take away your happiness, sweetie," he murmured, "but I killed her yesterday."

Katie couldn't help laughing out loud. She knew that the entire situation was mad and unorthodox to the utmost degree – but she didn't care. She just laughed, and pressed her forehead to Axel's. Then she kissed him.

"Don't worry, Daddy," she said. "That makes me even happier."

He squeezed her hand again, and smiled into her face, as the sound of running feet crunched towards them across the gravel. By the time the cops got there, though, Axel was dead. His eyes were closed, and his face was peaceful. All the madness was gone from him, now. Now he was who he was supposed to be.

One of the cops laid a hand on Katie's shoulder, trying to make her get up. But she shook him off, and bent down over her father, sobbing miserably.

She wouldn't move until she heard a familiar voice behind her. Someone knelt down by her side, and touched her cheek.

"Katie."

She looked over with a tear-stained face, and saw Cora kneeling there beside her. Her father's head was still lying in her lap, so she lowered it gently to the ground, and then turned to Cora with shaking limbs.

"It was my father," she whispered. "It was him all along – and now he's gone . . ."

She stared into Cora's face for a few seconds, trying to keep her lips from trembling. Cora's expression was perfectly heartbroken, utterly filled with shock and anguish for Katie's sake.

Katie fell down against her, and buried her face in her neck. She cried while they took her father's body away. She didn't want to see him go, so she didn't look.

***

A short while later, everyone from the asylum – both the staff and the patients – were grouped together in the front lot, their shoes crunching in the gravel as they shifted their weight from foot to foot.

Katie had been wondering how Detective Morgan knew what had happened, and as it turned out, this is how he heard about it.

Apparently, the orderly named Tim Reynolds wasn't as nefarious as he seemed. He was actually an ally of Cora's. He kept an eye on things for her, and reported back. When Diederich demanded that she join him that evening in his experiment room, she told Tim about it, and asked him to call the police a few minutes after she went into Diederich's office.

Tim did as he was told, and soon after Axel knocked Cora out, Detective Morgan arrived at the asylum. He didn't really know what to expect, and he was probably pretty shocked when Axel came flying out at him. He'd been badly wounded by Axel's knife, but he was alive. Right now, he was lying on a gurney inside an ambulance that had arrived a few minutes ago.

The lights of the ambulance flashed and swirled, creating a strange effect on the faces of the moving, fidgeting crowd. It made them all look like red-faced demons.

Katie took a deep breath, and passed a trembling hand over her face. She was sitting on the front steps next to Cora, watching the crowd, waiting for someone to come and question her.

Cora moved closer to her, and laid a hand on her knee. "Are you okay?" she whispered.

Katie looked over at her, and tried to smile. "I am as well as can be expected, Dr. Halstead."

Cora smiled back weakly, and squeezed Katie's knee.

After Detective Morgan was injured, it was deemed appropriate for everyone inside the asylum to be evacuated, so that policemen in front of the building could keep an eye on them. Now, there were dozens of people out in the gravel lot, some sitting on the stairs, some milling around aimlessly. Katie watched their faces, and saw a multitude of sad ghosts that were very similar to the ones with which she herself was so familiar.

It wasn't long before a policeman came to speak with her. She was relieved to see that it was Officer Humphreys.

He stood there in front of her, frowning sadly, inspecting her face for signs of trouble.

"Hello, Katie," he said quietly.

The sound of his voice was comforting, somehow. As if the life she'd lived before – the life that was divided by her arrival at Greystone – hadn't completely vanished.

"Hello, Officer Humphreys," she returned politely. She felt strangely numb, the way a shellshocked soldier must have felt. There were noises buzzing in her ears, but they were far away, somehow, much farther away than they actually were. She couldn't even feel the stone step underneath her. It was as if she were floating in midair, waiting for someone to throw her to the ground.

"I have learned that your father was involved in what happened tonight," Humphreys said. He didn't say, *I heard your father was a lunatic murderer,* or *I just found out your dad killed three people, and then stabbed a detective.* He said what he said, and he said it with kindness. Katie was grateful to him for that, but even his kindness couldn't put back any of the blood and flesh that had been drilled out of the hole in her heart.

"Yeah," Katie muttered, turning her eyes down towards the ground.

"I will have to speak with you soon," Humphreys said. "But we won't do it here. I'll bring you down to the station. I'll get you something to eat, and let you rest a while. There's no rush."

His remarkably sweet behavior touched Katie's heart, but she felt as if she were a boulder full of magnets, heavier than a Titan, and being slowly drawn down to some dismal metal surface below the ground.

"All right," she said simply. She thought for a moment, and then asked, "Where's Diederich?"

"He's already been taken away," Humphreys answered. He looked at Cora, and added, "I'll need to speak with you about Dr. Diederich." His voice was somewhat pained. He had been very fond of the doctor, after all. "I need to know exactly what he was doing," he said. "The details of his experiments, and all that. And though I don't believe that you had anything to do with it, Cora – I'll have to make sure."

Cora nodded stiffly, but didn't reply.

Katie glanced at Cora, and pressed her hand. Then she looked back at Humphreys. "Cora didn't have anything to do with it," she said resolutely. "She tried to save me tonight. If it weren't for her, I'd be dead."

Humphreys smiled softly, and said, "I appreciate your saying that, Katie. But you have to bear in mind that your word won't hold up with my superiors." He lowered his voice, and said regretfully, "You're a convicted murderer, after all."

"That may be," Katie said, "but it's the truth." Humphreys frowned, and thought for a moment. "Is there anyone who can testify to that?" he asked.

"You might want to start with Marcus Bickford," Katie suggested. "And Dr. Wilkins."

Humphreys nodded, and then went quickly up the steps, obviously trying to get back to his work. He was shaken by these shocking revelations concerning Dr. Diederich. He was like a little boy who'd just learned that his favorite football player popped steroids and had sex with underage women on the weekends.

Before Officer Humphreys reached the front doors, they swung open of their own accord, and two more officers came out into the red flashing night, each one gripping a Holloway twin by the arm.

Katie frowned. She had forgotten about them.

They came down the steps with the two officers, not offering any resistance at all, smiling their familiar, blank smiles. Their thin white lips were stained with blood.

When they got to the bottom of the steps, a policeman came forward out of the crowd, and spoke to the twins' escorts. "Are we bringing them to the station?" he asked. "What'd they do?"

One of the officers frowned, and rubbed at a wound on the side of his neck. "They were locked up in the room we found Diederich in," he said. "Me and Williams went to unlock their chains, and they fucking *bit* us. I mean, goddamn it – look at the bite she took out of me!"

He turned his neck towards the flashing light, and the policeman who'd questioned him grimaced. "Here," he said. "Let me get Thompson, and we'll take them for you. You need to get that looked at, Jones."

Officer Jones nodded grimly, wiping at the blood that was flowing onto his black shirt collar.

But the twins weren't paying attention to any of the policemen. They were staring at Katie.

"We remember your name, now," they said in unison. "Hello, Katie."

Katie didn't answer. She stared up at them wordlessly, wishing a hole would open beneath their feet, and licking flames would spring up to drag them down to hell.

"Were you telling the truth," one of them said – and the other one finished by adding – "when you said you didn't kill your sister?"

"Yes," Katie said slowly. "I was telling the truth. I've never killed anyone."

The twins frowned, then sighed together. "That's too bad," one of them said. "There was something we liked about you," the other one added.

Katie shivered as the twins were dragged away from the steps.

But then, a small approaching group made itself apparent, and Katie looked towards them in confusion. It was Marcus Bickford, Midge Hampton, Carmen Rodriguez and Elizabeth Parrish.

"Hey, Katie," Marcus said, looking shy and nervous. "Are you all right?"

"Yeah," Katie replied. "I'm fine."

"What happened?" Midge asked curiously.

Katie thought for a moment, and pressed her knee against Cora's. Finally, she sighed, and answered, "You probably wouldn't believe me, even if I told you."

Midge smiled grimly, and said, "It doesn't matter, anyway. As long as that psycho German is finally getting what he deserves."

Katie nodded in reply, but couldn't help glancing at Carmen, who was shuffling her feet, and looking at Katie from under her eyebrows. Katie watched her in confusion for a few moments, and then asked, "Is there something you want to say to me, Carmen?"

The young woman hesitated for a long moment before speaking. "I guess I wanted to say –" (she swallowed thickly) "– I guess I wanted to say I'm sorry for being such a bitch."

Katie knitted her brows, and frowned. But the strangely contrite expression on the young woman's face soon made her smile.

"All right, then," she said. "After all – I've been through a hell of a lot worse than *you*, Carmen. So whatever, I guess."

Carmen nodded, still shuffling her feet. "Cool," she muttered.

Mrs. Parrish was the last to speak. She stepped up close to Katie, and said, "I know you did something to stop what's been happening here. I know you did."

She leaned forward, pressed one of her old knees to the stone step, and took Katie's hands in her own. "Thank you," she whispered, tears streaming from her eyes. "Thank you for saving me."

Katie looked at her for a moment, feeling a poignant pang of sympathy. "You don't have to thank me," she said. "I don't know anything about you, Mrs. Parrish – but you shouldn't have had to go through that."

The old woman's eyes opened wide as the trapdoors in the bottoms of rainclouds, and she wept over Katie's hands. "It doesn't matter what you say," she murmured. "I'm still grateful to you."

"Then be grateful to her, too," Katie advised, knocking her knee against Cora's, and jerking her thumb towards the other woman. She looked into Cora's face, and smiled. Then she said to Mrs. Parrish, "Dr. Halstead's the one who made sure the police got here when they did."

Mrs. Parrish looked earnestly into Cora's face, and said, "Thank you, Dr. Halstead. I'm forever in your debt."

"No one's ever in anyone else's debt, Elizabeth," Cora said, smiling lightly. "We're only lucky when we get to help each other from time to time."

Mrs. Parrish nodded tearfully, and turned away, staggering off into the flashing red lights.

Which left only Marcus, Carmen and Midge. The two women seemed to quickly realize that they had nothing more to say to Katie, so they nodded as politely as they could, and started off across the crunching gravel, looking for their places in a place where there were no places to be found.

"I haven't seen Lamberto," Marcus said in a worried voice. "Have you, Katie?"

Katie looked miserably into his face. It was hard for her to find her voice.

"I'm sorry, Marcus," she murmured. "He's gone."

Marcus hung his head, and sighed heavily. "Poor guy," he muttered. "I sort of liked him."

Katie nodded, and dropped her eyes to the ground. She was thinking of Jacob Barlow, and how there didn't seem to be anyone around to miss him. It made her feel like someone had hit her in the gut.

But then, she thought of something Officer Humphreys had said, and she looked up at Marcus.

"Listen," she said quietly. "There's going to be an investigation into what Diederich was doing. Cora and I have told them what we know, but you're going to have to vouch for us. You and Dr. Wilkins."

Marcus hesitated for a moment, but then nodded, and reached out to press Katie's hand. "I've got your back," he said. Then he glanced at Cora, and added, "You too, Dr. Halstead."

Cora smiled and nodded. Katie looked into Marcus's face for a moment, thinking about the tragedy of his life – thinking about the tragedy of human life. "I wish you the best, Marcus," she said. "No matter what happens."

He nodded again, and smiled. "Thanks, Katie," he said, squeezing her hand once more.

Then he walked away, and found his place beside Dr. Wilkins, who was standing off at the edge of the red flashing lot. He leaned against the doctor; and Wilkins put his arm around him.

Katie smiled. She took a moment to look around at the trees illuminated by the flashing lights, and she felt a strange sense of calm. Trees had always brought her that feeling of calm. That's why Mallory Kent had bought her the woodland scene by Shishkin. She'd ended up hating Mallory; but she'd loved the painting. She actually would have liked to have it back.

She looked at the trees – she thought about the trees, and all the memories they harbored – but her pleasant thoughts were disrupted by the arrival of Dr. Marina Salvador.

Cora looked up sharply. She looked at the other doctor, the expression in her eyes inscrutable, her shoulders rigid, her back stiff as a board. Katie looked from her to Marina, feeling sick.

Dr. Salvador spoke Cora's name, and the sound of it was filled with an indefinable emotion, a strange combination of longing and anger.

"Hello, Marina," Cora returned stiffly.

"This is quite the production," Dr. Salvador announced. "Don't you think?"

She looked meaningfully into Cora's face.

"I suppose so," Cora agreed. "But it was bound to happen sooner or later."

She paused, and added, "We both knew that."

Dr. Salvador cleared her throat significantly, and ground her stiletto heel into the gravel, looking unwilling to admit any wrongdoing on her own part.

"If you say so," she said simply. But then she thought for a moment, and added, "Why are you sitting all the way over here?"

She looked curiously at Katie, and her expression turned sour. She looked back at Cora, and said, "Why don't you come and get a cup of coffee with me? They've got a little stand out behind the ambulance."

Cora watched her for a moment, obviously thinking hard. Katie hated to wonder what she was thinking about.

Finally, Cora said: "I don't think so, Marina. I've got things to see about." She paused, then added, "But I hope you enjoy your coffee."

Dr. Salvador glared at her, then turned on her stiletto heel, and marched off across the lot.

"You don't have to stay with me," Katie said quietly. "They're going to come back soon, anyway. They'll probably take me down to the station, like Officer Humphreys said."

Cora looked at her steadily, clearly still thinking deeply about something. She stared into Katie's face, and her eyes were wide and round. "Katie," she said slowly.

"What?" Katie returned in an anxious voice.

Cora paused for a moment, but then reached out and grabbed hold of Katie's hands. There was something very momentous about it. Katie looked down at their twined hands, and frowned. Then she looked up.

"What's the matter, Cora?"

Cora hesitated for a long moment, looking terrified. Katie squeezed her hands, and looked pleadingly into her face.

"I want you to come with me," Cora finally whispered, her hands still tangled up with Katie's. Her hair was a mess from the night she'd gone through, and her eyes were bloodshot. Her age was more apparent than it had ever been before – but to Katie, she looked absolutely beautiful. She looked straight into the older woman's face, and her breath caught sharply, sticking in her chest like a boot in mud.

"I can't come with you," she said simply, her voice breaking. "I couldn't do that to you. You'd never be free. They'd always be looking for you, Cora – don't you know that?"

"Of course I know that," Cora snapped, squeezing Katie's hands tightly, and leaning forward in a desperate motion, so that Katie could feel her warm breath on her face. "But I don't care."

"I can't do that to you," Katie said staunchly. "I won't put you in that position."

Cora stared into her face for a long moment, obviously considering the words to say. Finally, she leaned down, and pressed her forehead against the backs of Katie's hands. Katie could feel her tears against her skin.

"Katie," she whispered softly, laying her cheek against the young woman's wrist, "I love you so much. I never thought I could really love anyone. I married my husband, and I hated him. I slept with Marina, and I hated her. And there were – oh, there were so many more. I don't think – oh, Katie, I don't think I've ever loved anyone before. I'd understand if you didn't want to come with me; I know I'm almost twice your age. I have nothing to give you. But I love you so much, I'd try for the rest of my life to give you whatever I could."

Katie stared at her in disbelief. She couldn't believe she'd just said all that.

"Before I kiss you," she murmured thickly, "we'd better go somewhere no one can see us."

They rose up from the stone steps, their bottoms and thighs chilled with the cold air of November. They walked hand-in-hand down the steps, and around to the parking lot. And no one noticed. Everyone was either too busy feeling sorry for themselves, or discharging their imaginary duties. Imaginary, because they did no good. Detective Morgan thought he'd been doing good, but then Lydia Brock had died anyway. Katie almost wished she could have seen him again. But no – it didn't matter. He'd have to deal with it himself.

Katie and Cora walked around to the staff parking lot, and Cora pointed out a shiny but humblelooking Hyundai. Katie thought of Mallory Kent's showy Mercedes, and murmured, "I love you more every minute."

They got into the car, and sat silent for a moment, looking around to make sure no one was nearby. "There's a back road that leads to the highway," Cora said. "As long as no one sees us leaving, it'll be a while before they put it all together."

"But they'll trace your license plates," Katie said worriedly. She hung her head, and felt incredibly guilty. "I can't ask you to do this, Cora. You're going to get caught, and you're going to get in trouble. Just let me go back."

Cora caught her hand, and held it tightly. There was such intense emotion in the gesture, Katie looked over at her in surprise.

"If you leave me," Cora murmured, "I'll never live another day. Every day will be like a little death. I'll never breathe properly, never feel properly, if you're not with me."

Katie looked wonderingly into her face. She was so amazed to hear those words, and so amazed to see the truth of their expression in Cora's face, she was momentarily dumbstruck. She felt as if she'd just been punched in the face.

"I'd feel better if you could do it without me," she murmured.

Cora looked desperately into her face, and said, "I can't."

Katie sighed, and threw herself back in the seat. "How are we supposed to live?" she asked. "I have money, but they have all my cards. They would know if I tried to withdraw any of it."

Cora looked at her slyly, and said, "I've thought of that."

Katie knitted her brows. "What do you mean?"

Cora laughed, and said, "I withdrew the balance of my savings account."

Katie didn't say anything. She was looking at Cora reprovingly.

"Five hundred thousand dollars," Cora murmured. "It's in a suitcase in the trunk."

Katie wiped at her tears, and looked away through the passenger window. "Then please take it, Cora," she said. "Take it and start somewhere new."

"Without you?" Cora asked.

"Yes," Katie replied stolidly.

"No."

"Yes!"

"No."

"Goddamn it, Cora –"

Cora threw herself across the seats, and draped her body over Katie's, burying her face desperately in her neck. "I can't live without you," she murmured. "I can't *be* without you. Please don't make me try."

Katie looked seriously into her face, and couldn't help smiling. "I might be able to make a withdrawal of my own," she said. "Let me try calling Marty Walsh. He might be able to unfreeze my account long enough for me to get my money."

"I don't care about that," Cora whispered, kissing Katie's neck frantically, moving her lips up her throat, and kissing her cheeks.

"Well, I do," Katie said. "If we're going to be together – we're going to do it right. I'll have to get a burner phone to call Walsh. After I get my money, we can go wherever you want."

Cora laid her head against Katie's chest, and asked, "Where do you want to go?"

Katie thought for a moment, and said, "Mexico would probably be best. Under the circumstances, that is."

"Mexico in November," Cora murmured, tilting her head to catch Katie's lips with her own. "Sounds good, doesn't it?"

"It does," Katie replied, with just a touch of melancholy in her voice. "If we can pull it off."

Cora looked at her seriously for a few seconds, then asked, "You want me to send you back, don't you?"

"Yes," Katie replied honestly, looking into Cora's face with earnest eyes.

"That's how I know you love me," Cora said, kissing Katie's mouth one more time, and then resuming her place in the driver's seat. She looked around to make sure there was no one in the parking lot. But it was empty. Everyone was either in the front lot, or inside the asylum itself.

"Ready to go?" Cora asked, turning the key in the ignition.

Katie looked into her face, and couldn't help smiling. "Sure," she said.

The engine started with hardly any noise, and Cora put the car in reverse, rolling back in the gravel.

"When we get far enough away from this place," Katie said, "will you pull over?"

"Why?" Cora asked, looking around warily as she slipped quietly out of the lot.

Katie laid her head back against the seat, watching the other woman's beautiful face in amazement. She felt like she'd died and gone to heaven.

"So I can kiss you properly," she said simply.

Cora navigated the car between the trees that marked a back path to the highway. While the red lights flashed behind them, and the darkness of uncertainty loomed before them, she glanced over at Katie. "I'd be a fool to refuse an offer like that," she murmured.

So they drove on, on and on into the dark night, not knowing if someone would come to stop them, not knowing if fate would come to hinder them.

All that mattered, really, was that they were together.

And Katie was just waiting, waiting and waiting for Cora to pull over, so that she could finally kiss her properly.

THE END.

Author's Note

Dear Reader,

I just want to take a moment to thank you for reading my story. So many people have so many stories — so many people dream so many dreams — it makes me feel very fortunate to think that another living person has dreamt this dream with me.

Readers like you mean the world to writers like me.

TO CONTACT THE AUTHOR:

Email: camablackwood@gmail.com

Follow me on Twitter & Facebook.

23039803R10174

Printed in Great Britain
by Amazon